BLOOD
DANCE

James
William
Brown

BLOOD
DANCE

HARCOURT BRACE JOVANOVICH, PUBLISHERS

NEW YORK • SAN DIEGO • LONDON

Requests for permission to make copies of any part of the work
should be mailed to:
Permissions Department, Harcourt Brace Jovanovich, Publishers,
8th Floor, Orlando, Florida 32887.

Portions of this book previously appeared in different form in
the following publications: *Epoch*, the *Dublin Magazine*, and
Shankpainter.

Lyrics on pages 101–102 from "First Rain"
by Mitsakis, first recorded 1948.

Lyrics on page 138 from "I'm Going to Send
God a Letter" by Babakis, first recorded 1950.

Library of Congress Cataloging-in-Publication Data
    Brown, James William.
    Blood dance: a novel/James William Brown.—1st ed.
      p. cm.
    ISBN 0-15-113214-3
    I. Title.
    PS3552.R68566B57   1992
    813'.54—dc20   92-28374

Designed by Lydia D'moch

Printed in the United States of America

First edition
A B C D E

To the memory of Zelma and Brownie
Ἄς εἶναι ἀλαφρὺ τὸ χῶμα . . .

and for Jane

CONTENTS

ACKNOWLEDGMENTS

The author wishes to thank the following for their support: the National Endowment for the Arts; the Wallace E. Stegner Fellowship at Stanford University; The Fine Arts Work Center in Provincetown; the Montalvo Center for the Arts.

For help in determining the accuracy of details historical, sociological, or musical, I am grateful to the following sources: Richard and Eva Blum, *The Dangerous Hour* (Chatto & Windus, 1970) and *Health and Healing in Rural Greece* (Stanford University Press, 1965); C. M. Woodhouse, *The Story of Modern Greece* (Faber and Faber, 1968); Marjorie Housepian Dobkin, *The Smyrna Affair* (Harcourt Brace Jovanovich, 1966); Joy Coulentianou, *The Goat-dance of Skyros* (Ermis, 1977); Peter Gray, *People of Poros* (Whittlesey House, 1942); Kevin Andrews, *The Flight of Ikaros* (Weidenfeld & Nicolson, 1959); Katherine Butterworth, *Rebetica* (Komboloi, 1975).

No gossip ever dies away entirely
if many people voice it;
it too is a kind of divinity.

—Hesiod,
Works and Days

I THE WOMEN

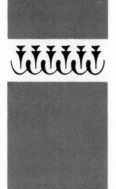

Wherever she went she heard it. Up the steps that led past our houses, up the hill through the village. It was here she heard it, and here too. In the courtyard where the lion fountain dribbled water through the yellow afternoon and in the branches of the fig tree near the church. It's above the village, in the fortress, she probably thought. For we had thought that once too. But she paused under one of our windows, stood still, perfectly quiet, and listened, listened. Then down she went, back down the long steps to the sea. Now she'll run along the beach hoping to find it there. And the men in the cafés will see her and smile at one another as they turn their beads over in their hands, pressing one against the other.

We had heard it too. But not now—not since we were young, of course. Not since we were about her age. Though some of us had heard it younger, others not until we were heavy with our first children. To some it seemed a cry, a sexless voice calling out. A terrible sound, because only you could hear. No one else seemed to notice at all. Though later, after it all, each of us women understood that all of us in the village had heard it. But each by herself, separately, in her own time. And to each it sounded different. Some said it came from far out at sea and was like a drum—a vast drum being beaten just below the horizon.

What was the sound to her? From the tops of our houses, halfway up the hill, we could see her walking on the beach, stopping a moment to listen, holding her head just so against the wind. We were hanging out our wash on the flat roofs and admired her walking far below, her young body, the sea breeze blowing her hair. Amalía, the daughter of Grigóris. Growing up, becoming a woman. She would be just like us soon. She didn't have to tell us she could hear the sound. We knew from her eyes, from her searching: All the young girls of our village hear it eventually and later their eyes change and they braid their hair and knot it behind their heads as we all do here. Together we do our washing in the courtyards; we hang it on the roofs.

But Amalía was different from the other girls. We might have expected it of Grigóris's daughter. She had read all those books, and not the sort of books girls read for school. She and her friend Maroula, the butcher's daughter, were always reading books with titles we couldn't understand. Amalía got them from the post office where the clerk said they came through the mail from foreign countries. It was his job to open them, of course. But they were in other languages. Some of them were grammar books. Did she plan to leave here? Did she need a better language than ours? Our children were her schoolmates until they finished high school. And they all said that when she got higher marks than they, it was because the teachers felt sorry for her because of her father.

Grigóris was of our most respected family. It was they who helped start the revolution that drove the ill-fated Turks from our land 150 years ago. Grigóris was the last son of the family and the shop he ran was the best the island has known. You could find anything there: rice for pilaf, beautiful cloth for dresses, scented soaps from the mainland, vegetables without soft spots. Even if we needed nothing, we found excuses to go there. For Grigóris was tall, taller than any other man in the village, taller than the great rolls of cloth stacked on his counters. He smiled at us from behind them, head and shoulders over the topmost roll. His eyebrows were heavy and nearly ran together. We knew what that meant. When we spoke to him our voices shot up suddenly; we dropped our eggplants on the floor.

We waited on the other side of his counter for years. But he turned away from us to make his own bad match. Katína was of our blood but she was not from here. She came from Smyrna where she had escaped from the Turks. A well-formed woman with copper skin and the blackest hair twisted into a thick plait that fell down her back. She brought her own ways with her, the secretive ways of one who has lived among enemies.

With Grigóris's money and Katína's education, we had to look up to them, to respect them. They were the best family. But from such a height there is only one direction to go.

One day Grigóris saw two boys fighting by the sea and went to break it up. One of the boys picked up a sharp stone and threw it at him. It hit Grigóris just in the side of the head, at the temple, and he died at once, leaving Katína alone with Amalía, their only child. We were shocked at first, that such a respected man should die so strangely. People felt sorry for Amalía and her mother. We pitied them openly and talked about how death entered the grand door of their big house just as easily as it slipped through the shutters into our bedrooms. They had always carried themselves so proudly. What could anyone expect?

Amalía had only a single friend as she grew up. She lived in the house with her mother after the death of her father. Death was everywhere, the fishermen said. The world was eating itself—this they understood from news shouted at them across the water from the boats of fishermen of other islands or of the mainland. Man killed man in places whose names we had never heard before. But the sea kept its secrets, the stars turned across the sky, wheat rose gold and fell before the scythe. We were alone. There were no ferries from the mainland, no new supplies. Be still, we said, and the world will not know we're here.

Widow Katína ran Grigóris's shop, sold us beans, sold us rice, sold us tallow for candles. Look how she makes money from our bad times, we said. Look how our gold sovereigns are swallowed by her money drawer that snaps open and closed like a mouth. Oh, toward the end, just before boats came again and we learned that the killing was done, the world's hunger for itself finished at last, Widow Katína gave us what was left—soap and oil and tins of meat—as if, we said, she hopes now to win us with easy ways. The men made jokes: Where can you get your bread baked? Widow Katína's hot oven. Ach! Such are men.

Amalía came to look much as her mother had years

before when she first came to the island. But Amalía was more beautiful. The oval face, great dark eyes, heavy-lidded. Nose and lips as fine as those on any icon in the church. Several young men were after her but she showed no interest. At Carnival time each year she led the other girls in their dance across the square. She danced well, skimming around the square with the grace of a swallow. She was the best dancer in the village, as her father had been before her. The men watched her from under the eucalyptus trees and sucked in their breath as she danced past. Everyone knew that young Nikos, the son of one of the fishermen, wanted her but he couldn't even catch her eye when they passed in the street.

Then last winter a stranger came to our village. He was tall and blond and very good to look at. A tourist, we supposed, though tourists don't often come here, so far away. He had a little book in which he wrote things. Most of the time he stayed up in the old deserted fortress above the village, where he had a tent inside the walls. We supposed he was trying to find out things about the fortress, such as how old it was and who built it. Those are the things that usually interest foreigners. We knew things about the fortress but why should we have told him? So he could have written it all down in a sentence or two to amuse his friends at home? No. We kept to ourselves. We would not be reduced to a line in a foreigner's notebook!

The fortress belongs to us. It's always there, just above the level of our eyes. If we look up from our washing, glance up from our marketing, we see the fortress. It has always been there, crumbling away above the village. So many stories are told about the king who lived in it. Some people believe the stories; some do not. The young people believe nothing at all now, but they will when they're older. They'll tell their children about the king who wanted to prove that his language was the original one spoken by man. He believed that his was the first language to exist.

Some shepherds told the king about a wild boy who had been seen in the mountains. He was a child who had been abandoned and isolated. He preyed on goats and lizards and had probably never heard a human voice. The king had the boy captured and brought before him in a cage. But the boy only snarled and growled and would not accept food or drink. Finally the king ordered him released inside the fortress. The boy leapt onto a window ledge and one of the shepherds tried to grab him. A soft moaning sound came from the boy's lips and then he either jumped or fell out the window and died on the rocks below.

Inside the fortress everyone agreed that the boy had spoken a word of the king's language before he died. But they disagreed as to exactly what he had said. Each person put into the boy's mouth a word generally considered to be important to the king: *war, courage, love, wisdom.* But the king finally announced that only *he* had understood the sacred word the boy had said. The word was so holy, the king said, that it could only be repeated to the heir to the throne. And each king would pass it on to the next.

Of course, everyone has forgotten what this word was. But some say you can still hear it, a soft moaning sound, when the wind blows through the windows in the crumbling fortress wall. It has become part of the sound of our village. But only a part. For the village speaks to us, when we are young girls, with many voices.

But how could we tell all this to the stranger? He had

put an ugly tent there in the middle of the courtyard. And he was so much taller and fairer than our men. When he walked along the sea all the men stared at him as they usually stared at girls. They talked about how he walked as if he belonged here, as if he might stay for a long time. We never knew exactly where he was from, though some northern country seemed likely.

It became known that the stranger swam wearing nothing at all. Po-po-po. There in the cove on the other side, not far from the road where Mad Manólis passed with his donkey carrying the day's load of village rubbish. Where the priest walked to church. Where children from outside the village went to and from school. Mr. Diamándis, the headmaster, said that the children had covered the blackboards with terrible drawings of what they saw. Some of us hid behind boulders in the cove to see if the children were right—in order, of course, to decide what should be done.

But what could we do? We couldn't speak his language. We didn't even hear him talk much because Amalía bought him everything he needed. He met her just after he arrived in town. They managed to understand each other somehow and he was always looking for her when he came down from the fortress.

Some people said that they knew Nikos climbed the fig tree outside her house and entered her bedroom at night. There, so they said, he proposed to her, declared his love, and warned her that the stranger's ways were not our own. But she did not accept him and finally, without doing anything to her, back down the fig tree he would go.

Imagine how it looked to see Amalía strolling with the

foreigner through the village! Most of our girls would not walk around with even one of our own men unless they were engaged. At first we said she will marry him just to show us she is better. And some people said this would be good because she was almost as much a foreigner as he. Better that they marry each other than our people. But then, we said, perhaps they will go away together. It wouldn't be right for her to leave the place where she was raised. They acted as if they were married already. We knew she went up to the fortress with him sometimes.

We were sure her mother knew nothing of this since she seldom went out of the house. So finally someone told her. And then the neighbors could hear Amalía crying. Nikos and several of the men who work for Spyros Galánis at the tomato factory went up to the fortress one night and burned all the foreigner's things. We could see the flames just over the edge of the old wall. By the next day the foreigner had gone.

When we first saw her after that, she looked as though nothing had happened, as though the stranger had never been here. It was time for her to be married, we said. Everyone told Nikos that he must take her. He must find a way, as our men had found ways when we were young, when we dreamed foolishly of going away to the city, to another country even. Going to a life different than that of the village. Bad dreams. For the men made us understand that our way is right. The Church made us understand what is expected. And our mothers taught us the work of a wife, the holy work of a wife. We listened to the wind and to the sea, to the water in the lion fountain, to the clicking of the beads in the hands of the men. And slowly all these sounds became one sound.

Perhaps one night you woke up suddenly, unaware of what had awakened you. It was the night before you had to make a decision—about marriage, about money, about the family, perhaps. And you were young and the men watched you when you walked by the sea. You sat there looking out the window and listening. Did you hear your name? Did you hear a drum beating? Did you hear music like none you knew calling you to its source? Perhaps you heard something else. Only you know. But you tried to follow the sound, to find it, either sitting there in your bed or running, running through the streets, up the hill, along the seashore. Beating on doors, perhaps, asking people could they hear, did they know what it was?

But the men looked at you strangely and the women just smiled mysteriously and said no, they wouldn't know what it was that *you* had heard. Yet the sound continued, circling around and around in your ears. And everything became part of it. The priests chanting, the market women crying out their fresh figs and pomegranates. There was nowhere you could run to shut it out. Who knows what it meant to you, how it changed you? But change it did. For finally the sound departed; the decision was made. You braided your hair and knotted it behind.

We could see it happening to Amalía as she turned on the beach and ran to where the fishing boats lay banked. Looking out to sea—what did she hope to discover? We said that she was not so different after all; she was really just like us. And one of us flicked soapsuds into the wind and another danced a bit and one marched around and pretended to be young again with her body straight. "Come help us with the wash!" we cried to Amalía from the roof. "Let the soap make your hands red like ours!"

But she paid no attention to us, for just then the men began to run out of the cafés and to leave their nets. They ran toward Amalía but they were not interested in her. Not far from her a great sea turtle had come ashore and was scratching at the sand. The females often come at this time of the year to lay their eggs in the sand. This one was as big as a small boat. The men hate them so. Sometimes the turtles become caught in the nets at sea and, in trying to escape, tear holes and free the catch. There is more than this to the fishermen's hatred, but as women we are not meant to understand.

We ran to the beach and called the children back. Such things are not for them to see. It was better for them to be behind closed shutters with us. But some of us looked out to watch our men do what they had to do. Only *she* remained, staring at the men who had gathered around the turtle. She should not have been there but she stood as though unable to move. The men at the edge of the group began to bring stones and gave them to the others, who threw them at the turtle. It tried to turn back toward the sea but the men surrounded it. It lay there watching, the great mouth opening and closing. The men ran farther along the beach for larger stones, shouting ugly things as they ran. And flocks of birds screamed and flew off. The stones fell more rapidly but still the shell was not broken.

Then Amalía turned and ran. She climbed onto the wall overlooking the beach. From there she must have seen Nikos jump onto the great shell. One of the men passed him a huge stone which he held over his head. He threw himself down with all his weight on the stone and the men cheered as the shell cracked. And the great mouth opening and closing as if it were speaking. She turned and ran

12

again, ran up from the beach, away from the sea, up the long steps through the village. Nikos ran after her, his clothes stained from the turtle. The men continued to stone the turtle as Amalía ran faster and faster up toward the castle with Nikos pursuing. We could see them higher and higher until at last they ran into the fortress and out of sight.

On the beach one of the fishermen ran to take a harpoon and the others fell back from the turtle to watch him. The mouth was open, locked open, and the eyes open. The man aimed at her and all was quiet. In that quiet we heard a cry, a voice calling out, then cut off quickly. It had come from behind the old walls. The fisherman ran at the turtle and plunged the harpoon deep into its throat. A great shout went up from the men as they gathered around the turtle to finish their work.

In our kitchens that night we made soup from the turtle. We were thankful the men had killed it. It was a good omen. Fishing became better that season and many children were born. The turtle had become part of us.

In a few days the marriage of Amalía and Nikos was announced. It is time for them to dance their dance, we said, and later she will braid her hair and knot it behind. We thought only that the first rains would come, bringing out the snails and the cyclamen. And the men in the cafés would talk of other things as they turned their beads over in their hands, pressing one against the other.

II

KATÍNA

It was late afternoon of a winter's day that I came here, a young woman with pockets stuffed full of drawing pencils, and saw the island rise up from the sea.

The sky and the sea were equally gray so that heaven and earth seemed all of a piece with no horizon dividing one from the other. The shape of the island rose slowly for an hour or so as the ferry made its way toward the small harbor. But the shape too was gray and indistinct. Then suddenly the sun slanted through a hole in the sky and lit the village atop the great rock of the island. The village seemed suspended there, glowing. The white cube houses were stacked at odd angles to one another up the side of the rock and seemed whiter than anything I had ever seen. A circle of crumbling fortress walls crowned the rock. And above them gleamed the gold cross of the chapel within.

Suddenly the sky closed; the sun was gone. The island went completely gray and seemed to move back. The vision of it had lasted just a moment or two, not long at all. But time enough for some old longing inside myself to settle there.

I walked the cobblestone streets in my city clothes and was stared at by the old women in black who stood in their doorways with hands folded over their aproned bellies. A room had been found for me in a private house high up in the village, not far from the fortress.

I had come here to be a part of my first archaeological dig. It would also be my last. I was assigned this temple site by the archaeological school in Athens, whose museum employed me as an assistant draftsman.

The temple itself, dedicated to Athena, was scattered all over the village. The capital of a beautifully worked column had been used to prop up a stable. In one wall of the church was plastered the statue of a man—or was it a god? It had been used as a way of saving stones. There was a bulge where the plaster had fallen away and you could see the shoulder of the statue. Other pieces of ancient marble were to be seen here and there in the middle of brick walls or as paving stones in the street. The team from the museum was carefully uncovering the ancient foundation within the fortress walls, next to the modern chapel. It was there I spent my days, measuring, drawing. Just below the fortress, on the side facing away from the village, lay the present cemetery with its neat rows of white tombs under cypresses. And farther down the slope, in the place that had perhaps the most beautiful view out to sea of anywhere on the island, was the village rubbish dump.

"It's a place of bad luck," an old woman in black said to me. I had wandered into the central village shop, a kind of gathering place where women gossiped over rolls of cloth and men drank coffee as they sat on chairs in front of the refrigerated case full of goat cheese and sheep butter.

"She's right," another said. "Why go up there, so near the bones of our grandparents?" Others joined her, pushing forward until they were all around me, eating me with their eyes, reaching out to touch my dress. In those days, the time between the wars, young women did not travel alone, did not have any kind of work other than that of the wife. And tourists did not come here then as they do now. The only people who visited this isolated island were archaeologists, male archaeologists.

"It's not good, that place near the tombs and the dump," one whispered to me through ancient yellow teeth. "Only Manólis and his donkey go there to empty baskets of trash. There it is always smoking, always smelling."

They all talked at once or interrupted one another, and they moved around, dipping their hands into bags of beans, of rice. Some carried heavy wicker-covered jugs of oil, of wine. I explained that we had come to look at the stones. That we could, well, read them. Read stories of the past in them.

They nodded. "Like Lilliána," someone said. It was the first time I heard her name.

"She's crazy," another said.

"No, she isn't," a third said. They were all talking.

"She understands everything about our lives from the stones."

"She's an old fool."

"She is not."

"You're an old fool."

"The wind blows, hens lay eggs, everyone's a fool."

This Lilliána, it seemed, knew the custom of telling a fortune by casting stones on the floor and reading past and future from their positions. No, I said, the stones we were interested in were from the buildings built in other times. I told them how we dug them up and then I drew pictures of how they must have looked long ago.

"So much trouble, the past," the shopkeeper called out from behind the counter. Grigóris, my life. Hair so thick I didn't see how he could ever get a comb through it. Dark blue eyes. He was enjoying this scene of me surrounded by the old women, trying to explain.

"Yes, it is a lot of trouble," I called back.

"What good does it do you?" one of the women asked. "You can't eat these stones. You can't plow a field with them."

"No, I suppose you can't."

"Or catch fish with them."

"Or wear them."

"They don't cover your head in the winter or protect your flock from the *eye*."

"You can't make babies with them."

"Maybe *some* can," Grigóris shouted and winked at me. It was not a funny comment but there were screams of laughter from the women. Mouths flew open, gums bit gums, yellow teeth stuck out from under leathery lips and gray tongues waggled.

"So why save the past?" he asked when the laughter had died down.

"Yes, why?"

"Why?"

"So as not to forget," I said. "Not to forget."

"Eh, my friend," Grigóris said, "You should listen to them. They are right. What is the past? A lot of old stories no one wants to hear."

"And you a woman," someone said to me. "What work is this for a woman? How does your father allow you to travel so far from his home?"

"I came out of Smyrna," I told them. "I lost my father, my mother, everything. That is my 'old story.'"

One touched my face saying, "Poor child, poor child."

There was silence. To break it, I took out my pad and did some quick pencil sketches of the women. They gave little cries of surprise as they recognized themselves on paper. None had ever been drawn before. The sketches were passed from one to the other.

"Ah," Grigóris said, coming from behind the counter. "These are wonderful. You have this power to press us onto the pages of a book. Please, I hope you will accept these as a gift of welcome to our island. You honor us with your visit." He held out to me a few student copybooks. "For your drawings," he said, putting his other hand on his heart and smiling such a smile as most of the island girls probably would have given their birthrights for. As I accepted them, he touched my wrist, then took my arm and escorted me around the shop, pointing out the rolls of cloth, the bags of tea, the packages of soap. He steered me around the women as if they were barrels of olive oil. "Anything you need," he said, "anything at all, come to Grigóris."

Much of the business of the village took place in the shop. Land passed from hand to hand, funerals were arranged, dowries were discussed and a season's olive harvest was bought up for half its value, or double—who knows? What a shop it was. Then, it was the only one and was much more than a shop. "We'll discuss the matter at Grigóris's," people said to one another.

Grigóris flattered women into buying. He would lean across the counter and say to a fat, red-faced housewife, "How beautifully a dress of this cloth would suit you." She would blush and giggle like a schoolgirl and buy enough of the cloth for a score of dresses. Or, speaking to me one day as I bought some toiletries, "Oh, to be this lucky bar of soap you're buying. What journeys it will make." And then there was always a little touch, you know, just at the wrist as you were accepting change, or a squeeze of the shoulder as he adjusted your shawl. What a peasant, I thought, to treat me as if I knew nothing of the world but these narrow streets.

His had been the oldest and most respected family on the island. He was alone then in the big house. His parents had died years before. And every girl on the island wanted to be the mistress of that house. Grigóris, with his little compliments, his touches and his attentions, gave each the feeling that she had the best chance. It was a game he played cleverly and well. His cash drawer was always full.

It was difficult to keep away from the shop that summer. I was disappointed with the work at the dig. For a long time I had dreamed of an excavation, of seeing golden spears and masks brought out of a darkness last breathed by men of royal line centuries before. But I remembered going to digs with Papa and seeing that most of the work of uncovering ancient stones was dirty, dull and painstaking. The trenches opened around the base of the temple contained little more than chips of marble and porous limestone. Some of the potsherds found had been burned and were mixed with scorched earth and the charred bones of small animals. All these I sketched as they were uncovered and I did countless excavation plans. I was good at my work. I could look at a handful of potsherds and draw the original pot, could rebuild on paper an ancient wall from the sight of a few stones. Piecing together the past. It was this skill that had given me a life. Not just a salary, though there was that too, of course. I had learned how to take the burned fragments of my past and make something whole out of them.

When I was a child in Smyrna, the soldiers came. Silent as ghosts, they moved through the streets of the city of my birth, far across the Aegean from this island. Their dead eyes looked neither left nor right as they passed along the graceful avenues, then turned down the coast to await evacuation back to Greece. We gave them bread, for they were our own Greek soldiers retreating. Some told us of the avenging Turkish army that had driven them back to the City, the enemy that would soon follow with the scent of blood in its nose.

With the soldiers came Greek and Armenian refugees, fleeing the Turkish towns of the interior before they got caught between the two armies. Trains pulled into the station with people swarming on their roofs. The carriages were so crowded that those who had died on the journey had to be passed over the heads of the living and out the windows at stations along the way. Refugees came by the thousands, sleeping in churches, schools, mosques, streets, offering whatever they could for passage on boats that left for the nearby islands. Through the refugees moved our ragged soldiers, like men walking in their sleep.

Beaches and casinos emptied. The merchants and ministers from all over the world who had made Smyrna a great commercial center, had been the first to flee. Along the seafront you could no longer hear the mingling of languages, see every shade of skin and kind of costume. Instead there was the chaos of refugees and boats, and over it all, like a memory of other summers, was the scent of roses that had made the area famous. That's what they called Smyrna, the Great Rose. Ships had come from all over the world as if drawn by its fragrance. But that summer they fled from her, for the scent of roses was mixed with that of death.

August 22, 1922, was the date written at the top of the last page of the notebook I kept that year. The rest of the page was blank except for the burn across the bottom. The notebook was all I saved from the fire, the only tangible thing I saved of my life there on the other side of the sea. Years later I would tear out the partly burned pages, folding them small and sewing them as charms into the hem of Amalía's wedding dress. I wanted those powerful pages from the end of my own childhood to make the old women of this village powerless. They had always been there at the edges of our lives, watching with hearts chewed ragged by envy, jealousy.

There came a spring day, just before the summer of the soldiers, when I was younger than Amalía is now but just as proud. My class went on an excursion to the ruins of ancient Ephesus, down the coast from Smyrna. You could smell the earth and the yellow flowers that grew among the old stones and broken columns. The bees drove you mad, they buzzed so loudly. The sun pounded and the sweat ran down my sides, making me shiver in the heat.

I never was one to follow the leader and soon I wandered away from my teacher and classmates. I came upon the ruin of a great temple. What god had been served there, I did not know. But his power still existed among the stones. I had never before felt what I felt that day. The sun burned me and I crouched on the floor of the temple and ran my hand through the groove that one of the huge temple doors had made in the stone. A lizard darted across my hand. And I knew that the place wanted me. It seemed alive and I felt things so strongly then. No man had yet taken me. I didn't know what was ahead—the soldiers and the collapse of our lives.

The Greeks and the Turks have faced each other across the Aegean for many centuries and only the waters between them know the truth in all those years of troubled history. The graceful city of the roses was the last piece of a Greek empire that once stretched deep into Turkey. The Greeks, Armenians and Turks had tried to live together there. Many of the old grudges had been rubbed out by the dailiness of life. They had to earn their bread, as did we. We did not always get along, but what marriage is ever free of troubles? It would go on forever, I suppose I thought, if I thought about it at all.

I felt my smallness before the huge stones of the temple. And the strength of the place poured into me, filled me. Worship here, the stones seemed to say, worship here.

A stork flew over and I thought of my plans for the summer ahead. The wings of the stork seemed to gather all those plans and scatter them across the sky. When I tried to leave the temple, the weeds pulled against my skirt and rubbed yellow pollen on my legs. Something had happened to me there, and I carried away some of the temple's strength. The place had claimed me.

Later I wanted to tell Papa about this feeling, for we

often sat in the courtyard of the house in the evening and talked of other civilizations. He was the curator of the museum. But he had become more and more vague over the years. Remembering him now, I don't know how he kept his position in the museum. His mind had clouded and the scholar had been replaced by a gentle, wistful dreamer murmuring of forgotten times, lost places. I never did tell him; I wrote about the temple in my notebook instead.

Days added to days. They packed down neatly all the way into summer. I swam with my friends and our skins turned pink, then brown, then mahogany. We rushed in and out of the sea and lay on the sand beneath the tall palms. When we took walks, we would hear the tinkle of glasses and spoons as people sat in courtyards eating sweets made of rose petals, sipping liqueurs.

And then in August we heard that the latest attempt at negotiations between Greece and Turkey had fallen through, mostly because of the bumbling government in Athens. Some months before, it had ordered Greek soldiers out from Smyrna in an attempt to cross much of Turkey and seize the Turkish capital, Ankara. This was all part of what they called The Great Idea—to reestablish the Greek Byzantine Empire. What fools, what horned cuckolds there were in Parliament then! It was they who brought the Turkish soldiers down on our backs like hornets. We were sacrificed to the foolish dreams of politicians hungry for places in history. Here we were, Greeks on a Turkish coast with our backs to the sea. It was so easy for the Turks to punish us for the mistakes of the government in Athens. Ach, politics—the Greek passion, as we say.

But it is more like a dagger we use to stab ourselves again and again.

There were promises of safety from local Smyrna authorities and many believed them. Slowly the glorious summer days filled with retreating Greek soldiers.

I went with my friends one day to watch them. On the way we passed the shop of Cousin Vangelis and noticed something odd: Above the door was the Turkish flag. Now, Vangelis was one of the most patriotic people I knew. He could spend hours (and often did) telling you how he was related all the way back to the most ancient of families. He was the first to bend to kiss the bishop's ring, the highest jumper when he danced the *Kalamatianó*, the most enthusiastic speaker on national holidays. Actually, I thought he was red eared and boring. But I could not understand why he had that flag.

So we went into the shop and asked him about it. His ears became very red as he looked at us. Then he began to shout, "You get out of here! You don't understand these things. Get out of here and tell your families that if they're clever, they'll put flags over the doors of their houses, just like my wife and I have done. Now go away!" And he slammed his cleaver into a piece of mutton.

We ran out of the shop, worried and upset. But as we walked home, we noticed more and more Turkish flags over shops, on the fronts of houses. What could it mean? I asked Papa.

He did not answer directly but only turned the pages of a book he was reading. I was not to worry. Not to think about these things. He turned the pages. He would need to return to the museum soon, he said. There were many problems. Fragile objects were being packed, hidden away. Where to put them all? Where to put them? He turned the pages of the book.

Mother was more practical. She took me into the garden and we sat under the plane tree. She smoothed the wrinkles of her dress and said quietly, "In a few days the Turks will come. Everyone says there will be no trouble for us. Perhaps they are right. But perhaps not. Do not talk to your father about this. We'll pretend that there will be trouble and we'll make a plan. Of course if nothing happens, and probably nothing will, we can just laugh about it this time next week."

I felt very important as she explained it all to me. It was to be a secret between us. If any Turkish soldiers came to the house, I was to run to the garden and get over the wall. There was a well on the other side. Inside it, stones stuck out at different levels so that someone my size could easily climb down. I was to go into the well and wait there until Mother came to fetch me. I practiced a few times until I could do it quickly and easily. We treated it like a game. She kept saying that of course nothing was going to happen. It was just a secret we needn't tell Papa. Whenever I imagined the soldiers causing trouble, I thought of them tearing up Papa's books or making us give them food or something like that. Perhaps they would ask us for money, but then we didn't really have much. So I thought they would go to the big houses of rich people and leave us alone.

Two days later the Turks arrived in the City. I was writing in my notebook when one of our neighbors ran up the street in tears. Mother went out and talked to her. The shop owners masquerading under Turkish flags were among the first to be attacked. A mob bent Cousin Vangelis over the very block where he had butchered so many sheep and calves over the years. They cut off his nose, his ears, and his hands. Then they carved him up and hung the parts of his body from meat hooks in the window.

Our neighborhood went into panic. Some families began moving out their furniture and possessions. But of course there was nowhere to move. The army was pouring in from the country on one side and the city faced the sea on the other side. Our neighbors dragged chests and boxes, gilt mirrors, piles of clothes out of their houses and then carried them back in again. Some left treasures in front of their houses as if the soldiers would take only those and go away. Others simply fled into the center of Smyrna from where we could see clouds of smoke beginning to rise. What a people we are. Clinging to our little bits of land, we had watched most of our soldiers sail away and organized no real defense, convinced that the promises of safety were sincere. Pah! What a people!

Mother tried desperately to convince Papa that we should flee to the harbor and try to buy our way onto one of the foreign ships. But he refused to leave. He seemed unable to understand the seriousness of our situation. Mother gathered a few belongings including some pieces of jewelry and some gold sovereigns into a small bag. She pleaded with Papa hour after hour. But he stood at the window looking out through the cracks in the shutters. The soldiers would not bother us, he said calmly. He had always got along very well with his Turkish colleagues at the museum. His only preparation was to gather his diplomas, degrees and other papers together. He said he would show them to the soldiers and then they would leave us alone. As if such soldiers could read—or would care!

Mother and I wept and pleaded with him. But it was hopeless. He would not leave, could not leave. And we had lost so much time. We heard the sounds of glass breaking, of shouting from the other end of the street. And then there were screams. Mother took my hand and we ran into the garden. She lifted me partway up the wall and I climbed to the top. Just as I turned to help her climb up also, two Turkish soldiers appeared at the gate. Instead of climbing up the wall, she turned suddenly and fled back to the house.

I screamed for her, but afraid the soldiers would see me, I climbed down the other side of the wall and into the well. It was difficult balancing myself for more than a few minutes on the stones that jutted out at intervals all the way down to the water at the bottom. I was sure that I was going to fall into the water at any moment. My legs trembled from fear and they ached because I couldn't change position without losing my balance. From all over the neighborhood I could hear screams and shouts, gunshots and explosions, more shattering of glass. But I closed it all out. I concentrated on not slipping and falling into the water. For the splash might bring the troops. After a while I could hear fire destroying wood. Smoke covered the hole above my head and I knew our house was burning. Mother and Papa? Had they gone? How would I find them? I began to sob and the well echoed my sobbing. The sound coiled around me and frightened me as if it came not from me but from the dark water below. There were no tears, just dry sobbing, for they were gone, gone where I could never find them. I imagined my notebook burning, the summer burning. My foot slipped off the stone and I scrabbled to hold on but fell into the water below.

The shock of the cold water stunned me. When I came to the surface, I paddled quietly to the side of the pool that lay in the shadow of the rim above. No one came. But it seemed to me then that if I just waited, Mother would come as she had said she would. They had gone to my aunt's house near the harbor, of course. There was a police station near there. They would be protected. I reached for the jutting stones and began to pull myself up and felt, suddenly, that I was at the ancient ruins again. The strength of those stones ran through me. I got a foothold and was out of the water. The fields, the bees, my schoolmates—they all came back. But most of all I felt the stones of the great temple. I clung to them and they filled me with their strength.

How long was I there? After a while there was no sense of time. There were only the stones and the cramps in my legs. Hours must have passed but I cannot remember them. Not a single thought went through my mind, or so it seemed. As if I slept, but I could not have slept. The hole above my head blackened and I knew that night had come. The outside noise was farther away. Slowly, I climbed out of the well.

As I peered over the rim, I could make out strange shapes in the darkness: the smoking remains of our house and the other houses on the street. There was no movement anywhere except for the smoke circling in the night breeze. I eased myself out and lay in the dust beside the well, rubbing my legs, breathing in the hard char smell. When I tried to stand, my legs would not support me and I fell back to the ground. I lay there some time; perhaps I dozed off. I don't know. It was still dark when I was first able to get to my feet but the sky above the center of the city was aglow. The walls of our house stood out in the dim orange light. I walked into the rubble and sat on the bottom step of a staircase that led up to nowhere. Perhaps the bodies of my parents were there, just near me. But I did not think of them.

At some point I found myself in what had been my room at the back of the house. There where the window had been, where I had sat so often and gazed into the garden, was a pile of schoolbooks only partly burned. I nudged them with my foot and recognized the shape of my notebook. I seized it and held it to me. It was to be all that I would save of that life, of those times. Holding it then, my mind cleared suddenly. I understood that I had to get to the harbor and board one of the foreign ships. I had to leave and I had to do it at once. Pushing the notebook into the front of my wet and filthy dress, I ran.

The streets were full of bodies. A few houses were still burning and in their light the faces of the dead wore expressions of pain and terror. Some were horribly mutilated. A young woman hung from a plane tree, her nose and breasts slashed off. Most of the bodies were those of women or older men. Later I was told that our younger men had been herded into the countryside to rebuild villages destroyed by the Greek army. They were never to return. Others were massacred immediately in the streets of Smyrna.

As I neared the center, the noise, heat and light all increased. I tried to run through gardens behind houses but the residential area gave way to shops and I was forced back onto the streets. Rounding a corner, I nearly ran into a group of soldiers. I jumped back into the doorway of a burned-out shop and crouched there, terrified. The soldiers had cornered an old man and were talking to him. The man had thrown up his clasped hands in an attitude of supplication. One of the soldiers split his hands with a sword, cut them off at the wrists and chopped the old man down.

From the other direction came another group of soldiers moving slowly up the street toward me, carrying bloodied clubs. There was nowhere for me to run. I shrank back into the doorway, but one of the soldiers had seen me and he shouted something. I pushed against the door and it fell open so I fled into the gutted shop. Tripping over the rubble, I tried to make my way toward the back wall which had partly collapsed, leaving an enormous hole. The soldiers were behind me, crashing across the burned floor. I moaned as I ran and cried out, "No, O God, no, O Mother, O God, oh no, oh no." I was nearly at the hole in the back wall when the silhouette of a soldier appeared there.

I froze. They stopped too, four on one side and the other blocking the only way out. I began to tremble as some handed their clubs to others. Belt buckles snapped open. More soldiers, probably the ones who had finished with the old man, poured in the door. They looked at me, laughed, and nudged the others aside. There was scuffling as I backed against the wall, shaking uncontrollably.

Suddenly there was a loud cracking noise as the weakened floor gave way under the soldiers' boots. Several of them crashed through to the cellar, screaming. In the commotion, the soldier at the back wall ran off, perhaps expecting the wall to collapse. I darted through the hole and down the alley.

Sheets of flame rose at the end where buildings were burning on both sides. There was nothing to do but go forward. My dress was still damp from the well water and I covered my wet hair with my hands, aimed myself between the two buildings at the street beyond, closed my eyes and ran. The flames seared my face and I prayed the buildings would not collapse on me. I shot out into the street with my dress smoking, my hair singed, my eyebrows and lashes gone.

I was on the wide street parallel to the quay one short block from the water. Across from me was the French consulate with mobs of people trying to get in. French marines were holding them back. I was sure that this meant there had to be at least one available ship in the harbor and everyone wanted passage on it. I could speak some French. I had been one of the best students in languages in my class. But how would they take me for French with my filthy clothes, my singed eyebrows and no passport or papers of any kind?

One of the marines came into the street and looked anxiously at the nearby fire. I ran up to him, "Please," I said, "let me enter. My papers, everything, lost in the fire. Please let me enter. I want to go home."

He looked down at me. I tried to cry but I could not. That would come later, much later, the mourning, the keening. But there in front of the marine, I could only sniffle unconvincingly. He did not believe me, I could tell. But he told me to follow him and led me through the mob.

"I was here first!" a woman screamed. "Don't let her in. I have children, babies, my old mother. Let me in first!"

"Hours we've been here, days even . . . ," others cried.

"For the love of God, let us enter!" The marine passed through them all, nudging them gently out of the way.

"Soon," he said. "Soon." And to the other marine at the door, "Raise your hand and let her enter."

Inside I joined a line in front of a table. As the line crept forward, I rehearsed my story: My father, an archaeologist, and I had come there to examine the ancient ruins. Our luggage was burned when the soldiers set our hotel on fire. The line moved slowly and I heard my people struggle with this other language, struggle to convince the foreign officials that they were not from here, that they needed passage home. At last I reached the table.

"Passport?"

"Burned. The fire . . . all our luggage. We were in the hotel, you see, and . . ."

"Age?"

"Eleven."

He looked at me and smiled. "Your accent is good. Where did you learn it?" Before I could answer, he gave me a paper good for passage on a troopship flying the tricolor flag. "Do not lose this," he said. "I can't give you another." A marine came forward and led me with a group of several others to the door.

Outside, the streets were littered with so many swollen bodies that it was difficult to walk. Buildings were burning, everything was burning, and the soldiers were shooting into the flames. They glared at us and muttered but when they saw the French flag carried by the marine, they let us pass. Finally the marine turned and led us over the one block to the quay, where we were to board whaleboats that would take us out to the troopship. We emerged at the far end of the quay.

The Smyrna harbor was shaped like a crescent. It was a solid wall of flame two miles long. Later it was said that sailors far out at sea, too far away to see the flames, mistook the smoke from the city for a high mountain range. On the promenade, with the flaming ruins of grand houses on one side and the sea on the other, were packed thousands of people. As the fire swept down toward the quay, it had pushed the people before it. Many had fallen or jumped into the water and tried to swim out to the foreign ships. The commercial vessels had already left. Only a few ships from the navies of various nations remained and most of them could not pick up refugees because they were under strict orders from their governments to remain neutral. The waters bobbed with bodies of the drowned.

Turkish cavalry rode along the crowded waterfront, forcing people into the water, then shooting at them as they swam toward the ships. Mothers drowned their babies. A young woman sang and danced in madness.

The whaleboats went back and forth and our numbers increased rapidly when the French consulate was evacuated just before it caught fire. I was in the last boat that moved slowly over the gory sea. From the deck of the troopship, across the copper red water, we watched the tongues of flame writhe a hundred feet in the sky. Against them were silhouetted towers of churches, domes of mosques and the flat, square roofs of houses. Ammunition stores were exploding and out of the warehouses rose black, oily smoke that hid the moon.

And there was the screaming. As if the people wailed and keened for Smyrna which was dying. It tore from thousands of throats as the people stretched out their arms to the departing ships.

And screamed.

The dead are more fortunate than the living, I thought later in the mainland Greek refugee camps. Many escaped the fire only to die later of typhoid or pneumonia. Some were too deeply in shock to know that they were ill. They were blessed.

Those years after the troopship were like the narrow corridors at the Home in Athens where someone was always crying. I don't remember going there. I was told that I had been found crouched in an overturned barrel, delirious with the fever of pneumonia, in one of the refugee camps near the harbor. They were probably the longest years of my life and yet I remember them the least. I knew that we slept three to a single bed, boys and girls together, grateful to have a bed at all, and comforted each other as best we could.

School was escape. I was far ahead of others in my year because of the good school my parents had sent me to in Smyrna. I had also spent long hours in the museum where Papa was curator and on digs with him around the city. In Athens I won school prizes in history and drawing and spent all my free time at the great museum downtown. It was the closest place to home in this new land of my ancestors. Most weekends for several years I practiced my drawing in front of the glass cases. There I watched the reflection of myself as it grew taller, fuller, softer. And saw it circled with young archaeology students. Even before I finished the gymnasium, I was given a part-time job as an archaeological illustrator with the museum. My girlfriends were worrying about the size of their dowries then and whether or not the fat middle-aged businessmen their parents had chosen for them would notice if they were maids, as they said, on their wedding nights. If I had no family, no dowry or groom, at least I had a small flat, a smaller salary, and the attention of the scholars who swarmed around the museum as if, with its grand halls and courtyards, it were the ancient palace they dreamed of discovering. And I within, keeper of its secrets.

There was a dank room in the basement of the museum for my work. There I sat long months, drawing under the fluorescent lights, longing for a chance to get out, to work on a dig. Finally I was told of the excavations of an island temple where a draftsman was needed.

And so it was that I came to hold in my hands the charred remains of sacrifices made at this island temple, as if they were the pieces of my life and the lives of my parents. But what were their lives sacrificed to? The decisions of politicians? Is that the new god of Greece? Pah! We would have done better to stick to Athena and her wisdom.

The name of Smyrna does not appear on the modern maps of the area. And I have not said it for many years. But the great stones of that other temple at Ephesus must still be there, as I am still here, head of the House of Sarrás, strong with the strength I gained from those stones one spring day.

The stones of this island temple kept bringing me back to the vicinity of Grigóris's shop. I was trying to draw the stones and statues used as supports for the foundations of other buildings nearby. And I would wander in for a break. It was there I met Spyros, closest friend of Grigóris. The old thief of a money lender, he was a big man, rough in his ways, smelling of the fields. He was always ready to lend money happily but insisted on interest, for, as he said, "You lose both your money and your friends without interest." If he lent enough to buy a dozen hens on Monday, the loan had to be repaid the following Monday at the price of thirteen hens. "This is fair," he would say, gesturing to a boy to bring coffees that an agreement might be concluded. "For there is no place in business for friendship." In this way and with the help of a clever marriage (he was engaged to the daughter of a rich landowner) he would come to own over half the fields on the island, many thousands of tomato plants and the factory that sends island tomato paste all over the world.

He and Grigóris had been boys together and sometimes still were, punching one another, embracing, laughing and playing tricks on each other.

"Eh, Grigóris!" Spyros would shout, thundering into the shop. "Tomorrow I go to the mainland. You too, eh?"

"Pah! With all this work?"

"Work? What work? Tomorrow is a holiday."

"Pah!"

"Yes, it is. Have you forgotten, my poor friend? You see," he would say to the others in the shop, "what too much work does to my friend here. Melts the brain."

"Soft as honey," one of the women said.

"Empty as a cracked water jar," laughed another.

Grigóris moved among the women, repeating orders as he wrote them on a pad. "Three kilos of sugar, one hundred grams of salt, half a kilo of broad beans . . ."

"Ninety elephants," Spyros continued, walking behind him, writing on an imaginary pad. "A woman with orange hair, two crippled cats, one melted brain . . ."

"No!" shouted Grigóris.

"Listen, my friend: The sun bakes us; winter freezes our bones. God is an old lady with bad breath."

"No!"

"And tomorrow is the Holiday of the Mad. You! Me!"

"No!"

"I'm glad you agree with me. Here are the ferry tickets. We leave at five. Don't forget to bring one of those bottles of old wine you keep hidden in your storeroom. Your health!"

"Your health!" everyone would shout as Spyros left the shop. After siesta the next day the Closed sign hung on the door.

Many were the stories of their adventures on the mainland. The tavernas they visited, the money they spent, the wine they drank, the women they shared. But they were also rivals in all things.

Grigóris was usually in the lead for his family was the older, the richer. This meant everything to him—the House of Sarrás. Spyros of the House of Galánis was always trying to catch up, to outdo Grigóris of the House of Sarrás.

"They eat each other's lives," the women told me. "Always it has been so between their families."

Every time I came into the shop, the women asked me the same questions again: Why are you here? How is it that you are a woman alone, away from your father's house? I found myself giving the same explanations over and over again. But the next day the questions would be repeated as if never asked before. Why are the stones important? It seemed they believed nothing of what I said. If they just asked me often enough they would wear me down and the unbelievable stories would fall away, revealing what? The story behind the story? And what was the story they sought if not the one I told them?

They talked of the old days. A time that present days could not compare with. "Ach, Katína," one would say, "then was the time to be on our island."

"Melons grew bigger than water jars."

"If you crossed yourself and threw a line out to sea you could catch a fish big enough to feed the whole family."

"Bees gave tubs of honey."

"Grapes were so fat they fell into baskets without being picked."

"Wine never turned to vinegar."

"Saints came to the doors and healed good people. No one was ill."

"But what about the others?" I asked.

"What others?"

"The people who weren't good."

"There weren't any."

"But if everyone was good and everyone was healed by the saints, then no one ever died. Where are they all?"

"We are they."

"Oh."

Most of them have since died, good or not. But others seem to take their places. Their numbers vary little over the years.

Sometimes Grigóris would take me to one side to show me some new material that had arrived on the boat. "And there are more wonderful fabrics that I have in my storeroom. But you know how it is." He would lower his voice here: "These women, they cannot appreciate such things. They don't know good imported material from local quality. So why show this to them? Yet I cannot show it to you without them seeing us. I do not want to insult them. So perhaps if you could come tonight, after the shop is closed. There is a back door. No one will see . . ."

"What you do not understand," I said, "is that not only the women fail to appreciate the difference between local and imported quality. You too have such a problem. Good day." I walked out of the shop and did not return for several days.

But what could I do? It was the only shop. There was no choice. I could not take the ferry to the mainland whenever I needed something. Would I meet him in the olive grove behind the church? The rocks along the shore? Finally, just to show him who he was dealing with, I agreed to meet him one night under the fig tree beside the lion fountain. But I didn't go.

"So you think you can test me," he whispered as he wrapped up some drawing pencils for me the next day. "Pah! You have hurt me; you don't know how you have hurt me." And he looked at me with those great pirate's eyes full of false pain. I paid without comment. But I admit I liked these games, playing him for the fool as I thought I was. At first it was the game that excited me and then I understood that it was Grigóris himself.

Nights, we went to the taverna, the others from the dig and I. The women and girls of the island were shocked that I, a single woman, spent my evenings in such a way. I knew they said awful things about me. But I knew also

that women who came from the mainland never behaved
as village women did. The island women would have to
get used to it.

Like the shop, the taverna was the only one on the
island. We ate grilled octopus and tiny squids fried crisp.
The coarse local wine was strong and heady. The men from
the tomato fields drank oceans of it, then danced, kicking
away the plates we smashed at their feet in admiration.
Spyros was always there, and Grigóris. Both sent pitchers
of wine to our table, as we did to theirs. The dancers cast
shadows under the unshaded bulbs that hung on cords
from the ceiling. Outside, the old women in black peered
through the windows and shrieked with laughter when one
of the dancers stumbled or fell. The dancing grew wilder
as the smoke and noise increased. The men with outstretched arms were like ungainly birds trying to land,
swooping around the tiny space in front of the tables.
Spyros danced with them as everyone cheered and whis-
tled. There was much joy in his dancing but he was a big
man and when he thumped to the floor after a leap, the
whole room shook. He didn't seem aware of his lack of
grace. With sweat running down his face, he hissed and
turned, shouted, "Oh-pah! Oh-pah!" and ended his dance
to loud applause and cheers.

Late of an evening and only after he had been asked
repeatedly, Grigóris would dance. As he was the best
dancer on the island, Spyros had nicknamed him the
"President."

"Eh, Mr. President!" he would call out to Grigóris.
"We are waiting for you."

"Go to the devil!" Grigóris would answer, ordering

another pitcher of wine, lighting another cigarette. He liked to draw it out. Someone else would dance, but later, after the applause, would come the cry again.

"Eh, Mr. President! We, your people, unclean as we are, with big feet that smell bad—we wait for you."

"I can't dance. I am ill. My government, you know how it is, has made me sick."

"No. It cannot be. Shoot your prime minister!"

"Hang him!" others shouted.

"Burn his house!"

"May the earth reject his bones."

"Ach, Mr. President." Spyros was standing now, bowing in the direction of the table where Grigóris sat alone. "Your government is, how shall I say it, kaput." He drew a finger across his throat. "The people offer you their love."

Applause. Grigóris, smiling, pushed his chair back and walked to the center of the room. More applause. Sometimes he and Spyros danced together, side by side, each with an arm thrown across the other's shoulders. A few simple steps forward, close, tense, then back. The private, concentrated dance of two friends.

But it was for Grigóris alone that we, the people, waited. Where did it come from, this melancholy that rose out of the man who was otherwise cheerful, attentive, pleasant? For when he began to dance, a kind of grieving rose up in him. Eyes on the floor, body tense and slightly crouched, arms loose at the sides, he began to move slowly, deliberately, around some fixed but imaginary point on the floor. Snapping his fingers to the rhythm, he doubled a step or held it for two beats, always circling around the point on the floor, the center of his concentration. The tension grew until, with a shout, he leapt into the air and seemed to hang there longer than was earthly possible, slapping one of his heels with the palm of his hand midair before his feet touched the floor. Sometimes his concentration, after a leap, would center on a table which he could lift with no hands. He bit down hard on the corner, locking it in his jaws, lifted the table and danced around the room with it, spilling none of the wine from the glasses on top. And always his arms balancing him and moving, cutting shapes in the air.

I thought him magnificent those nights—a kind of local god, perhaps the one to whom the temple had been built, his the shoulder that supported the wall of the church. The others would watch in silence, hardly breathing. Even the old women were quiet as they watched through the windows. Graceful and economical in every movement, he bent slowly backward from the knees, moving his hips to the music, all the way back until his head and hands touched the floor behind him and rested there, his long body arched across the floor. His trousers were stretched tight by the angle of his body.

Then he pushed himself up gently, as if his spine were made of tallow, unbent until he was upright again. He still swayed to the music, arms outstretched, fingers snapping, his face shining with sweat. We cheered.

"Let me show you the island," he said when he had joined us at our table and we had drunk to his skill as a dancer. "Always you people are working, working with some old stones. You will leave here knowing nothing of our island." He was sitting next to me, his arm on the back of my chair, his hand touching my back.

"But I've seen the island," I told him.

"No, no, you've seen nothing. Tomorrow. Yes? Take

the day off. I will put the Closed sign on the shop and we will walk everywhere." His fingers stroked the small of my back gently, then firmly.

"Yes," I said. "Yes."

From the hill we looked down at a bay with a sunken harbor. Once ships passed there from all over the world, he said, and sat in the harbor loaded with spices, with gold and slaves. And then the bull shook his horns, as they say—an earthquake. And for hundreds of years after that no one lived there. "Look, you can see there—the old pier, walls of some of the houses. Then my ancestors came and little by little, others. Merchants. We are everywhere, like ants. But come—you haven't seen the butterflies."

There was a valley where a kind of yellow butterfly rested by the thousands in the branches of trees. No one knows why they come here, Grigóris said. When he clapped his hands, the butterflies rose up from the trees, clouds of them filling the sky then fluttering back down to the branches where again they sat so still you would have thought them leaves or blossoms.

It took us more than one day to cover the island—the secret coves where fish swam in emerald waters, the light that bounced off the whitewashed buildings so that even a stable seemed dazzling. The heat resting in the olive trees.

All this was new to me. I was a child of a city. And though Smyrna was the Great Rose, so also was it crowded with camel caravans and the carts of vendors, a city parched and dusty, loud with cries of men and animals. Papa was always busy. There had been little time for travel to islands or even into the countryside. Then too there had been the feeling that we Greeks sat on the edge of land not quite ours, land that could be pulled from under us at any moment.

Later, on this side of the sea, had been the refugee camps and the relief home in Athens. When you have been wretched in a place it is hard to feel good about it, no matter what happens there later. Even when I walked from my flat to the museum, I passed corners where I had once begged money for cigarettes. I stood next to a man on the trolley from whom I'd stolen food in the home years before. Everywhere was something to remind me of that terrible time. But here, the silence, the stillness of the island was a kind of balm. I came to dread summer's end, the return to the dank city museum. This island summer was a gift served up to me, I thought, as if to make up for that other summer whose burned pages I've sewn into Amalía's wedding dress. You have only one island summer in a life, I think. And though I was still young, I knew enough of this earth and the winds that blow over it to seize that summer.

Nights, after the dancing, Grigóris took me down to a cove where we sat in a sandy hollow just near the water's edge. I let him run his hands over me and I longed to feel his weight on mine. Every time I saw him dance, saw his hard body moving to that music that opened in him wells of darkness, I wanted to take him inside myself and hold him there. "Why not here?" he asked. "Why not now?" And the sea sucked at the rocks below us.

But I was no fool. Look, I had already said to the mirror, what is your life? Do you want to grow old drawing pots in a museum? For it seemed unlikely that a woman with no more education than I would do better in those times. I had no family to look after my interests, to inquire into the reputations and incomes of suitable young men. I would bring no dowry with me, neither fields nor gold sovereigns. An old man who wanted a wife to nurse him —that would be my fate. Oh, there were the students, the scholars at the museum. They talked of love enough but when it came to marriage they chose women of families known to their families, women who brought with them the deed to a house, or an apartment and a good family name.

The effects of the Depression had started to be felt in Athens. Poor Greece, in debt to Washington and London for all sorts of loans for stalled projects such as road construction and land drainage, was falling apart economically. There was no money anywhere, no jobs. The funding for the dig would end with summer. It was not a good time to go back to Athens.

Life in the village, however, seemed to go on just the same. With a few crops of its own, its own wine and fish and bread, the island seemed cut off from the world.

The wife of Grigóris would be respected here, I thought. Pah! I didn't know then how respect is laced with envy, jealousy. Grigóris wouldn't need to worry about dowries. I didn't love him but I was not so silly as to believe love necessary for marriage. Anyone knows that if you marry sensibly, love will come later and be far richer for the wait. I was fond of him and his island. Of course my parents would have called him a peasant, and that he was. But we're all peasants if you look back far enough. We've all scratched around in the dust and planted our potatoes by the light of a new moon. But I was not such a peasant as to lose a man by lifting my skirt too soon.

Marriage was in everyone's mouth then. For soon Spyros was to exchange wreaths with his bride. The women talked of nothing else.

"Clever Spyros. What a dowry she has!"

"How much?"

"Seven fields."

"And hundreds of gold sovereigns."

"A block of flats in the city."

"And with no brothers or sisters, she'll have her father's house when he is gone."

"Clever Spyros."

I saw the poor creature in the shop with her mother. Froso, she was called—a skinny thing, toothpick arms and no chest at all, her eyes always cast down at the floor, following her bossy mother like a mouse. She coughed from time to time. I thought, Well, they're getting her off their hands while they can, poor thing; she won't last long. And she didn't. It was the winter damp that was to take her before she and Spyros had been married a full second year. If it hadn't been the damp, I'm sure she would have died in childbirth. Those hips would never have been wide enough to push out a child by such a bear of a man. Spyros was to leave the island the year after her death, not to return those many years.

Neither Grigóris nor Spyros could do anything that the other didn't try to equal or top. Grigóris couldn't stand it that Spyros was to marry. But at the same time he was pleased for this friend and many pitchers of wine were drunk in celebration at the taverna.

"She's not beautiful," Spyros said of his fiancée. "But she's a good girl. Everyone says it."

"Of course she's good," said the women in the shop.

"With such a face . . ."

". . . how could she be bad?"

Good or bad, she was to be Spyros's wife. I could see Grigóris examining the village girls as they passed through the shop. But Spyros had taken the best of the lot. The ideal girl had three benefits: good name, good dowry, good looks. No man on the island really expected three out of three. Most were lucky to get one. Spyros's fiancée had two out of three so Grigóris could settle for no less. The other village girls, if they were good, were poor and ugly. The beautiful (there were few of these) were all poor and had long ago lifted their skirts too soon. The only other girl with a good dowry (not as good as that of Spyros's fiancée) was said to have known a merchant marine, a second cousin, who had sailed away. With her dowry, she would have no trouble finding someone, but with her name, he would not be of the House of Grigóris.

"From the collar or the cuff," the fat woman wheezed at me outside the door of the shop.

"What?"

"Come, come along." She motioned me to walk with her. "From his collar or his cuff."

"What do you mean?"

"The thread. It must be from his collar or his cuff."

"What thread?"

"Don't be stupid. You want him, don't you? Well, give me a thread from his collar or his cuff and you can have him." She smelled of fish as she swayed down the street, plucking at a head scarf that barely contained knots of hair. I had seen her before.

"Lilliána!" A woman rushed up to her. "The chicken foot! It worked. Alékos got out of bed this morning by himself. Please take this." She handed Lilliána a bag of flour.

"Oh no," Lilliána said, "I do the work of God."

"Please."

"Well, just to pay for the chicken."

"Your health, Lilliána."

"And yours."

So this was Lilliána, reader of stones, worker of spells. When the women had gone, Lilliána said again, "The collar or the cuff. It doesn't matter which. Better hurry if you want him. They've all come to me, you know, they've all asked me. What can I do? I'm a poor woman alone. But you are the one. The stones say so. And you'd better hurry. The collar or the cuff. Now go away. I have some patients to see." She turned into a courtyard.

I knew what she meant. I remembered Mother telling me about it long ago—the old custom of stealing a thread from the collar of the man you wanted to marry. You were supposed to give it to a wise woman, who, I thought, burned it in front of an icon. Or was it that she ate it? Years later I asked Lilliána, "Just what was it that you did with that thread I gave you?"

"What thread?"

"The one I snipped from Grigóris's collar in the shop. Mother of God, I was terrified he would see me that day."

"You gave me no thread."

"Of course I did. You remember."

"No, the thread never works. I don't use that. It's all a lot of rubbish."

There was no arguing with her. What does it matter if the thread worked or not? We exchanged wreaths in the autumn, just a few days after Spyros, in the same church where tomorrow Amalía and Nikos will walk around the altar. Grigóris got two out of three, same as Spyros. I was more beautiful, he said, than any village girl. Everyone thought of me as exotic, he liked to think; not quite foreign, for I was of the same blood, but not in the same class as a skinny local girl. No one else had a wife like me, certainly not Spyros. Grigóris told everyone of a dowry seized by the enemy soldiers across the sea years ago. And of a family of position. It was true, more or less. And no one could check. As to good name—I had come to take Grigóris away from the island girls, the women said. That was the story behind my story. What could I answer? What is said about us is often what we become.

"Why did you marry me?" I asked Grigóris, teasing, months later.

"Because you wouldn't let me lift your skirt until the wreath was on your head." He laughed and reached for me again, the third time that day. Ach, Grigóris!

Who can say? Maybe it *was* the thread.

The house of Sarrás was one of those overdone neo-classical things, built in the time before everyone started to settle for whitewashed cubes. It was made of wood, common then but rare now. There were two stories, and balconies off most rooms, some held up by copies of cary-atids from the Acropolis. When I drew the curtains and opened the windows onto the pines outside, the house was filled with light. It sat at the highest point in the village, just under the fortress, and had views over the roofs of the village houses and out to the sea beyond. I loved the garden with its lemon trees and oleanders. And the huge old parlor with its aging velvet curtains, chairs and sofa.

Around the walls ran molding in the shape of flowered garlands held aloft in the corners by plaster of paris cupids. A gigantic sentimental painting of a ship in harbor was hung on one wall. It wasn't an island house at all, but rather a place put together by merchants who had traveled and admired something here, something there, and each had added what he liked to the house left behind by the generation before.

The women of the family had sat in the parlor and offered candied fruit, coffee and cool water to visitors. And I, no longer a visitor, served the same to the island women who came to call on me. I enjoyed watching their eyes travel over the antique copper and brass trays that hung on the walls, the imported pottery on the mantel. I was of the House of Sarrás.

Shortly after we were married, I went with Grigóris to the mainland on a buying trip. I took him to the museum, for he had never been to one before and I wanted to show him where I had worked. He was like a boy as he wandered amazed among the glass cases where lay the gold death masks, the drinking cups with lions, the rings whose seals closed royal documents thousands of years ago.

"But Katína, who did all this belong to?" he asked, stunned.

"Kings and queens, warriors, priests . . ."

"Dead kings."

"Very dead."

I was filled with the sight of him, his eyes wide, the color of his face reflected in the gold mask of a king. He was as finely made as the statue of a libation bearer who held a jar for sacred oils in the next glass case.

I took Grigóris around to the offices where we met

some of the people who had been at the temple dig in the summer. It was good to see them all but I really hadn't missed them. There was a man at my old job in the dank basement office.

Later, on the ferry home, we stood on the rear deck in the wet wind, watching the gulls swoop and scream behind the boat. Grigóris was quiet for a while, and then he said, "Those kings, I can't stop thinking about them. Did they know that they would die but that the things buried with them would just go on? That the plates they ate off, even the chairs they sat on, would live longer than they would? Did they know that, Katína?"

The question (or was it the wind?) made me shiver suddenly. I stood close to him, my arm around his waist, and thought of the treasures brought out of the black earth. I had made my choice: the bearer of sacred oils beside me over the one in the museum. Already I was sure his child was inside me and, shivering, I suggested we return to the lounge. I had no answer to the question.

Amalía was born with open eyes. When the midwife held her up to me, Amalía looked startled, then angry. For months she screamed and waved tiny fists at me in rage. She will never forgive me for having borne her, I thought. She accepted care from me but only in her father's arms did she find comfort. It was for him that she was first to fling open her own arms.

"You see," Grigóris said to me, "she likes me better. Didn't I tell you? Who do you like?" he'd ask her, and she'd hug him. When older, she hid from me behind pieces of furniture and rushed to sink her tiny teeth into my ankle. She spoke a secret language for so long that we worried she would never make words we could understand. Lilliána examined her mouth and advised we give her silent water—that which has been drawn from a spring by a mute—to loosen her tongue. But we thought that probably Amalía had nothing she wanted to tell us yet.

One day as I was bathing her, Amalía stood up in the tub and said, "The water is too hot. Change it." Later the same week she hummed the opening three notes of Rachmaninoff's Prelude in C-sharp Minor. It had been playing on the radio the night before. After that she spoke in complete sentences and hummed music. She seemed to prefer Chopin.

Grigóris often took Amalía to the shop and sat her on the counter where she charmed customers by shrieking when old ladies pinched her cheeks. She pulled the beads from the hands of men and flung them to the floor. They only laughed.

"What a pretty child."

"May she live for you, Grigóris."

"Health to you, my child."

Amalía was the daughter of the House of Sarrás, the oldest on the island. The village shook its finger but always forgave her.

"Look, look!" she'd say, turning around and around as he came in the door from work. The radio was on; there were ribbons in her hair. "I made up a dance just for you."

"Ah, my little apple, my pomegranate." He'd lift her in the air. "I could eat you up like bread. Not a crumb would be left." She'd shriek and laugh and drag him off to her room to show him her dolls, share her secrets with him. He teased her, bought her necklaces and ribbons and countless dolls, then pretended not to notice her. She would act out a story with herself in all the roles and win back his attention. She seemed to have been born with a sense of men, a feeling for them. I had lost that to her along with the very edge of my spirit, leaving me, at the end of the day, too tired to draw Grigóris's attention away from Amalía, back to me.

I worked through the tasks of running the big house. There were sturdy village girls to help with the cleaning, the laundry, the preparations for feast days. I ran all day, it seemed. But everything got done; I could deal with chaos. I'd had practice. Everything had to be right to protect us from the jealousy and curiosity of others. The girls, I knew, reported all that they observed. Our deeds, our clothes, our food, and sometimes, I felt, our very thoughts must be in everyone's mouth. I worked harder than any village woman, I the outsider, that nothing might be said against the House of this man whose life was braided now with mine. But he often closed the shop at the busiest times, turning away business to come lie in the garden under the lemon tree while his daughter wove wildflowers through his hair.

Amalía was to be our only child. When, after a few years, no others came, I went to an Athenian specialist. That Amalía's birth had been difficult, he didn't have to tell me. But her birth had destroyed all possibility of others to follow.

Grigóris quickly changed toward both of us after I'd told him this news. Amalía was no longer his peach, his sweet plum. "Go play now," he'd say. "Get out of here. Go away. I'm tired." It became a circle. The more he pushed her away, the harder she tried to come close.

"Look, Papa, look!" She waved her drawings at him. "This one is of you. See how beautiful you are, Papa. Look at the big smile I made for you." He hardly glanced at them. He no longer took her to the shop and he came home after she was in bed.

"You're hurting the child," I said to him. "Why behave so?"

"Hurting? Such is the way of fathers and daughters. She must learn. What is a daughter? A dowry to be raised. A threat to the honor of our name until her wedding day. Pah! And when the earth has eaten my bones, what will be left of the name, of all I've worked for?"

"But what is ever left? The earth eats everything, good and bad name alike."

"Don't speak of it!" he shouted and went off to the taverna to meet his friends.

It was the idea of the Son that we all suffered from. In the shop I overheard a visitor to the island ask Grigóris if he had any children. "No," he said, "but there is a daughter." To him, as to all the island men, only sons counted. He was the last of his line. The name would die. Poor Amalía. Poor Grigóris. The absent Son crippled them both and I was in the middle, trying to comfort first one, then the other.

They pulled away from the house, from me, and turned to friends. Of all her schoolmates, Amalía was close only to little Maroula who had always followed her like a kitten. Where Amalía was willful and noisy, Maroula was silent, calm. Both were not the sons their fathers longed for. Maroula's father owned the village butcher shop and it was his wish for a son to work beside him that would eventually force Maroula into a marriage with a distant cousin. The shop was a poor one then in a time when few could afford the luxury of meat. Maroula worked there after school, the poor child, cleaning the counter with bloodied rags as she does even now; for she has become again a child. She was always the steady one, always quietly loyal to Amalía who taught her to take risks, to dare.

I used to find them naked in the garden, comparing their bodies behind the oleanders. Maroula wasn't much more than half Amalía's size though they were the same age. They decorated each other with flowers and weeds. I didn't mind until Amalía began to invite boys into the bushes. I sent them home and beat Amalía with a switch off the same bush. She screamed with anger and tore the bush to pieces. After that I could hardly look around without seeing the other oleanders tremble, without finding Amalía there with other partly undressed children, mostly boys. I cut down all the bushes so there was no place to hide.

I didn't tell Grigóris and he didn't even notice the change in the garden. He seemed to live in the shop and the taverna. I would lie in bed at night, sleeping and waking, and hear the music of the bouzouki, the shouts of the men. The noise crossed the village in the still night and I knew Grigóris was turning through clouds of smoke, a cigarette clamped in his teeth, leaping to slap his heel, bending to kick away the pieces of plates that others smashed at his feet in enthusiasm.

"I tell you, Katína," he said one morning after a long night, "some days I cannot stand it. I think I will drown myself. You know what I mean. Days when your whole life rises up and takes you by the throat. I drink wine and suddenly I am dancing. Throwing it all out, the anger and bad thoughts, so I can breathe again."

"But what anger? What bad thoughts?"

"I can't speak of it. Women can't understand."

He left the house. I couldn't comfort him for I didn't know what it was that made him hurt.

"Ach, Katína, they're all like that here," Lilliána told me. We were in her evil-smelling house at the edge of the village. Years of stale incense were in the air and candles burned everywhere. She had so many icons that you felt you had died and gone to meet the saints. But if the afterlife is like the inside of Lilliána's house, I think I'd as soon not have one.

"All the men here, they look for night devils to throw themselves at. Men eat them, swallow them. But then it is the devil's turn. He starts to eat the man, slowly, from the inside."

"But what are these devils?"

"I should know? Each man has his own." She picked at knots of her hair. "There is *Stringlos* whose hoarse voice cries out before someone dies. And the *lamías* that live in the bellies of boy children. Or the *kalkes* who steal fire and leave men cold and shivering inside. It's all because the men are thieves here."

"Thieves?"

All the old families came from thieves, she explained. They called themselves landowners or merchants, but they were nothing but thieves. Pirates washed onto the land, full of blood and seawater that would not drain into the soil.

"The earth rejects them. They have no home. Always they talk of their House. But they have no home."

"All that was long ago."

"You think time matters so? The night devils know nothing of time, of generations."

Whatever it was that ate away at the men here—the rivalries, the hatreds (devils of a kind)—they were deep and violent and marked one's House for all time. Someone moves a boundary stone a few inches onto his neighbor's land and the great-grandchildren of both families still suffer from the deed a hundred years after.

Danger comes not only from enemies, Mother taught me. There is jealousy in the admiration of neighbors and friends. Magic in wine can change dark thoughts into deeds. All this Mother knew when she talked of the *eye* to protect ourselves and those we love. Of course I think she might have laughed at Lilliána's night devils but she would have understood just the same. For she always taught me to respect the essential powers of the unknown.

"Don't worry about me and their devils," Lilliána said, heaving herself out of her chair. "There is nothing women can do about it. Even if we could rid Grigóris of his devil, he'd only find another to throw himself on. He is a man. Women may lie with devils but we don't search for them as men do. We know where they live; we can let them alone."

She sighed as she walked across the room. Out of her came a great blast of fish and onion odors. "It's Amalía you should worry about. She's not like the others."

"She's strong willed like her father."

"No, it's more than that, I tell you, Katína. You can't see it because you're too close. She could do anything."

"Amalía?"

"Yes. She's going to need protection, need your power.

When she's a woman, when it is the time of her leaving, sew something of your past into her clothes."

"But there is nothing left of my past."

"There is something. I know there is. You must find it."

"But why?"

"Because the stones say so. Come let us read them." She took a cardboard box down from the shelf. Inside were many small stones of the kind found along the shore. Most of them fit in the palm of the hand and stood for people in the village. "This one is you," she said. "Here, hold it." There were other stones that represented fates, mysteries. The box contained the world of the village, its good and its evil. She took back my stone, rolled it around in the box with the others, then cast them all on the floor.

"There see how the small stones of the sea spirits are grouped around the stone of your House. It is Amalía they protect. But they are not enough. I saw this yesterday in the stones also."

I remembered the notebook, the burned notebook I had carried out of the fire and I saw again the windows of our house where I had sat writing and looking out at the garden. The window. I remembered that view of orange trees and rose bushes and it seemed to me that I had been outside tapping at that window, trying to get back in all my life.

"What's that?" Lilliána asked. "Those dark stones all clumped together over to the side?" She knocked them apart with her stick. "Pah! They mean war."

"What is it, my child?" I asked Amalía that night. A night full of rain.

"I want to feel it," she said, dancing from room to room, touching the walls.

"Feel what? Come away from there. Here, cut some pictures out of these magazines." But off she'd go, up the stairs to the bedrooms then back down, sighing, laughing, sucking in her breath. It made me angry to see her so unafraid when lightning cracked above our heads as a storm rubbed itself against the great old house. I poured myself a brandy and when she waltzed again into the room I shouted, "Stop it! I won't have it. Stop it now!"

"But Mother, it's in all the walls. You can feel it, you can touch it."

"Touch what? Sit down before I have to make you."

"You can't." She laughed. "I'm part of it." And she danced out of my reach, out of the room again.

Poor child, I thought, it's all this nonsense at school that is making her crazy. Everyone said the students learned nothing anymore. They spent all day singing patriotic songs and learning to march and drill. It was all the fault of that dictator, Metaxas. He kept trying to drag Greece into his own idea of the modern age. He even tried to limit the number of goats in villages so he could reforest the hillsides. This is the kind of thing leaders worry about. And all the while the world rushing toward war. Well, if he takes Germany's side, we all said, then it will be time to get rid of him.

The problem with the insects and other creatures began at the time of the death of Grigóris. I was to find them—spiders, worms, crickets—in the pockets of Amalía's clothes. Some crushed, some still crawling. As if death alone were not enough, with it came this sign of its entrance into our lives. I was standing in the kitchen making a marketing list when I saw a green spider run across the floor and wondered how it had got into the house. Then came the pounding at the door.

Mad Manólis, the rubbish collector, stood there. Sometimes Grigóris used him as messenger and sent him to bring me to the shop if business was heavy. But not now during the winter rains when there were no visitors on the island. And Grigóris had left for the shop only half an hour before. Manólis has never been clear in the head and he can't speak when he gets excited. He could only gesture for me to come with him.

I followed him down the street, down the long steps to the beach where gray waves were booming after a storm the night before. Shutters opened as I passed and women looked out at me. Where was I going? they asked; what had happened? I said, "Am I to know?" and hurried on. At the café men stopped talking as I passed and came to the door. A group of women were waiting on the beach, talking quietly. They came forward to meet me, hands folded over aprons, saying nothing. There were schoolboys there too, crying, and the old doctor. I heard a voice say that the priest was coming. Someone is dead, I thought, but why did they come get me? And I knew the answer before the thought was even complete. They stepped back. Grigóris on the sand with the purple mark there at the side of his head. Dead from a stone no bigger than a child's fist.

The women shrieked and closed around me, clawing at their hair. Several people tried to explain. Boys fighting on the beach. Throwing stones. Grigóris dead. Later I was told that I tried to beat the head of one of the boys against a rock and it took three men to pull me off.

Ach, Grigóris! Bearer of sacred oils. Lifter of skirts. Eater of devils. Which devil was it that you swallowed who drove you onto the beach to break up a silly quarrel between schoolboys? The lost father in you? The good son of the House of Sarrás—a name you rightly said was all you'd ever own? An argument among three boys. Who knows what it was about? Some said sports; others said ownership of money lost, then found. Stones were thrown until you passed by and put yourself between the right and wrong of children. And left Amalía and me alone. I, the outsider, with no place on all the earth save this one where I will always be a stranger. Amalía not yet a woman, with no man to protect her from this sharp-toothed village. Oh, Grigóris, if like an ancient king you are outlived by water jars and chairs and cups, then I beg, beg you to take us with you.

But Grigóris had danced off, had been swallowed whole. I sent Amalía to Lilliána's house before the men lifted and carried him back to our house, where I washed that lean, long body with warm water and a soft sea sponge. I rubbed him with the piney cologne he bought whenever he went to Athens. Outside, the women crowded at the doors and windows, trying to get in, to help, they said, but really to touch the nakedness of the last male of the House of Sarrás. Only when I had finished dressing him carefully in his best suit did I open the door to the coffin maker, to the women who had brought tall candles. And when he was lying in the parlor among their flames, the village came and went all day and through the night, drinking wine and talking about the tomato crop—would it rot from all the rain? And which boy had thrown the stone

that mattered; how should he be punished? "Never tell
me his name," I said, "never tell me his name."

"A door closes," the women said.

"And another opens."

"The oil ran out in Grigóris's lamp."

"So it will be with us all."

"His House will be his memorial."

I am the House. Already I looked like the others in
my black dress. There is a place where they burn the widow
with her dead husband. Here they seal her alive in the
tomb that the House becomes.

Sleeping and waking. When I closed my eyes at night,
for many days I saw the stone that struck him down. I saw
it as Manólis threw it into the seaswell where it sank beneath a plume of water. I saw the whitewashed tomb, like
a tiny village house along the lane of cedars. The little
window in it with the oil lamp and the photo of Grigóris,
his shirt open, laughing in the sun. I lay with my hand
between my thighs and thought that never again would I
have the sleep that only Grigóris was able to bring me to.
Even if I kept the sanctity of his house, its secrets, its
business and raised his daughter and married her well and
wore black forever and kept my eyes lowered in the marketplace, even then I would never again draw from those
lean thighs the peace that only they could give me.

In the night came noises from the bathroom. I found
Amalía there, retching. In the toilet were the remains of
insects. Some had been swallowed whole.

"Why?" I asked her. "Why?" She said nothing but
sat on the floor trembling, looking so ill, her face white as
the tiles. I took her hand, pulled her up and held her for

a moment. "Go to bed, my child. We won't speak of it."

The next night I heard her creep downstairs and into the garden. She didn't come back for an hour. I lay there, aching for the weight of Grigóris, imagining Amalía putting insects in her mouth, tiny legs brushing the back of her throat, wings beating against the roof of her mouth. And then there was the retching but I didn't go to the bathroom.

The girls refused to do the laundry after one of them put her hand in the pocket of Amalía's school uniform. I went to see Lilliána, then followed Amalía downstairs the next night and stood beside the dark shape of the house while I watched her pluck crickets off the leaves of the lemon trees. Before she could get them to her mouth, I rushed out and slapped them from her hands.

"Hurry!" Lilliána had said. "Amalía is in danger. She's trying to swallow death, her father's death. Make her drink this."

"What is it?"

"Just take it to her."

Amalía tried to pull away from me. I nearly dropped the bottle and the mixture spilled across our nightgowns. I took hold of her hair, pulled her head back and poured some of the liquid into her mouth. She choked and gagged and I let go of her, then she spat the mixture at me.

"Let me be! Go away!"

I slapped her. "What is all this? Your father dead only a few days and already you're trying to kill me with this behavior." I held her head again and this time made sure that she swallowed some of the mixture. She tried to bring it up, but I held her tightly and half carried, half walked her to the house. "Let's hear no more of this before the memory of your father."

That night, fever set in. She called to her father in her sleep and tried to rub herself, as if she were dirty or had something crawling on her. She awoke in a dream of spiders. When at last the fever ran out of her, covering her body with sweat, I held her to me. And then she slept.

We began to live together more smoothly after that night. There were the two of us in the big house. We still argued; we still fought. But I found no more insects. Why did she swallow them? I was never to know. We didn't talk about it or of Lilliána's liquid that I felt sure had brought on the fever. The fact that I did not understand all this became itself a kind of insect that I had swallowed, one whose legs and wings fluttered alive whenever Amalía willed them to.

"What was in that bottle of liquid you gave me for Amalía that night?" I asked Lilliána later.

"Liquid? What do you mean?"

"The liquid that brought on the fever."

"I know of no liquids with such powers. That fever was the passing over of death."

There were many storms in the winters to follow. The house stood groaning and complaining beneath the pines. The years turned slowly, as the pines held their branches stiffly as if war had never come and cities never fallen. Metaxas finally stood up for us—his finest hour—when he said, "No!" to Mussolini and briefly held him back at the Albanian border. But the Italians and their German friends came anyway.

Troopships passed our island in the night but seldom entered our little harbor. The larger island groups—the Dodecanese and the Cyclades—got most of the enemy attention. But there are so many islands scattered through the sea like fish. How could they catch us all? We're so tiny and so far from Athens. What use would we have been to them? No one came to occupy us and no ferryboats visited us. We were cut off from the world. Fishermen still went out but not far and when they returned they said the sea was deserted. Only in the night did we see lighted portholes passing. A boy swam out to a ship, hoping they would pull him aboard and give him a uniform. But his body washed up on the beach a few days later, half-eaten by fish.

The War and enemy occupation left the mainland and larger islands in a state of ruin. Greeks fighting Greeks for control after the War further decimated even larger segments of the population. We heard of starvation, reprisals, the disruption of all communication and transport systems. I think Greeks killed far more Greeks on the mainland in those years than the Germans and Italians had managed to kill during the War.

How can a country learn to live with itself and the world after such horrors? But there is no alternative. Just as here on the island no fisherman may go to sea in a boat alone. So a village Communist and a village monarchist may have to row out together. Each will silently toss a net from his end of the boat, as if he were alone. But, as everyone here says, under the water the fish don't know one net from the other. They feed us all.

We could supply most of our own needs. There was mutton and there were vegetables. The grape and olive harvests were good. The shop's big storeroom was filled with barrels of flour and beans, salted fish, candles and kerosene. I became a merchant and stood in Grigóris's place behind the counter, scooping beans, weighing sheep butter, measuring cloth. This was not the way Grigóris's ancestors would have liked to see a woman of their House, I knew. But these were strange times, calling for strange deeds. I sold and traded, then gave the rest away. And so we lived. They hated me the more for my generosity. Weekly I made my way to the lane under the cypress trees and refilled the oil in the lamp of Grigóris's tomb, nodding to the other widows. All of them watching me and each other for a clue that all desires had not been buried with the dead.

Outside the house the boys were beginning to collect, hoping to get Amalía and Maroula's attention. They kicked balls in the street, chasing one another, shouting. In trousers tight as skin and in half-buttoned shirts, they waited for the honor of being ignored by the girls. Andréas, Takis and Nikos, always Nikos, with his hungry eyes.

But Amalía and Maroula lived in books, my old books of history, art. They spoke a secret language of foreign words and phrases all mixed together, which they had learned from language texts ordered through the mail back when the ferry still ran. Amalía's English was very good; in fact she seemed good at languages in general. And she, like Maroula, was turning into a woman beneath her cotton dress. There were still days of boyish running and tree climbing. But they had begun to leave them behind.

"Amalía is not like the others," Lilliána warned. But fewer were the days that Lilliána left her house to say anything at all. Suddenly she was old. She had always been, it seemed, at the same impossible-to-guess age. But almost overnight her face grew as lined as an old road map and her mind became cloudy, confused. Not many went to her for cures and advice. She mixed everything together, muttering about stream spirits and black dogs while prodding the stones around her floor. I brought her food when I could. "The sea lifts and falls, Katína," she'd say.

The fig tree beside our house grew taller and tapped at our windows as if asking to come in. The house too, complaining of its years, tried to tell us its tales and if Amalía understood, she did not tell me. I looked at the walls and thought, For all their years, how weak they and all walls are. How quickly they could burn, sending us into the night. For in fact we are naked, backed into our houses, waiting for soldiers to free us with their torches. But soldiers were never to come.

After the War, the fishermen heard there was lots of dynamite to be had cheap. All they had to do was toss it lighted into the sea and up would shoot a fountain of stunned fish—more than a week's catch for the nets. Then they just scooped the fish into their boats. For a year or so the sea exploded everywhere you looked. And so the seabed around the island came to be destroyed and fish no longer came to feed, except those who found the many arms and legs of fishermen waving gently like seaweed among the rocks below.

Fishermen were driven back to the land where the tomato fields and factory awaited any man wounded by the sea. The old factory had been part of the dowry that came to Spyros at the time Grigóris and I were married. Spyros hadn't lived here for years and the old building was deserted. But at the time of the dynamite he sent workers and managers to replant the tomato fields, to install machinery for the canning of tomato paste. Most of the men of the island came to work for him. They bent in the fields or grasped a machine control with the one good hand. Clever Spyros.

The island grew richer. There were more ferries and bigger boats too, carrying away the crates of tomato paste. Business at the shop was good and I also had a manager now. Never again would I stand behind the counter weighing beans, measuring cloth.

When I told Lilliána (who spent more days in bed than out) of the changes in the village, she said, "What is this to me?" and turned her face to the wall.

"How good of Amalía to show our island to the foreigner," the old woman said. I had gone to the shop to look over the books, check on the supplies and make sure my manager knew I was watching over his shoulder. Supervising others can take more out of you than doing the work yourself. I always tried to escape before the women poured their poison in my ear. But this time I was too slow.

"Foreigner?" I said. "What foreigner?"

"The yellow-haired one," another said.

"Who is he?" they all asked. "Why is he here?"

"Am I to know? I haven't seen him."

"But *you* came here from outside. We thought you would know."

They never let me forget (as if I could) that I am not of this place. They think everyone in the outside world knows each other. And I am held responsible for those few who step off the ferry here.

"You could ask Amalía. She would know about him."

"They say she goes to his tent up in the old fortress."

"Who says this?" I asked.

"Who?" each asked the other. "Who? Who?" Like

owls, they passed the word back and forth. A name was mentioned, then denied, then another, no, not that one, well someone, anyone.

"Mad Manólis saw them when he was taking the garbage up on his donkey," one said finally. "They were picking flowers."

"He picks hers," another giggled, "and she picks his."

That night Amalía turned from the mirror where she was brushing her hair. "What do I have to say about *what?*" It was just past her seventeenth name day then. Her figure was slender though her breasts were full under her white nightgown. She still seemed far from being a woman to me. She loved to run in the tall grass at the edge of the village, gather lemons from the top branch of the tree in the garden or play with an old mongrel dog, laughing, always laughing. But already I had stopped seeing her as she was.

"You know what I mean. Have you forgotten that you're of the House of Sarrás?"

She laughed lightly and said, "But I don't know what you're saying, Mother." She looked me in the eye as she spoke. She has much to learn, I thought. The obvious cover for a lie is the straight stare. "I would not shame my father's House."

"So you say, yet this is not what I am to understand. Your name is in everyone's mouth."

She went on brushing her hair, facing me now. "But that's always so. If not mine, someone else's. Don't worry, Mother. Did you see the moon tonight? How it makes the sea silver, as if the light came from under the water?"

"The moon? You speak of the moon? It's you whose name lights up the village tonight."

"Why speak of it?" She sat down on the edge of the bed. "Others have whispered in your ear and you have believed them."

"Ach! What a child I'm blessed with. You wait for me to make the first move as if we were bargaining for a donkey." Amalía looked around the walls of her room as if to find strength in the pictures of gods she had pinned there. Among them was the framed piece of embroidery I had given her—the *Tselapétina*, folkloric bird in the island pottery designs. She had always been more interested in gods of myth and folklore than in the Byzantine Christ who glared down from the dome of the church.

"Everyone says that strangers—foreigners too—are sacred," she said, turning back from her gods. "At least that's what people used to believe long ago. That we should welcome strangers as we hope they'd welcome us in their own land."

"So you do know what I'm saying."

"Then they'll carry away the good name of the island."

"Ach! So now I must give my daughter to anyone passing through. How generous I am. And I didn't even know it."

"Stop it, Mother. You know what I mean."

"Stop it? What words are these for you to use?" I crossed to her and took her by the shoulders. "Tell me what is happening and tell me fast. What do you think it is like for me to hear about my own daughter in your father's shop. Now! I want to know now. Is it true that you have gone with him to his tent?"

"Don't shake me, please don't. Yes, I go. But not as you think."

"Holy Mother of God."

"It's not as you think," she said. "Oh, what's the use of speaking of it? Look." She took my hands from her shoulders, holding them. "He's my friend. He's gentle. He wouldn't hurt anything. He's not like the boys here who throw a cat in the water and laugh to see it drown."

"I ask if you go to his tent and you tell me about animals. Am I a doctor of donkeys that I need to know this?"

"I like him, don't you see? That's why I go. I look through his books, his photographs. Oh, he's been everywhere, Mother. You should see some of the photographs. He writes songs about the places he's visited and he plays the guitar. It's also good to have someone to practice my English on. We don't always understand what the other is saying but usually we work it out."

"You can't get him out of your head, is that it?"

"Well, yes."

"As if there's no taste in your mouth anymore?"

"Like that." She laughed. "Oh, some of the places he's been! Where there are temples whose bells ring out across lakes full of fish as gold as sovereigns. Such wonderful places."

"Goldfish. My God. Now listen to what I'm going to tell you, Amalía." I explained that strangers come to Greece because they can live cheaply here. They like to take photographs of us because they think we're picturesque. We're all the same to them. We are charming, part of the charming landscape. Young men want to see the world and try the young women in it. But they would not like to meet us in their homes. Except, of course, when they need workers for their factories because they haven't enough men of their own, because many were killed off

74

in their War. They don't understand the customs here, what it means for a man to walk with an unmarried woman. "But you understand these things. Still you ruin your name in every good house on the island. Soon no one will respect you; no one will receive you. And he? He'll just move on to the next place. Or go home."

She didn't care now but later she would, I told her. I hadn't when I first came here. They would make her care, I assured Amalía. There are no friendships here between unmarried men and women. If she wanted to leave, if she wanted to go to the mainland to study languages, I'd see what we could do. "But until we make some decisions, don't slam doors shut here. Go slowly. Be cautious."

"I hate slowness. I hate caution." She let go of my hands. "I hate things that are halfway and careful."

"I'll have to ask you to stay in the house until he leaves the island. Go straight to school and come straight home again."

"But I have to help him. I translate for him. He doesn't know as much of our language as I know of his. How will he buy his food?"

"And who helped him in all these other places? The goldfish? It sounds as if he can get along on his own."

"I have to see him. I have to."

"Don't make me angry. I don't care about my own name here. But we live in your father's house and I won't have you shaming him. Or yourself. You'll behave as a daughter of this house is expected to behave. Why, do you know this stranger has been seen at the beach without any clothes on? Children, the priest, old women, they've all seen him."

"There's nothing wrong with it."

"Maybe not in northern countries where people are used to such things. But people here don't understand— and he should know that if he has traveled so much."

"He wants to free people from such ideas."

"Mother of God. One of those. And he's trying to free you too, is he? What does go on in that tent?"

"He plays the guitar or we talk. About life and death."

"And what do you know of either of them?"

"I know something of death." She looked at me hard. The legs of the insect kicked inside me. The wings beat against the back of my throat. "And a little of life, maybe nothing, I don't know. But it's good to talk to him. I can't talk to anyone else that way."

"And that's all?"

"What do you want to hear? We do ancient rituals naked while throwing babies over the fortress wall?"

"That's enough! Remember what I said. You're not to see him again."

"I'll see him if I want to."

She picked up the hairbrush from the bed and began to brush her long hair hard. I turned toward the door.

"See him again and you'll wish your father were here to show you mercy."

She threw the hairbrush at the wall where it grazed the head of the *Tselapétina*.

"Throw what you like. Remember what I said."

But it was never any use trying to cross Amalía or to talk sensibly to her. She has a will, that one. She'll take any risk, dare any dare for the object on which her whole person has fixed. There's something pure in that, I suppose. But try to live with it. It was no easier than living with Grigóris and his devils. Amalía is her father's daughter, no matter how much her father would have liked a son instead. The strength, the defiance—they are the same in both. Beatings didn't really help me control her much, though I gave her enough of them, thanks to God.

"Katína! My Katína!"

"Spyro! Mother of God!"

There he was at the door the next day, after years away from us. How well he looked—taller it seemed, but probably just because he was now more spare. Gone was that muscular field-hand look he'd had when Grigóris and I married. A full mustache, well tended hands. His clothes were carefully cut of the fashion I had seen only in foreign magazines. We had had news of him—now in Athens, now in other capitals, setting up markets for his tomato paste. It was a new world, a post-War world, and America had bought its way into our lives through the Truman Doctrine. We didn't know then that all that aid would turn into a knife at our throats. Businessmen like Spyros had opportunities and this seemed good for everyone. Occasionally he came here for Easter or another feast day. But I had not really talked with him these many years, not since he had left the island after his wife died. I knew he was back. Who couldn't have heard! Spyros on his gray horse, riding through the tomato fields while workers called out to him. Who could have imagined our Spyros riding a horse, so trim, so carefully dressed? Spyros who had stood in Grigóris's shop lending the price of a donkey to anyone who asked.

"*How* well you look," I said as we came into the parlor.

"And you, Katína, and you." He was being polite, for the truth was that I'd gained weight with the years. Oh, not an enormous amount, but enough, you know. I could still turn men's heads when I walked to market. But these island men, they like women with something to hang on to.

"What has happened to you? Can you be the same Spyros who left us for Athens?"

"Yes, yes, Katína. Don't be fooled. My toes still stick out of my socks." He laughed his old booming laugh.

"Thanks to God. At least you still laugh like an earthquake. What of your life? The village never sees you anymore."

"What is there to say? I run and run and never have time left to sit and talk with friends. As you know, the factory gets bigger. We're sending the tins all over the world now. Everyone knows the name of our island. Thanks to God, it all goes well."

"Very well, to hear the talk."

"What do they say?"

"That you've changed the life of the island, given everyone work."

"And are they happy with all this that has happened?"

"Well, they have money now. You know how it is. They don't have to look to the sea for their sovereigns. About happiness, who can say? But tell me what you've done with the years!"

He laughed again. "What they have done to me, you mean."

"They've made you rich, I hear."

"Ach, I too do not have to look to the sea, as you say, the way my father did and his father before him." Spyros had found men he could trust to run his central office in Athens so he could return here. He hadn't wanted to come back for a long time. After his wife, Froso, died, may the earth rest lightly on her bones, the taste for this place left his mouth. And he had certain investments to protect. "They were difficult years, yes? But we have all survived, eh? It is not good to be away from the place of your people so long. It calls you back, the place of your birth."

"Does it? Mine doesn't."

"My poor Katína. What can I say? There is another from Smyrna in my office in Athens. Always he seems to be alone, even with friends."

"Yes, I'm sure. I knew others, of course, when I worked at the museum. But we avoided one another. The only thing to hold us together was our memory of what had happened. Together we called that memory to life. So we never saw each other. But of course it is different for you—you were only in Athens. And anyway now you are back. Grigóris would be so pleased."

"Yes, yes." He smiled down at the floor. "I wish he were here to see it all. Our Mr. President. Remember how he danced? Ach, how he danced! It hurts to remember."

"Yes."

"You know I always hoped one day we'd be partners, work together. He was my brother."

"He loved you very much."

"And I him. How is business with his shop?"

"Oh, good, thanks to God," I lied. "Of course we have some competition now that other shops have opened. But never mind. It's good for us."

In truth the business was not so good. I knew my manager cheated me. The books weren't kept properly; supplies were not reordered promptly. When I shouted at the manager, he jumped and ran and did what I asked.

But I knew the minute I left the shop he relaxed, ordered another coffee from the café, and did as he liked. And then I had given away so much of our stock during the bad times when no one had money. It would take a long time to make up those losses. Amalía and I weren't starving. But I had to cash in a gold sovereign from time to time to make up for the shop's losses. I didn't want to tell Spyros any of that. It would have embarrassed Grigóris. Spyros probably knew anyway. There are few secrets in village business.

"And so," he said in a voice to change the subject, "you have put your mourning clothes aside."

"Yes, I wore them three years of the time Grigóris has been gone, may the earth rest lightly on his bones."

"So I've heard. Two years longer than customary."

"No longer than he deserved. And most widows here wear black all their lives."

"But you are still young. May you live many years."

"And you." We lifted our glasses and drank, then spoke of other things. Of Amalía. "She grows up while we grow old."

Spyros had no children. After the death of his wife, he had put all his spirit into business. "Investments, you know, dull things, loans, stocks." He waved them away as if they were nothing. But now he had plans for the island. He hoped to build a chapel to Saint Spyridon, his patron saint. There were roads to be repaired and he was working with engineers on a plan for a new harbor where freighters could dock to load cases of tomato paste and unload machinery needed in factories and fields. No longer would he have to deal with our little irregular ferry. I poured out more brandy as we talked. By the time he rose to leave, I was glowing and felt dizzy. As we stood at the door wishing each other health, he quickly slipped a hand behind me, grabbed a fold of flesh on my bottom and squeezed. He was out the door before I could say anything.

As bad as Grigóris! No wonder they had been such friends. At least, I thought, under that new manner and fine clothes, he's still Spyros. But with all that brandy, all I could do was laugh as I went to the kitchen to make coffee.

I didn't laugh a few nights later when he knocked at the kitchen door. To come alone to a widow's house at night when anyone might see him! "How can you do this?"

"I thought you might have a walk with me."

"A walk? At night? You've been away from the island too long. These are the ways of the mainland. Perhaps you had better walk there." I started to close the door.

"I mean no offense." He spoke softly. "We can take the path down to the sea. I've just come that way. There's no one there."

I said nothing. I was angry that he would act this way, as if he had rights. But the idea gave me a secret little pleasure. The suggestion was really modest, I told myself. It would be silly to refuse.

"Come." He held out his hand.

We took the back way out of the village and didn't meet anyone. The trees and weeds were full of singing insects. Now we'll see what he has on his mind, I thought; but he didn't say anything. We walked on in silence until we could hear the sighing of the sea at the shore below.

"If you've brought me to look at the moon on the

water," I said, impatient to see what this was all about, "it's lovely. But I must get back before Amalía finds that I'm gone."

He touched my arm and said quickly, dryly, "Katína, your needs are different from those of a dead man." Ho, ho. As I expected. "Grigóris has been gone, may the earth rest lightly on him, these five years now. You loved him; I loved him. But now it's time to think of yourself and Amalía. Do you know what they are saying about her in the village? Her good name will be ruined if she continues to behave in this way. And then who will she marry? You both need a man to manage things for you. This problem with the foreigner. It would never have happened in a house with a man."

I hadn't expected the conversation to turn to Amalía. But even if Spyros were right, it was not his place to say so. He was not of our House. "Don't talk stupidities. You know how it is here. They eat any good name they can."

"Believe what you like, Katína. But know that there is talk, angry talk. I have heard it from men in the fields and factory. If the foreigner does not leave soon, there will be trouble for him."

"Trouble? What trouble?"

"I don't know. But our island men do not like this, a foreigner coming here, going everywhere with one of our girls."

"What is it to them? Amalía is of the House of Sarrás. Who are they even to speak of her? Do you give them so little to do that they have time to make up poisonous lies about my Amalía?"

"Katína, I'm only telling you what's going on."

"I was like a foreigner when I first came here. I went everywhere with Grigóris. It's the same."

"Come, Katína. It's not the same at all, as I'm sure you know. Grigóris was a man, a man of our oldest House. And you were not an island girl. Amalía *is* an island girl and this boy, who is he? A tourist in dirty clothes taking snapshots. He lies on the beach with no bathing suit—here where the old people have been married most of their lives without seeing each other completely naked. The island is insulted by such behavior. Island people have their ways and they are proud."

"I *know* their ways, thank you." We walked on in silence. I wanted to say more but I would have had to repeat Amalía's own excuses. And anyway, what was all this to Spyros? Where was this conversation going?

"I know I've made you angry, Katína," he said as if he were speaking to the olive grove we were passing. "But I ask that you listen to all I have to say, that's all. The shop. It's not going well. No, don't tell me it's not true. I understand these things. This should not be your problem. Let me help. How would Grigóris feel to see the work of his family like this? Fire your manager. I'll get you another. I'll put money into the place and we'll drive these new shops off the island. There are better things for you to do than to worry about how many bags of beans you've sold this week, eh? Or who has his hand in the cash drawer. Ach, I can see from your face that I'm saying all this wrong. Come, don't be angry. I am a simple man. I can run a factory, send my tomatoes around the world—but I don't know how to say things. You understand."

"No, Spyro, I don't think I do." I stopped and turned

to face him. "Just what is it you want? Me? Grigóris's business? You ask how he would feel to see the family shop today. Well, how would he feel to know that you are in his business—that's the question. You two may have been like brothers but you were never partners. And did you think that you'd have both me and the business?"

"Be my wife. That's what I want."

There was a pause. Then suddenly I was laughing. We started to walk back. "Oh, come on, Spyro. You don't have to marry me just because you want Grigóris's shop. Surely that's a bad bargain, even for an old moneylender like yourself."

"I ask you not to insult me."

"And will you please drop that tone. As if you were at a funeral instead of proposing marriage. No, Spyro, I won't marry you. I thank you—but no. What do I need another husband for? Someone telling me what to do. Under my feet all the time. Rushing off to brood over secret sorrows. Ach! No. Men are fine when you need them. And that, I think, to be honest, is in bed. I didn't miss that little squeeze you gave me the other day. But as for marriage or business, no, these are other matters."

At first he didn't say anything but then slowly he began to laugh. He got louder and louder.

"Shhh! Just ahead is the priest's house. Do you want Panayóta, that vixen of a priest's wife, to hear us?"

"Katína, Katína, you are wonderful. I think I've always loved you." He pulled me to him, held me strongly in his arms. "It's you I want, only you."

"Don't lie to me." I was half suffocating, half laughing in his embrace. "What you mean is that you're willing to start with me and maybe you'll get the business later."

"How can you think this?"

"How can I not, you old moneylender? You've always wanted whatever Grigóris had. And he felt the same about you. If it were you lying in the earth today under the cypress trees, he'd be trying to get your tomato fields."

"You insult us both."

"You like it."

We pulled apart and continued our walk. "Think about it, Katína, please. And we'll talk again. But think *this*, Katína. You are alone. I am alone. Before the new generation comes and shovels us into our graves, let's comfort each other a little, eh?"

Back in my kitchen I sat over my coffee and thought, Pah, men and their schemes. As if women were not watching, listening. Poor Spyros. All that money, the fields, the factory and still he wasn't content. I'd always liked him but there's no better way to get to dislike someone than to marry him. I came to love Grigóris though there were times I didn't like him at all. No one could say I hadn't tried to honor his name: running the shop and keeping the sanctity of his house all those years as he would have liked it, wearing scratchy black dresses and telling myself to stop, stop wanting. Not that I didn't have chances—a widow with a shop, a big house. But who was there to choose from here?

I wouldn't mind having someone to laugh with. Grigóris always got angry when I laughed. "But it's funny," I'd say. "Don't you think the positions are funny?" He didn't. Next to love, I like laughter best.

There was a noise on the stairs. I went into the front hall just in time to see Amalía making her way carefully down the steps with a laundry bag held in front of her. She stopped midway.

"I thought you were out," she said.

"I'm back." We looked at each other for a long minute.

"I'm leaving."

"So I see. With the laundry."

"Don't. I haven't got a suitcase because I've never been anywhere."

"Will you tell me where you're going?"

"No."

"I think you'd better. At such an hour."

"I left you a note upstairs."

"Save me the trouble of reading it."

"I'll be back. But I don't know when."

"That's all it says? It doesn't say where you're going or what you'll do for money or who you're leaving with? You *are* leaving with someone, aren't you?"

"Good-bye, Mother." She came down the rest of the steps and started past me. Her eyes were steady, decided. She had given herself up completely to this leaving, its drama.

But she knows nothing, I thought, nothing about anything. And there's no ferry until tomorrow morning. They'll come down from the fortress together, walk down through the village to the harbor with everyone watching. There would be trouble, Spyros had said. I caught her arm.

"Mother of God! Don't you understand? They'll hurt him if you try to leave with him."

"Let go of my arm."

"No, you'll go nowhere tonight. I warned you not to shame this house. Your acts are not just your own. You carry a history with you."

She turned to me and said calmly, "You'll die one day, you know. Just like Papa. But I'll still be alive and that's when I'll come back here. I'll eat off your plates and sit on your chairs."

I hit her with my free hand. Her face, her ears, her arms. I raised and lowered my hand, flesh smacking flesh. I don't know how long it went on or when she dropped the laundry bag to the floor to cover her face with her hands that I slapped away. I was far heavier and stronger than Amalía. She never made it to the door. I pulled her up the stairs, hitting her hard, as she screamed, and forced her into her room where I turned the key that had lain untouched in the lock for years.

We spent the night together on either side of the door. She shouted words at me that I had never thought she could know. For a long time I stood, then I sat on the floor in the hall, empty, exhausted, all my strength gone. She talked through the keyhole.

"Mad Manólis was the first. I was thirteen and was up at the fortress picking poppies when he came along with his donkey and the rubbish baskets. He saw me there alone, came over to me, and opened his trousers. You should have seen, mother. Like a chair leg. Remember that spring when there were so many poppies? I kept bringing them home day after day. Remember?

"Old Petros—the fisherman that died last year. He used to mend nets over in the third cove where Maroula and I swim sometimes. One day he caught us without our bathing suits. Maroula was frightened, took her clothes and ran off. I stayed. Such a strong man, even though he was old. He bent me over one of those bundles of nets and tried to stuff a handkerchief in my mouth but I spat it out and said, 'It's all right, I won't scream—' "

"Stop! Stop it now."

"This is *my* history. Open the door, Mother. Let me go."

"Who knows? Who knows of these things?"

"It's nothing to me, nothing."

"Mother of God."

There were more such stories, more pleading for release. Then silence. To remain locked in the room that night was her punishment. To stay on the other side of the door was mine.

Oh, Grigóris, I thought, falling asleep, how could you leave me all these years among strangers? Spyros was right. All this would not have happened with a man there. But it's too late. Now all a man can bring me is laughter. You would not deny me that, my bearer of sacred oils? Ach, of course you would, old jealous-hearted one. To the Devil with you then.

When Amalía came out of her room she acted as if nothing unusual had happened. I had unlocked her door to bring her some breakfast, for it was day and, as my parents used to say, in the day deeds of the night are forgiven. We had to go on with our lives here in this house together if we were to face our hard-jawed neighbors.

I expected to see her with swollen eyes, crumpled dress. But when I opened the door she was sitting by the window reading a book. Her hair was neatly brushed, her face smooth, without emotion, and she wore a fresh dress. As I stood with a tray in my hands she said, "Good morn-

ing, Mother," addressing me in the plural as if I were a
visitor. "Thank you for the tray." She took it from my
hands, put it on the bureau, then went down the hall to
the bathroom.

What did it mean? From her window had she seen the
flames jump over the fortress wall? For when I had awakened on the hall floor in the early light, I had heard women
talking in the street below. I went downstairs to listen and
understood that the foreigner's tent had been burned in
the night. He was gone.

"Who did this?" I asked, standing on the front step.
"Who set the fire?"

"Are we to know?" one said.

"Some know," said others.

"Men from the tomato fields, they know."

"Nikos and his friends, they know."

"What they did was right. It was time for him to leave."

"He was too long in this place."

When Amalía came back from the bathroom, I started
to tell her what I had heard. But she looked at me as I
opened my mouth to speak and something in her eyes said
Don't. It was a look I was to see often after that. There
was an air of distraction about her, as if she stood apart
from the life around her. She walked around the village,
around the countryside, as if looking for something not to
be found. She would hurry into a room then stop, remain
fixed, as if looking at something no one else could see.
There were times when I looked in her eyes and felt I did
not know what a human being was.

Her presence was so fierce that even the girls who
helped in the kitchen and the laundry fell silent when

Amalía was near, though before they had joked and shared secrets. I did not go into her room often for I was afraid to find it swarming with insects.

Men from the tomato fields and factory had not burned the foreigner's tent, Spyros said. He had questioned his managers one by one. But then how could they know the actions of each man in the village? Perhaps they had done it, perhaps not.

"Ugly," Spyros said the next time he came to the kitchen door late at night. "All of this ugly. It is a black mark on the good name of our island. Our tradition is to be hospitable. I was afraid this would happen, but it is ugly."

"It's not a tradition I noticed when I first came here as a stranger. If I hadn't been able to draw their pictures, I think they would all have lined up with stones."

"How you exaggerate, Katína."

"How you forget, Spyro. You can't see it because you are of this place. They've never been hospitable here. Never."

"It's not true." His voice rose. "You don't understand. You expect too much of these people."

"These hospitable people of yours burned the personal property of a visitor and drove him away. I am glad Amalía is free of this foolish foreigner. But that does not make the deed a good one."

"Did I say it was good? Ugly, that's what it was. But it was your foreign ways—not being strong with your daughter as you should have been—that caused all this to happen."

So there again, we came to his same point: a House without a man to protect it is a house without a roof, exposed to every danger. I didn't tell him of Amalía's confessions—he would have used them to prove his point. But I came to depend on his advice, even if I disagreed, and to enjoy our arguments. It was good to have this strong force to fight against. The struggle sharpened each day, made me feel as if I'd been asleep for years.

It was not easy for us to see each other. I would see him from a distance, talking in the harbor with engineers holding blueprints. He rode his horse past the marketplace on the way to the tomato fields. Children ran behind; dogs barked. Everyone looked up to watch him pass. I laughed to myself at what a boy he still was, eager to impress, to be the most important man in the village.

His was the old family house at the edge of the village. He was enlarging it, making it more modern, planting the garden with fruit trees. He had asked the women of the island to advise him, pretending to know little of houses and gardens. They swarmed through his house, licking every corner, as they say. Shrieking that he must do this, not that, arguing with each other, bringing him cuttings for the garden. In this way the women got used to seeing others going in and out of his house and thought little of it.

"They want my house to be better than yours. You should hear what they tell me." We were sitting on packing crates in his parlor. Spyros took out his handkerchief and pulled it over his head, holding the corners under his chin. He wrinkled his face like an old woman—an old woman with a graying mustache. "Lemon trees!" he shrieked, poking his finger at me. "You must have lemon trees and pomegranates and pears in the garden, Mr. Galánis. Mrs. Sarrás has these, did you know? The best in the village.

But yours, hee hee, will be better. And this new window you're putting in . . ." He walked to the wall, bent over, and drummed his fingers on it. "Here it must go, with a view to the east. The parlor window in the house of Sarrás faces so. Is the house of Galánis to have less of a view?"

He was the old Spyros then, the Spyros who used to drag Grigóris away from work and off to Athens. He reminded me of how we both were in those days when I had just arrived here. I laughed and said, "What I like best, Grandmother, is your sweet mustache."

He rubbed his mustache as he took the handkerchief from his head. "And what *I* like is hearing you laugh. It doesn't happen so often. You don't have much to do with joy anymore."

"Pah. It is joy that has little to do with me."

It was afternoon when the rest of the village slept. Dust lay heavy on the roads and not even a chicken stirred. Later, upstairs the bedroom shutters were closed against the heat but where a slat was broken a stripe of sun came through and rested on the hairs of his arm where it lay thrown back across the pillow.

"You know," he said, taking my face in his hands, "you only have to say it, only one word, and before the whole village I will stand and take you as my wife. Only a word, Katína."

Carnival was coming. Wooden chests were opened and costumes aired from the branches of lemon trees in courtyards. From the schoolyard came the strains of the old songs of the island on the record player while Amalía and the games mistress led the girls through their dance. Each year on the last weekend before the beginning of Lent, the young people danced. First the boys at night in their goat-skin masks and later the girls in traditional island costumes.

The celebration is pagan, but no one here knows that. Its origins have long been forgotten or taken in by the Church. But under the thin Church blessing, you can still hear distant wailing of the pipes of Pan, still feel the earth tremble under the feet of masked dancers. In ancient times the island was known for its fine goats. Perhaps it was then the custom began of skinning newborn kids to make the frightening masks the young men wear for the goat dance. At the end of winter, a dance to spring, to good crops, to the birth of children. It is a dance to stir seeds in the moist earth.

The young men turn themselves into beasts. Sheep-skins are wrapped around their bodies and harnesses of bells placed on their shoulders. They dance through the streets once each year, their eyes peering through the goat-skin masks, bells on harnesses clanging. Later the girls put on the dresses passed along by mothers or grandmothers and make their way to the square.

I had no dress for Amalía as I was not of this place. But years ago we had repaired one that belonged to Grigóris's mother. A long gown, deep red with an embroidered panel down the front. Across the top were strung chains of coins in imitation of the old way of displaying dowries. Grigóris's mother had once danced across the square in it and Grigóris's father had seen her and wanted her. He asked his father to speak to her father to begin the talks that ended with an exchange of wreaths in the village church.

It was to be Amalía's last year to lead the dancers, as she had done every year for so many. She was the best dancer in the school but soon she would finish with the years of classes. Next Carnival another girl would raise and lower the scarf in front of her face as the line of dancers moved across the square beneath the eucalyptus trees.

"This year someone will ask for Amalía," Spyros said. "Wait, you will see. I am sure of it." It was not the first year I had opened the door to find a father on the step. Each year Amalía had danced, someone had asked for her. I drank coffee with each father in the parlor, talked of crops and weather, of fishing and seasons and finally of our children, our plans for them. But to each I said the same: She is too young. Her father would not have wished it so. And each in turn said he would come another year. As you wish, I told them all but I encouraged none.

After each I went to Amalía and asked, What do you think of his son? This one has two fields and a donkey, that one a house and thirty olive trees.

This one is foolish, she said, that one too short with a scar on his face. We often sat on her bed and laughed as she described the son of a father I had just entertained gravely in the parlor. "He talks like this, Mother." She'd put her tongue between her teeth and lips: "Thweet Amalía, will you walk with me bethide thee?" She could imitate anyone and get me to giggle. I told her stories of the young men I had known when I worked for the museum. One had recited nationalistic poetry. "O Motherland, to thy breast we press our lips." There was the way he looked at my tightly buttoned blouse as he recited.

Amalía and I would laugh so much that anyone coming into the room would have taken us for a couple of schoolgirls. "You don't have to take any of them yet, you know. You have land, this house, gold sovereigns. It's not as if

you're shoeless and must take anyone who comes along."
She didn't want to think about it then. Well, she is only
a girl, I thought. Ach—that's how much I knew. All this
was before the stranger came and left. After the night we
spent on either side of her door, there was no more laughter
between us.

On each of several weekends before the last one of
Carnival, people would go from house to house to drink
sweet vermouth, eat candied fruits and other sweets. It
was not the custom for them to stop at the house of widows
but a few of our family friends did, some in costume, some
not. One Sunday evening, as I was looking at the tray of
sweets the girls had prepared and wondering if anyone
would call, there was a knock at the door and in came a
masked pirate who seized me and danced me around the
room. Crazy Spyros. With a red handkerchief over his
head, a black eye mask and great cape. He'd taken ad-
vantage of Carnival with its costumes to visit openly.

"What if someone else comes?" I asked.

"You will say this is Mad Michaelis the masked pirate,
eh? Stealer of children, seducer of women."

"You're crazy. Let go of me before Amalía hears you.
You must be drunk."

"Never."

He had just released me when Amalía came down the
stairs, ready to go to a rehearsal at the school. She wore
the antique embroidered gown and had braided her hair
into a thick plait down her back. She could have stepped
out of one of the oil paintings from the time of the revo-
lutionary heroes.

"Ah, a beautiful island maiden," Spyros said. "I'll steal
her away."

She looked hard at him and then said, "Oh, hello, Mr. Galánis."

"There, you see," he said to me. "The perfect costume fools everyone."

"Sit down in the parlor, you two. Others may be along soon so I'll bring out something to refresh ourselves."

"Wait, wait! Here we must drink what I have brought." He pulled out a bottle from his cape and held it to the light. The liquid was black-red. "Black wine. The great one."

"I don't like wine," Amalía said.

"You must try this—there is so little of it left in the world. No one makes it anymore. Or even knows the secret of how the grapes are blended to get just this taste, this sweetness. It comes from an island on the other side of the mainland. Now deserted after an earthquake many years ago. Katína, will you bring us some glasses, please?"

Black, I thought on the way to the kitchen. Black. It had been years since I had it. My father used to love it of an evening after a meal when we sat around the table in the garden. He'd pour a little in a glass for me and I'd hold it near a candle to see the color.

"You'll like this," Spyros told Amalía as they sat on the sofa. He pushed his mask up to his forehead and poured the wine into the glasses I'd brought.

"I won't."

"Don't be rude," I told her. "Just try it. It's Carnival, after all."

"Health," Spyros said and we lifted our glasses.

It was delicious. Sweet but not very. It slipped down the throat easily and called back those evenings in the garden, the rose-filled summers. I could see that Amalía liked it but did not want to admit it.

"Well?" Spyros asked.

"It's all right."

"Just all right? Here, have some more." He topped off her glass and refilled his and mine. "Health."

"Health."

As we sipped the lovely wine, Spyros told us stories of delicacies he had eaten while traveling, setting up markets for his tomato paste. Shark fins and frog legs. Grasshoppers and bumblebees. He refilled the glasses. Amalía was drinking easily now, listening to Spyros's stories. "Once a businessman from the East took me to a restaurant that served wonderful little steaks. Very tender. Guess what they were."

"What?" Amalía asked.

"Snake. Boa constrictor. A kind of snake that gets so big it can squeeze people to death and swallow them whole."

Amalía squealed and said, "It's not true."

"Of course it's true. Would I lie?"

"Yes."

"And in some places they eat dogs."

"Ugh! How nasty."

"And cats."

"Stop! Stop!" She was laughing now. "I don't believe anything you say."

"Have more wine."

"No, no Spyro," I said. "You'll make the child drunk. She has to go to the dance rehearsal, don't you, Amalía?"

"Oh yes, is it time?"

"I think so."

When she was gone Spyros and I slowly finished the bottle of wine. "A lovely girl," he said after a long silence. "She must marry soon or you will have more trouble. All the boys in the village burn for her."

"I don't know what she wants. When I look at her, I think I don't know what anyone wants."

"She wants a man—a husband."

"That's what all men think a woman wants. Maybe she wants something else."

"What else is there for her to want?"

"Am I to know? She tells me nothing. But maybe she still wants to go away from here. She likes studying foreign languages. She could be a translator. Or a teacher."

"Women should not have careers. It invites men to take liberties."

"Listen to him! What do you think I did?"

"That's different. You were not a village girl. Amalía is."

"So?"

"She won't know how to act away from here. Men will try everything with her. Look what happened with the foreigner."

"She's clever. She'll learn, if she hasn't already."

"You think so?"

"Ach, let's not talk more of it. All day every day I am thinking of these things. And now the wine has clouded my mind. Listen, the streets are quiet. Everyone's gone home. You should leave now. It will look strange if you stay longer."

"But I'm masked."

"That doesn't hide the fact that you're a man visiting a widow when everyone else has gone home."

"It's not so late. Let's have a brandy. Just one, and talk of Carnival."

"What is there to say of Carnival?"

"What costume you'll wear when we go into the streets next weekend."

"Pah! A widow dancing with a widower in the streets? That would do much for the name of the House of Sarrás."

I poured us brandies. Spyros was serious. We'd be in costume and mask, he argued; no one would recognize us. It was our chance to be together without hiding in a house for once. When was the last time I had seen the Carnival dancers except by looking through the window? he asked. It would be fun of course, but I felt sure we would be recognized. Even Amalía had known Spyros as soon as she came into the room. He insisted. I said no. We had more brandy. And more again later as we continued to argue. Floating on a sea of it, finally, I knew I would say yes, knew I loved the risk as much as I had loved it the night Spyros first came to the kitchen door and suggested a walk. He was looking at me now, silly man, with his mask all lopsided on his head.

"What are you thinking?" I asked.

"You know."

"Now? Here? In Grigóris's house?"

"Yes."

"Mother of God. Amalía will be back."

"Not for hours, eh?"

"You look so silly in that mask."

"I know."

On the last Saturday night of Carnival, I looked out the window at the crowds as they made their way down to the square. There were costumes of all kinds but the ones that mattered were those of the goat dancers, the young men of the village. They were fearsome things, covered in shaggy pelts from head to waist, the face of a goat, the harness of clanking bells, the baggy shepherds' trousers. Where does it come from, this instinct in man to turn into a beast? Young men wait anxiously for Carnival, for their turn to wear the goatskin mask, as their fathers and grandfathers before them. And the island boys who have left for the mainland will do anything to return and dance their dance. Though it has never been much of a dance that I can see. It seems enough to be able to hop and jump inside the shaggy coat, held down by the weight of the bells. They balance themselves with shepherds' crooks that have bunches of wild narcissus tied to them. The night was full of noisemakers and horns and the narrow street outside the window was covered in confetti. Amalía had gone off with her classmates to follow the goat dancers from the square up through the village to the chapel inside the fortress on top of the rock. There they would remove their masks and Papa Yiannis would bless the dancers and bestow fertility on the tomato fields for the next year. Later, in the square, Amalía and the other girls were to dance.

When most of the people had gone down to the square and our part of the village was quiet, Spyros knocked softly on the kitchen door. He was already in his pirate costume but I had made masks for us that completely covered our faces. I pulled a handkerchief like this over my head and wrapped myself in a kind of cape I had put together from old blankets. I was sure that even Amalía wouldn't recognize us now. We went into the night.

"Only for a few minutes," I said.

"We'll see." He tossed some confetti at me.

"Yes, won't we!" I blew a toy horn in his ear and made him jump. We crossed the street as a group of children passed by throwing fistfuls of confetti in the air.

"Happy Carnival!" they shouted at us.

"Happy Carnival." They were neighborhood children but hadn't recognized me. A feeling of freedom went through me. They hadn't recognized me. I was someone else, someone unknown in this village and so was Spyros. We could be whoever we wanted to be this one night. This was the idea of Carnival; how stupid of me never to have understood it. The freedom of losing yourself! I could do, say anything I wanted and no one, save Spyros, would ever know.

We strolled along the street, arm in arm, as we had never done, and passed people we had known most of our lives. Some were in costume but usually you could tell who they were. The other widows were at their windows in their black dresses, their eyes moving over us. But how were they to know that we were not visitors to the village? For many came from the mainland to see our Carnival. I blew my horn rudely at the widows; Spyros threw confetti.

Men passed us with guitars, singing *rebétika* song:

> "You left in April and I was alone.
> Now you return with the first rain of autumn
> because poverty finally has found you.
> For months I longed to see you but couldn't.

You come now that it's started to rain
And water runs off the tiles of the roof."

Women in costumes ran past, throwing confetti at the men. One woman broke off the song to call out, "Meet us later behind the square and we'll sing a better song." A wine bottle fell to the street from a balcony or rooftop. Past us hurried the priest on his way to the chapel in the fortress where he would receive and bless the goat dancers and all who followed them. After him came Panayóta, his wife, the old shrew-faced one, who would light the candles and tidy the chapel. From below we could hear the sound of the goat dancers, their bells, the cheers of the crowd. We waited for them to make their way through the streets to us.

The first rounded the corner wearing a mask of spotted goatskin. His body, clad in sheepskin to the waist, was that of a shaggy beast harnessed with dozens of brass and copper bells whose clanking bounced off the walls of the houses. From the waist down he wore white woolen shepherd trousers and on his feet were sandals. He stamped and jumped to make the bells clank louder. Children ran after him, daring one another to get closer and then screaming in terror as he jumped at them, this sweating, hairy man-beast, snuffling for air behind the mask of skin, swinging his shepherd's crook above the heads of the crowds that followed him. Behind him came one peering from black goatskin, more energetic than the first, leaping from side to side, snorting, and stamping in the clouds of confetti that fell on him from people gathered on balconies and rooftops. The first two moved along but now there were others, four in the narrow street at once. The noise of the bells was terrible to hear. People were covering their ears.

In the old days the goat dancers sometimes fought, it is said. Disguised by the masks, men sought revenge for stolen goats, losses at cards or in love. They would beat each other with the crooks or with knives they would slash the harnesses that held the bells. Today they only acted this out, shaking their crooks, twisting their bodies so the bells deafened. Spyros and I moved back into a side lane between two houses, to avoid the crush of the crowd as the dancers moved up the street. When most had gone by, I started to go out into the street again but suddenly the space in front of me was blocked. Something huge and dark and smelling of rank man was there. I ran into it, a goat dancer. I crashed against the bells and fell back with a scream, my mask all to one side.

"What the devil . . . ?" Spyros shouted.

"Mother of God, we've run into someone in the dark. Quick, turn around, the other way." I was trying to get my mask on straight again. The goat dancer seemed stunned—his mask too was awry and he was struggling with it, leaning against the wall as if he had lost his balance, breathing heavily. I had to take my mask off in order to get it on again and just as I did so, he lifted his. The light came from behind him. My face was lit while his remained dark.

"He saw me," I whispered to Spyros as we turned away from the dancer and made our way out the other end of the lane into the back street. "He saw who I was just then."

"Did you see who he was?"

"No. The light was from the other direction. All I could make out was the white mask."

"White? Completely white? Albino?"

"Yes."

"It was Nikos."

"Nikos, which Nikos?"

"Nikos, the fisherman's son."

"You mean the one who's been following Amalía all these years?"

"That one."

"How do you know?"

Spyros said the albino mask was the tradition of Nikos's family. They killed an albino kid each year to make a mask. When Spyros had danced his own dance, long years ago, Nikos's father, Giorgos, had danced behind an albino mask. This year everyone knew that Nikos would have such a goatskin.

"Well, he has seen me, anyway, seen me with you, though your mask was still on. He knows that Widow Katina was in a lane with a man. Tomorrow the whole village will know."

"Perhaps not." He kicked the piles of confetti as we walked. "It was dark. He was confused. The sheepskins are heavy and when you turn and turn in them it is impossible not to become dizzy, even faint. Probably he didn't recognize you. He will say nothing."

We walked in silence for a while. There was the noise of the crowd above us as it neared the fortress. The goat dancers would be pushing one another back with their crooks, each hoping to be the first at the chapel, the first to seize the ropes and ring the bells.

"Nikos," I said. "Yes, of course he is a young man now. I remember how even as a child he followed Amalía like a puppy. But he never interested her. He was clumsy.

He dropped things at her name-day parties. I think he pushed her into the sea once. How angry she was."

"He will ask for her this year."

"What? How do you know this?"

"I told you I was a friend of his father, Giorgos. I baptized Nikos."

"He's one of your godsons? I didn't know. But you have so many."

"Half the island, I think sometimes."

"The father told you?"

"Yes."

"She won't have him."

"He thinks she will."

By the time we were home the bells were ringing out above the cheers of the crowd. Lent was beginning, forty days of fasting before the dead God would rise. It was Nikos, I thought, Nikos who rang the bells.

We didn't go to see Amalía dance in the square. My unmasking by Nikos seemed a warning. Spyros and I returned to the house and closed the shutters against the roar of Carnival. I heard the next day how beautifully she had danced, how the heads of the men had turned to watch her lead the line across the square. All the men. I understood that if she were to stay here unmarried, the women would not stand it. Would they drive her from the village as the men had done to the stranger? Their revenge would be double for through Amalía, they'd come to me.

As Lent moved along, spring opened the earth and the smell of soil moist from winter rains rose in the air. There were kites in the apple orchards and the young men walked the streets one way calling out to girls who walked the other way giggling. At night the singing from the taverna cracked the village silence, for everyone ate little during the fasting and men drank too much on half-filled stomachs. They were hungry and restless so there were quarrels over bets made, money lost and gained. It seemed the dead God would never rise from the sun-warmed soil.

Amalía continued her wandering whenever she was not in school. Spyros saw her at the seawall one day. When he was finished talking to his engineers, he went over to her.

"There was no one around so I spoke to her."

"About what?"

"I asked her what she was looking at. She said that women here always look out to sea. Didn't I know that? Yes, I said, but not young women. She told me it had nothing to do with age. 'Then what?' I asked. But she just smiled."

"Then?"

"Then we . . . She said nothing more, so I left." He paused. "But what is it that women look at?"

"Ach. Something inside themselves, their lives, the lives of their men. Am I to know? When I was Amalía's age I had to fight each day just to stay alive. There was no time for dreaming. But here in the islands something different happens to girls. They search the horizon for—what? A ship? A bird? A sign of some kind."

On Easter Sunday morning early, Amalía and I hurried home from church cradling the Holy Light of our candles against the wind that we might light the lamps in front of the icon of the house and, thanks to God, eat like humans again. (Not that I hadn't broken the fast more times than there are raisins in pudding. I had grown fatter. Spyros liked me that way.)

The earth turns, the door opens, fathers are on my step, one by one.

"Our Christos will have fields next to your Amalía's and our house is nearly as old as yours. My great-grandfather baptized the grandfather of Grigóris."

"Fotis is a good boy. He works hard at the tomato factory. We are not rich but our name is good."

"Amalía would bring honor to our family. And there is not a boy on this island as clever as our Dimitrios. He and Amalía will have the taverna when I am gone. The best food in the village! Our stuffed eggplant is known everywhere."

To each I replied, "It is good that you have come. I will speak to my daughter on behalf of your son."

"This is not the way," they would tell me. "She will respect your judgment, as all good children respect the judgment of their parents. She will do as you say."

"This is *my* way. You have honored my house with your visit. We shall talk again."

"Fools, all of them fools," Spyros said. "Give her to none of them."

"It is she who gives herself or not."

"She won't have any of them." He was right.

"I'll throw myself into the well before I'll marry Fotis," Amalía said. "And may I die the day I exchange wreaths with Christos or Dimitrios. I think Christos should marry Dimitrios and then they can stuff each other's eggplant."

On the morning of the day of the turtle, the women came to me in the marketplace. Figs? they asked. You look for figs? No, it's not their season yet, I said. They were still green and hard.

"Some like them that way," one said.

"Young men do," said another.

"Sons of fishermen, they like the fresh new figs."

"What do you mean?" I asked.

"You should know," they said. "Beside your house grows the biggest fig tree in the village."

"And?"

"And there Nikos climbs at night. All the way to the top branch beside the upstairs window. And then he goes inside, to eat figs, the new green figs." They laughed. "Ask Amalía. She'll know. Ask her about the figs."

Mother of God. Could this be true? If Amalía had seen Nikos in the house and all the village knew, then it was decided. He would ask for her this year, as Spyros had said.

"And talking of fruit," one said, "does Amalía like apples?"

Now it begins, I thought, for everyone knows that the apple is the fruit of virginity. When a young girl gives a man an apple with a bite missing, it means she wants him to take her. "Yes, Amalía likes apples. But I'm sure she hasn't bitten into as many as have your daughters."

"No, no one in my house eats apples," said one. "There are no apple trees in our garden."

"You have to go to the mainland," another said, "to find the best apples."

"Is that why your son drives a taxi in Athens?" I asked her.

Suddenly with a crash a cart of peaches tipped to the ground and the fruit shot out around our feet. "Fool!"

shouted the merchant at Mad Manólis, who had run into
the cart. "Don't step on my peaches! Don't bruise them!"

"Turtles!" Manólis called out. "Turtles in the water!"
He ran among the fruit stalls waving his arms.

"What about my peaches, fool? Who'll pay?" The
merchant was on his knees grabbing at the rolling fruit.
No one cared about his peaches. The marketplace began
to clear. From the shops and cafés men rushed down the
steps toward the sea. Even the old ones, taking the steps
sideways like crabs, hurried toward the beach. Some carried boards with nails in them. Others had clubs.

I made my way home. "They're early this year," I heard
women say as they pushed their children into houses,
closed doors and pulled shutters tight. Each year the old
ritual, the new sacrifice. Where was Amalía? By the time
I got home the village was quiet, waiting. But from below
you could hear the shouts of the men gathering on the
beach. They had left the tomato fields by then; the machinery in the factory would be idle. All the men of the
village would be there, even Spyros, watching.

The fishermen say that the turtles tear their nets, letting
the fish escape, but I don't believe them. They've ruined
their own fishing, these men. Ruined it with dynamite. But
they cannot admit that.

Amalía was not home. I went up to the flat roof where
the girls had hung the wet laundry in the sun. From there
I could see the men gathered far below on the beach, could
see the figure of a woman standing by the seawall. Amalía.
No other village woman would have dared be there. The
younger women would stay inside the houses with the
children.

The wind rose up from the sea and slapped the wet

sheets behind me. I couldn't see the turtles from there but I guessed the men had at least one of them within their circle and were doing things that no one would speak of later, after the remains had been thrown back into the sea. Come home, Amalía, I thought, come home. These men are filled with blood lust. I was unable to move. The sheets slapped and cracked behind me and threw drops of water across my back. I told myself to go to her, bring her away, back here to the house of Sarrás, safe under the shadow of the fortress, away from what was happening there below. My urge was as ancient as that of the men. But still I could not move.

Suddenly she was running, away from the seawall, into the streets between the houses. Nikos ran after her. I could see them and then I couldn't. The roofs of houses blocked my view but I saw them run across the open place by the lion fountain before I lost them again. The village took them in and hid them from me. The wind brought the sound of running feet on cobblestones, now from this direction, now from that, as if to fool me. I lost them for a long while, lost them completely, as if the village had taken them both away. I went from side to side of the roof but there was no sound other than the wind slapping the sheets on the village rooftops. Bed linen was out all over the village and waved like banners from every roof. The women were there too, the old ones. Black against white sheets. They were looking down into the same streets as was I. But they were also watching me silently. And I felt for once that there was sympathy in their stares, kindness even. They understood what was happening, as daughters, as mothers. Perhaps they had understood more than I all along. We stood there, we the women, watching, waiting.

A scream. From the fortress. Then I was running, down the stairs and out into the street. But I couldn't move so fast anymore. I am an old, fat woman, I thought, short of breath and worn-out. "Amalía!" I shouted. "Amalía!" And stopped beside a closed door to still my heart, then ran on. "Amalía!" The arch in the crumbling stone wall was just ahead. Where to look first—not in the chapel, no, nor at the site of the temple whose few stones I was sent here to draw years ago. But just as I passed through the arch into the great courtyard, I saw them standing over by the ramparts facing each other; not touching, yet close to-gether, still, as if they had been standing there a long time, years even, with the wind moaning along the ramparts behind them and columns of dust moving between them and me, moving and dying and moving again.

I stopped. I became part of whatever it was that had been going on so long. We stood like that, the corners of a triangle, the dust in my mouth, my nose. And then I began to walk toward them slowly, coming from a great distance away.

"Amalía," I said. "Come home."

"Here is Giorgos, Widow Katína, come to visit you," said Spyros formally on the front step, as if he were no more than an old family friend. "And he has brought his son, Nikos."

"Welcome," I said, "welcome to our house," and showed them into the parlor as if the visit were a surprise and the liqueurs and preserved sweets not ready in the kitchen. I in my best silks and Amalía in a new dress. Old Lilliána, ancient and half-deaf as she was, had been propped up in a high-backed chair. The three men crossed the room to greet her for she was now the oldest person in the village and respect had to be shown.

"What is it to me who marries whom?" she said as one by one the men kissed her on both cheeks. "Will I never be finished with you all?" They laughed and wished her health, but stepped away quickly, for the dignity of years had not rid Old Lilliána of her bad fish smell.

She had not wanted to leave her bed. But I had begged her to come so the two Houses would be of equal numbers. Spyros, as godfather of Nikos, came with the men for he had been asked to help the two sides reach an agreement. Old Lilliána said she would come only because she had something to tell Amalía, and then she hoped we'd all let her be. "Dying is as hard as living," she said. "It takes up all my time."

Two days had passed since I led Amalía down from the fortress under the eyes of the other women on their rooftops. And already all were asking, "How is it that no arrangement has been made?" We could delay no longer. I had made my plans with Spyros. Nikos and his father had sent word they would arrive at night, around ten o'clock, to escape the curiosity of the neighbors. Ach, as if no one knew what was happening.

The men next greeted Amalía who was standing beside Lilliána in a simple blue dress. Her hair was pulled back, woven into the usual thick plait and she kept her eyes to the floor. Giorgos took her hand with his one hand, for his other sleeve was empty and tucked into the pocket of his jacket.

"How grown-up your daughter is, Widow Katína." His smile creased a face leathery from years of sun. "You know what they say: When a woman is in the parlor, your house becomes a garden, yes?" He laughed as if he had invented the saying himself.

"Your son has grown too," I said. Nikos was a well made young man. I had never really looked carefully at him but now I saw that he was strong and lean, his skin dark above the collar of the cheap striped suit. A mop of black curls tumbled onto a face where I saw cleverness, perhaps even intelligence. There was a kind of animal satisfaction in the way he stood, a certainty that he would get what he wanted from this earth. He's wrong, I thought, but he probably won't realize that until years from now and by then maybe it won't matter. Now it was Amalía he wanted and from the way he looked at her, I knew he had always wanted her.

"I'm sorry," I said, observing the usual courtesy, "but I wasn't expecting you so I haven't prepared anything special. Still, you must have something to refresh yourselves."

"Thank you," Giorgos said. "We were taking a walk and I said, 'Let's go visit Widow Katína and her daughter. All these years doing business at her shop—let us stop and wish her health.' Yes?" He laughed again.

"You honor my house. Please sit down. Amalía, will you offer our guests something, please?" She went to the kitchen as Giorgos and Spyros sat on the sofa under the painting of the ship in the harbor, facing Lilliána. "Niko, you can sit here." I had put a pair of chairs for Amalía and Nikos to one side and I sat in a high-backed one next to Lilliána. Men faced women.

There was a pause. Spyros touched his cuffs and smiled

to himself. His suit was light gray, foreign cut, perfect. He looked up, saw me watching him and winked. It was time to begin. He cleared his throat and leaned forward.

"Children grow up and elbow us into the grave," he said, opening the discussion. "And so we must plan for them, try to foresee their difficulties. My wife, Froso, and I were blessed with no children, sadly; but it is good to see the health of my godson Nikos and of Amalía, daughter of my great friend, Grigóris."

"Wonderful health!" Giorgos said. "Nikos is in wonderful health, Widow Katína. Look at him! See how healthy he is." He jumped up and slapped his son on the shoulder. Nikos threw us a grin.

"This is true," Spyros said, taking over from Giorgos as if on cue. "And Nikos doesn't play cards or drink. He's steady in his ways and loyal. Already at such an age he has earned the respect of all the village. Any village girl would be pleased to have his attention." His eyes did not meet mine.

"I know that this is true," I said to Spyros. "But as we know, Amalía is of the oldest House. She is not *any* village girl."

"She can cook!" shrieked Lilliána, suddenly alert. "She can sew!"

"This is good," Spyros said, humoring her. "She has to know how to cook and sew."

"What?" asked Lilliána.

"Cook and sew," Giorgos said.

"Nikos cooks and sews too? What work is this for a man?"

"No, no," Giorgos shouted so Lilliána could hear. "Nikos is clever at mathematics. He was first in his class."

"At what?"

"Mathematics. Numbers!"

"You mean he can count?" she said sourly. "What ideas people have about marriage today. As if it mattered anyway, marriage. Centuries of it and no one's the better . . ." She trailed off, said something no one could hear, and stopped.

In fact Amalía could neither cook nor sew. She burned omelets and stuck needles into her fingers rather than cloth. She had no time for such matters and said that those who did were fools. But then Nikos was probably no better at mathematics and who could say *he'd* be steady in his ways?

What Amalía was good at was the serving of refreshments. It was the tradition of the daughter of the house and when she came into the room carrying a tray, I could see she was enjoying the attention of the men. The tray was carefully laid with a lace cloth and tiny plates of thinnest china. Each had its silver spoon and curl of preserved orange peel. There were three glasses of cold water and three cups of sweet coffee on saucers. She served the spoonsweets and waited to one side while each of the men finished his. Nikos could barely get his down for staring at Amalía. Giorgos and Spyros too held spoons in their mouths, eyes on her. When they had finished, Amalía returned the plates to the tray and served the coffee and cold water. Giorgos and Nikos sipped noisily as Spyros silently drank his. While Amalía was taking the tray back to the kitchen, the men clicked their cups down on the saucers almost together, as if to say, Now let the serious talk begin.

"It is necessary for us to know," Spyros said, "if you've spoken with your daughter."

"Yes, I have talked with her and I shall tell you what

she said. But first let us speak of other important matters.
If we are to come to an agreement, the most important
thing that Amalía would bring to it is the good name of
the House of Sarrás."

"Yes, yes," Giorgos said. "It is better to lose your eye
than to lose your reputation, yes?"

"But if this were true, then surely Amalía would be
half-blind by now because of the acts of your son."

Giorgos reddened. "What does this mean?"

Spyros, as arranged, broke in here. "Widow Katína,
these are dark words you speak. And yet I think I know
their meaning. Giorgo, my friend, if I may." He spoke into
Giorgos's ear while Nikos shifted uncomfortably. I studied
the floor as if searching for something I had dropped.

"No!" Giorgos said in mock surprise and anger. As if
no one knew that Nikos had climbed the fig tree to Amalía's
room, had chased her through the streets of the village to
the fortress, as if no one had heard the scream. "How can
this be true?" he demanded of Nikos. "Tell us now, Niko,
here in front of everyone that we may all know the truth."

"I . . . I . . ." he stuttered, then chanted the line he
must have prepared. "I have respected the honor of this
house."

"But you see," I said to his father, "it is not a question
of honor. My daughter tells me that our honor is intact.
It is our good name that may not be. And just as you would
not want to join your House with one whose name is in
question, so we would not want to force you to do so.
Amalía and I have talked of moving to the city where she
can continue her study of languages."

Silence. Nikos looked at his father, who looked at

Spyros. What is this? their looks said. We have come here for this?

All the way down from the fortress, Amalía had said nothing. Her face was smooth, without emotion, the way it looked that morning I opened the door after our long night. We came into the parlor away from the eyes of the village and faced one another.

"We'll have to leave. It wouldn't be wise to stay here now. Pah! What a place. Well, never mind, don't worry. We'll close the house and go to the mainland. There are language schools everywhere and we can get an apartment near the museum. You can study. I hear there's a need for translators, for language teachers . . ."

"I don't want to."

"What are you saying?"

"I don't want to go to a language school."

"But you can't stay. You'll have to marry Nikos if you do. They say he has come into your room at night. Is this true?"

"Yes."

"And you think you can stay here unmarried after that? After the fortress? Do you know what it is to be a woman without a man in a village, a woman of bad name, mocked by everyone? You'll have to face the other women and if you are still here after that, you'll grow old in these rooms. The only men who'll ask for you will be ones with things wrong with them."

"But I'm of this place, Mother, can't you see that? It's you who are the stranger."

"Even you call me a stranger. But don't tell me you

don't want to leave here. I remember talk of temples and goldfish, don't you? Have you forgotten?"

Her eyes narrowed. "My life has changed."

"Your life? You speak as if you've lived a hundred years."

"Perhaps I have."

"Listen to her! You wear away at me with this nonsense. You mean you want this marriage?"

"I'll have it."

"That is not what I asked."

"But that is my answer. I have already told Nikos. Just now in the fortress before you came."

"Mother of God. So it is done."

"It is done."

"Then why did you scream?"

"To stop him from coming near me. To tell him it was all right, he didn't have to force me. I had made up my mind already."

"Why? Why? Is it because of what happened those other times, the times he came to your window?"

"Oh, stop it. Nothing happened. Nothing has ever happened between Nikos and me. Just because of what I told you that night you think I've been with every man in the village."

"Wasn't that the idea you wanted me to have?"

"Have any you like. But know this about Nikos: he came to my room, he talked of marriage, I told him no."

"And that's all?"

"That's all."

"But why now . . . ?"

"I've changed my mind."

"Like that. You've changed your mind."

"Like that."

"Why?"

"It is what should be."

"Don't be a fool. There is nothing that *should* be. Nothing is written. You get the life you make. What do you think you'll get, married to a leaky boat and a few mended nets? I'm not even sure you like him. Don't be a fool, Amalía!"

She said nothing. She had come into herself. Calm, focused. I was the one shouting. She could have been discussing the weather. I made a last try.

"It was Nikos who did it. You know that, don't you? Nikos burned the foreigner's tent that night. Everyone says so. Everyone knows what kind of person he is. You want a man such as this?"

"Why Mother, you've become one of the old women. Backbiting, gossipy. Look at yourself there in the glass."

She pointed at the old picture of the ship in the harbor, the picture whose glass has reflected generations of life in the Sarrás parlor. In it I could see Amalía pointing at us, at me—fat, a little bent, my face red, angry—all I needed was the black dress and a head scarf. I turned back to her. "Answer me. Do you know it was Nikos who drove away the foreigner?"

"It wasn't Nikos. But it might as well have been."

"It was. Spyros and the others had nothing to do with it."

"I don't care who it was. It doesn't matter. It's done. Even if it had been Nikos, it still wouldn't matter."

"You would marry him anyway?"

"Yes, yes, I *will* marry him."

She was her father standing there, dark, intent on some

devil I would not be given the chance to understand. "You and Grigóris, both of you with your secrets, your darkness. You're right. You're part of this place just as he was . . ."

From the outside came the noise of children, of women. So the turtle was dead. They would take pieces of her flesh for soup before the men threw her back into the water, where the sea slugs would feed on her. "Marry Nikos," I said, "marry anyone you like."

"My good friends," Spyros said to everyone in the parlor as Amalía returned and took her place next to Nikos, "this talk of honor and name is unnecessary. Both Houses are respected by all the village. What is needed is a wedding to wash everyone clean. Mouths will close once an agreement between families has been reached. We must speak of details. It is right that young people should know what they can count on and," he paused, "what they cannot. Widow Katína, will you begin?"

It had come to this: "The daughter of Grigóris and Katína Sarrás will be assigned three fields, a total of six hectares, that are, at present, leased to the priest. Good wheat land, level, without stones. On the day of the marriage, the groom will receive eight linen bags, each containing one hundred gold sovereigns."

Nikos sucked in his breath.

"There are the personal items. Blankets and rugs woven by women of six generations of the House of Sarrás. The embroidered bed linens and towels. More than one hundred cooking pieces of copper, four sets of china and silverware and of course the personal clothes and jewelry."

They looked pleased but expectant. They waited for me to go on. I didn't.

"Towels!" Old Lilliána laughed. "China and jewelry. Pah! As if these can help, as if they can hold back the evil hour, the black dog. Take my stones, Amalía; read them well. They speak without tongues."

Amalía raised her eyes and smiled at the old woman.

Giorgos looked around the room, then studied his fingernails. "The dowry you have mentioned, Widow Katína, is most generous but are not there other . . ."

"You speak of the house, of Grigóris's shop, I know. You have the right to know. It is my decision that these will remain in my name until my bones are laid next to those of Grigóris. At that time, Amalía will have them in her name. And of course—did I say?—the fields that pass from my hands on the wedding day will be in her name, not that of her husband."

I had told Spyros that I wouldn't have a son-in-law of mine sitting in a café all day eating his way through Amalía's dowry. He'd have to have some kind of work and *not* picking tomatoes. I also wouldn't have them living in Grigóris's house; I didn't care what the custom is here. So they'd have to have another place to live, something respectable. Amalía was still of the House of Sarrás, after all. But there in the parlor I wondered how many insults Giorgos and Nikos would swallow to make a marriage. They were not without weapons of their own. The honor of our House had suffered from Amalía's relations with the stranger long before Nikos pursued her to the fortress. And there was the Carnival night when my mask fell in front of Nikos. His eyes met mine and we weighed each other's strength. He was young and strong, full of his own grace. And I an old woman, as Amalía said, but still filled with the strength I gained one spring day from the temple of an unknown god. We each felt the steel of the other.

"But," I said, "the gold sovereigns are the groom's to use as the beginning of the couple's new life." I paused. "Of course, none of this is final, for there is still the possibility of further studies for Amalía and marriage put off for some years yet," I lied. Nikos would take the marriage on any terms.

"And now," Spyros said, "it is right that Widow Katína hear what the other House brings to such an agreement." Not much, it seemed, as I had expected. The boat, the nets, eventually their small house.

"And how," I asked carefully, "is the groom to make a living?"

"I have offered my godson work in the tomato factory," Spyros said, as we had planned. "Not as a worker, you understand, Widow Katína, as a manager. And of course he may move up. There will be other openings—in Athens or abroad. Remember I have no heirs. My godchildren are important to me."

"He won't have to pull his living from the sea, Widow Katína," Giorgos said, "and worry about accidents." Everyone looked at the limp sleeve. "No, a life on the sea is no good these days. The turtles, you know, they tear the nets."

Spyros explained that a small house went with the position. Usually he brought managers here from Athens and had to give them a place to live. Nikos looked proud, happy. He thinks it will be all right, I thought, looking at him as he sat there, pleased with himself, casting sideways glances at Amalía. He thinks she is accepting him for himself. But no, there is another thread there, one neither he nor I can see. Wait till he tries to live with this dreaming daughter of mine who cares not how one day, with its little failures, hardens into another till suddenly a year has passed, then ten. She will not comfort him for she will be intent on something else, something he cannot see. But life belongs to them now. There in the parlor they took it from our hands.

"I told you that I have talked with Amalía. She will tell you herself. Amalía, is it your wish to marry?"

"Yes."

"Does Nikos please you?"

"Yes, he pleases me." Her eyes were still on the floor.

Giorgos then asked his son, "Niko, does Amalía please you?"

"Yes, she pleases me." His eyes on Amalía.

"Someone help me out of this chair," Old Lilliána said. "I want to go home. He can count and she has gold sovereigns and all the while stars are driven across the sky by the mad moon. Oh, why am I old? Come, Amalía, help me home."

I sit and sew, as women have always done. I fold the yellowing pages of my burned journal in halves, in quarters, in eighths, and sew them into the hem of Amalía's wedding gown. These pieces of that last glorious summer will protect her when she wears the charmed white gown and stands in the church among the islanders, the old jackal women with their barbed minds.

Amalía looks at the yards of satin spread across my lap and onto the parlor floor. The gown is stylish. I saw it in a foreign magazine and had it copied by a seamstress on the mainland. She took so long with it—all those seed-pearl buttons—I was afraid it would never arrive. But did

Amalía worry about it? Ach, she would have gone to
church in a dressing gown if I had let her.

"There's so much of it that I'll trip over it," she said.
"And the shoes hurt my feet. Do I have to wear it? Nikos
won't care."

"Nikos will care. It would surprise you, the ideas men
have about matters like weddings."

"Then I'll have to change his ideas."

"Listen to the bride! We'll see who changes whose
ideas. And for now, let's have no more talk about not
wearing this gown. It cost a lot of your father's money,
may the earth rest lightly on his bones. Everyone has talked
of it. You must look perfect tomorrow so that no word
may be said against you."

She is lovely, my Amalía. Grigóris would have been
proud of her as she stands, slim and dark, her hair as black
and thick as his. In the gown she is no longer the village
girl who ran barefoot as a peasant, talking loudly to anyone
at all, singing island songs. Once again she has changed,
become someone else. Far more than the son of a fisherman
deserves. But what can we do? The old women are right
when they say that marriage is mostly a matter of luck.

It is impossible to see the places where I've sewn in
the pages and ironed the hem flat. No one will put the *eye*
on Amalía in church tomorrow, protected as she is by two
gifts: a summer, a box of stones. But how will they protect
her from *me?* There is something that bothers me about
this wedding and I cannot quite locate or define it. I intend
to find out the *why* of this marriage, to know the reason
the thought of it fills my throat with the beating of tiny
wings.

I came out of the fire, crossed the sea in refugee boats,

withstood the women of this place with the strength of the temple of Ephesus within me. Now (can it already be 1954?) I plan still to live long years, perhaps even to take Spyros's hand and walk along the beach when we are old. Day adds to day and we will become just another layer holding up the present. To my grandchildren, I will be an artifact, a charred bit of pottery from the past. Excavate, I will tell them, dig until you find me. I am here beneath the layers, waiting for you.

III

NIKOS

I cracked the seed between my teeth, eased out the kernel with my tongue and spat the shell to the floor. The others scribbled in their copybooks and glanced up at Mr. Kotzias, the teacher. He was reading a newspaper. Amalía sat by the window with a clip in her hair. She had finished her exercise; she always finished first. Her hands on her desk, she stared out the window at the orange tree. I had not finished and I would not. I spat more shells to the floor.

The newspaper moved; Mr. Kotzias's head appeared. "Two minutes," he said. My copybook lay open. I did not understand what to write in the blank spaces. I felt lost when I looked at them. There were no words in my pen, no verbs with endings remembered. I was not like the others who stood and said their words, said their numbers while the teacher smiled. I rushed away from all blank spaces. Down I dived, scissorkick down and drowned sailors waved to me with their hair. My arms were circled with gold and on my head a crown glistened in the green light that falls down through the sea. I was the king of the drowned sailors and my robes trailed after me like seaweed. Pink-eyed fish fled from me and great clams closed as I swam past.

Time was up, the exercises finished. I passed around oranges that I had stolen from the tree outside the window. From hand to hand they went, under the desks, while Mr. Kotzias collected the copybooks. His gray back moved slowly up the aisle. No one was to throw until I gave the signal. He stopped next to me, staring at the seeds on the floor, at the empty copybook. I flung an orange across the room, for I was king of the drowned sailors. Then everyone threw oranges. Mr. Kotzias shouted and dropped the copybooks while we ran screaming, shrieking out of the classroom door and down the street, down the hill past the white houses, down the steps to the sea.

We darted past the lion fountain and scattered into alleyways. I caught up with Amalía at the seaside where she was breathing hard against the damp sea air. When next to her, trying to catch my breath, I had nothing to say. But I had to speak or this would become another blank space. Already I felt lost. She buttoned her coat. She closed me out. She did not notice that I was there for she did not need me. She was unlike the others who drowned without me. So I feared her.

She walked faster then, for she knew I was there. Some of my books fell as I hurried beside her. They were not neatly held by a strap, like hers were. But I didn't care. "Did you see," I asked, "did you see how the teacher looked when I threw the orange?" She turned away without answering.

I will kill her, I thought. She will be dead forever and

birds will eat her eyes. She will not despise me. I ran at her; I pushed. She fell backward, screaming, backward into the cold sea. She sat there in the shallows, crying, and then threw her wet books at me.

I didn't do that, I told myself. Run now. No, no, I didn't do it. Run up the long steps from the sea. No, not me. Through the alleyways, past the lion fountain and the old woman spinning in her doorway. Into the house that smelled of fish soup.

On the playing field we marched in pairs. We lifted our knees high as the teacher led us. Soon he would blow the whistle he held in his teeth. We marched past the girls who were sorry not to be behind a man with a silver whistle. I marched in front for I was the leader always and next to me, tall Ávgustos. Andréas was behind us, laughing at the boys at the end who were weak. They could not keep pace. Their faces were red with the effort and we could hear them panting. One of them had talked with Amalía the day before. On the field, I would kick him instead of the ball. He would cry but no one would come.

As we approached the girls they tittered and giggled. Amalía did not look up at me for I was a fisherman's son. She wanted to look but she pretended to watch the boys with the red faces. She would not look.

The whistle blew. We stopped and stood at attention. We sang the anthem and the proud words rolled out of our mouths. We were one voice, one body. It finished suddenly and we heard only our breathing. We listened to ourselves. But the whistle always rescued us. We scattered across the field, chasing the ball. Some day, we said, we would play for the great teams of our country. Magazines would print our photographs. Girls would ask us to sign our names on them. There would be fast cars and we would travel around the world. The ball went up, rolling into the sky. We cheered and rushed to kick it when it fell.

On the blackboard the teacher pointed to a map. Here was Athens and here was Sparta. Here the enemy was crushed and again crushed. The world respects us. Greeks are the bearers of the light, the teacher said.

I see myself as warrior-king, a lawmaker. I have covered the building of my capitol with choicest marble and raised a statue of the goddess in the inner court of the temple. I have marched and killed and marched and killed again. But I am wise. My laws are just. My people lower their heads when I pass; they reach out to touch me.

The teacher turned his gray back to us and wrote. And on this date and on that date. Years were stacked in columns on the blackboard. I did not learn these years as the others did. I did not fill my notebook with them. For I understood that it is not a matter of dates one on top the other.

In the church the priest talked to us of our great church, Aghia Sophia, now in the hands of Turks. Candles burned in front of icons. Saints were watching. Dull light gleamed from gold and the priest's voice boomed up into the dome like the voice of God. But I knew he was only the priest who lived next door to my family. His wife shouted at him and his children were stupid. He chased the chickens behind the house but couldn't catch them. He didn't fool me with his booming voice and heavy eyebrows. He was greedy and easily tricked. Once I made a fool of him over a pig. But I liked it when he talked of

the Church and how one day we would retake it. I slashed
off the head of an enemy with my sword and the Church
was ours forever. The Turks bled into the Bosporus and
its waters were red with our victory.

An invitation came. Amalía was giving her annual name-
day party. We walked in our best clothes to her house.
But I had fought with a friend and my tie was dirty. The
ribbon had come loose from the box of cakes my mother
had given me for Amalía. It was Amalía's name day but I
was afraid to enter her house. It was the best house in the
village and my mother had oiled my hair until it shone.
But I was dirty because I had fought. I hesitated by the
gate and asked myself, Should I enter? Or should I turn
and eat the cakes myself beside the sea?
　　Her mother called from the door, "Come in, Niko,
come in. Everyone is here but you." And she smiled. Inside,
my classmates were in the parlor sitting on big chairs in
their best clothes. They turned; they saw me in the doorway. They waited but I could not go in. And then I felt it
in the soles of my feet and it rose through me—their need
for me. They were waiting for me to begin. In the best
house of the village they were waiting for me. Without me,
they would drown. I was the king of all drowned sailors.
I entered the room. The party began.
　　Amalía came toward me, smiling. I handed her the box
of cakes with the ribbon that dangled and I wished her
years of health. As she thanked me, my friends called out
from across the room, "Eh, Niko!" How funny they
looked, sitting on high-backed chairs in a row along the
wall. Jackets and ties, hair parted neatly, noses clean. Opposite were the girls in fluffy dresses. They giggled as I

joined my friends. Amalía helped her mother add my cakes to the mound of sweets on the table in the middle of the room. There were flowers there too in vases, and a glass bowl of something red with sliced fruits floating on the top. A meadow of wildflowers was woven into the carpet.

Such a room I had never seen. At home we ate in the kitchen under a picture of the Crucifixion bordered with painted seashells, blue and orange. But here, behind the girls, was a wonderful picture of many colors. Almost as big as the wall. A ship had come into the harbor and the sun was setting, staining the clouds and the water pink. A lone man stood on a hill, looking down on the harbor. I was this man. I had come home, home to this house after years away. Rich now, for the ship was full of my treasures gathered at great risk to myself and my friends. But casually done, cleverly—the arrogant turn of a card, the nod of a head worth a fortune. I stood on the hill. I let the sun touch my face.

Little plates with little forks were handed around. And cakes, pink and chocolate and lime. We talked of serious things, of sports and airplanes and who was the tallest of us all. My fingers were thick. How stupid the forks were, so small, as if made for dolls. Then someone passed a poke down the line; a fist rammed into my side. I turned to give it back and my plate fell there to the side of the chair, there where the carpet ended. It smashed on the tiles. Three pieces. Cake was smeared on the edge of the flowered carpet.

The talking stopped. Everyone looked. Amalía said to someone in a loud whisper, "He always spoils everything." The walls moved forward to crush me against the table; the bowl was filled with blood. I was gone, up and across the floor, through the door and the gate beyond. My legs pumped, my heart pounded. I hated and again hated big houses and plates that break. Those people had no right to make me feel like this. They needed me. The wind slapped and the sea boomed as I ran beside it. I promised to make them all care. I promised the wind and the sea. Someday I would come home to that house like the man in the picture. I would stand on the hill with the sun coloring my face. I would sit in that same chair. Amalía would bring me plates, one, two, three, a hundred. I would break them all. Everyone would continue to talk; no one would look.

On the beach with my friend Ávgustos, I played with stick and rocks. He threw and I hit with the stick, *crack*, out to sea. Then I threw to him, *crack*; it skimmed across the waves. The rocks were sharp but my stick was strong and wide. It sent them out to their final splash.

We noticed a man on the beach, running, chasing two boys. They came toward us, shouting something. The boys were throwing stones at him, trying to make him go away. We laughed at them. He would beat them, we said, if they were not fast. We continued to play, knocking the rocks, *crack*. My friend threw a big one and I hit it hard.

The boys shouted again but we did not turn. And then they shouted louder. When we looked, the man was lying on the beach. They tried to pull him up but he lay still. He tried to interfere, they said, tried to keep them from fighting. But they had turned on him with stones. There was a mark just there, at the side of his head. Amalía's father.

Whose was the stone that killed him? We never knew. The boys began to cry. "We didn't do it, we didn't."

Ávgustos too. "Was it our stone?" he asked me. "Was it ours?"

"No, no, it wasn't ours, never forget that." I didn't cry but called to Mad Manólis, who was passing. "Look what has happened—bring help! Go to the Sarrás house, bring the women, bring someone, oh, bring someone, please!"

They came, crossing themselves, turning faces to heaven, cursing the ill-fated day. The priest, the women, Mrs. Sarrás. She threw herself down on her husband and the women closed around her. And one of us—little Kostas—peered through the legs of the women to see the new widow mourn. It was just something he had never seen before. But she looked up suddenly, saw him and understood (right or wrong) that his was the hand that threw the stone. Pushing women aside with the strength of a man, she was upon him silently and everyone upon her. They saved him from her but not from his new name which quickly spread around the village: He-Who-Threw-the-Stone. But I didn't, he said many times those months to follow. Ach! the old ones said, the widow picked him out. It was a sign.

The whole village followed the coffin to the cemetery beneath the cypress trees. Windows were shuttered lest death enter as the dead one was carried past. Outside the cemetery gate, the old women gathered and cried out, wild, birdlike noises to keep bad spirits from entering. Amalía was white, ill, as we stood under the cypress trees. She did not once look my way. After six months and after he had tried to drown himself twice, He-Who-Threw-the-Stone was taken away from the island to someplace where no one knew his name.

The sea pulled me away from all that, pulled me out with Father in the boat. The water was always black in the early morning when we pulled the nets up from the bottom of the world. I did not know where we were or where we were from. Everything was black. It was all one piece. As we leaned over the side, my hands touched my father's. His were huge and scaly, like those of some great bird. The skin was scarred and the nails as hard as blades. My hands will be like that too, I thought. I will take the lives of a thousand fish. But my hands were still soft then and the nets left marks in my palms.

There in the east was a line that divided black from gray. And then from blue. The sun eased itself above the line and the sea stirred and rippled. We couldn't see the shore. We were an island from an island. But I knew that somewhere the sea uncurled itself on the shore and there we would go. The nets were pulled up, slowly, heavily. Veins stood out on my father's arms and the nets pulled back as if to force me down into the sea. Pink-eyed fish flopped onto the bottom of the boat. There were never enough. Too many nets, Father said, over too many centuries. It was like a lottery—who would win a fish today? I looked down into the dark green sea. What would be left for me when this boat was mine?

Some mornings Orion was already fading in the sky and still the corks had not gone down, the nets had not filled. "Even the gulls," my father said, "even they have left us for other boats." And he would pull out the

wicker-covered bottle from the gear in the bottom of the
boat. "It's the will of God," he'd say. "We can't question
the will of God, now can we, Niko?" He'd take long pulls
on the bottle and after a while he'd begin to sing softly:

> "I'm going to send God a letter with bad words
> and tell Him to think about me a little too.

> "I'll talk to Him strong and straight and bold
> and ask why bread is given to so few."

Mother hated the song. We could hear him coming
back from the taverna singing it at night. She would lock
the doors, crossing herself. "Don't go near the door, Niko,
don't open it; let him rot out there in the rain. We've had
no soup, no oil for days, and he comes home full of wine.
Don't open the door."

Later, when the sound of his pounding had stopped
and her snoring had started, I would open the door and
let him fall back against me, into the room. Sometimes he
was not as drunk as all that and embraced me: "My good
son, ach, already you know that woman has no right to
bolt a man's door against him."

Still later I would hear him take her in the night, hear
the bed, her little shrieks, his bark of a laugh.

"Women," he told me in the boat after a few more
hard pulls on the bottle, "women are the seed of the Devil.
Don't tell your mother I said this."

I climbed the tree. Branch by branch, I grew taller. From
its top I could see the whole village wrapped around the
hill, from the sea below to the old castle on top. I lay on

a great branch and watched each leaf, each insect move over the bark as even then I was moving, month by month. I ran faster, jumped higher and my feet grew closer to the bottom of the bed. My body was harder, stronger, and I knew that the other boys imitated me. They even, when I wished, took their orders from me. And the weak ones admired me with their wet eyes. We were alone then in school for the girls had been moved to other rooms in other buildings. When we passed them in the street we did not speak, for we had become men and were strong and commanded respect. They would have to understand that life was ours, to be shared as we decided. Our fathers had shown us this, had given us this truth. My heels tapped smartly on the pavement as I strolled with my friends. Teachers feared us and our parents shouted at us. But we did not listen except sometimes to our fathers. Our mothers had become silly. They crossed themselves at every wayside shrine. They pecked and cackled. Food poured out of their kitchens endlessly, monotonously. "Eat," they said, "eat and eat and eat." A mother is a mouth. We ignored them and did as we chose. We seemed not to hear them and swore at them when our fathers were not home. Yet this is true too: we would kill an outsider who insulted them or our sisters.

Our fathers no longer bothered us. They had felt what we were feeling. Life had wounded them. When we saw them in the cafés sitting, always sitting, with their beads in their hands, we didn't question them. A man holds his pain close to his body. It is the mark of a man. Soon we would sit there too. Already we threw the dice down onto the backgammon board and slid the colored disks, *clack*, against the sides. We slapped our cards down on the table and let an extra one fall into the lap. We would cheat the gods, if necessary. We would be clever, wounded like our fathers though we might be.

As Father and I pulled in the nets far from the island in the morning, we saw another boat from the island to the west. We called across the still sea, "Health to you, good health. How goes the life?"

"Our lives go well. And yours?"

"Thanks to God."

"What news?"

"The world is eating itself. Germans everywhere. And Italians. They feed off us."

Troopships passed at a distance. Ávgustos and I watched them daily, tried to make out the nationalities of the flags.

"We'll go," Ávgustos said, "the two of us. What life is this here? Fishing, school, pah! What kind of life is this for us?"

"Yes," I said at first, "yes, we'll go." Ávgustos was so much taller, bigger. He must be right, I thought. Uniforms, guns, the edge of the earth. We'd go off like brothers.

"No," both our families said. They agreed with each other that death comes soon enough without seeking it out.

But we dreamed of battle, dreamed of blood. Bells rang out in the clear winter night and the moon swam in the harbor. Ávgustos threw stones at my window. "Now," he said, "a ship is passing. Let's take your father's boat."

But what will become of the boat? I thought. "If they take us onto the ship, how will my father get his boat back? How will he fish?"

He stood silently beneath the window with the moon turning his hair silver. Ávgustos, who marched with Andréas and me behind the man with the whistle, Ávgustos, who dreamed with us of fame and heroism as we kicked balls into the sky.

"Your health, then," he said.

"Your health."

I didn't go to look at the thing they found days later on the beach—the whitened, half-eaten person his parents said was Ávgustos, the thing Mad Manólis said was all that remained of the figure whose arms he had seen slicing through the reflection of the moon in the harbor, swimming toward a ship that passed without pausing.

I had become as tall as a young tree. Amalía and Maroula were taller too. Andréas and I passed them as we strolled the streets in opposite directions from the girls. We glanced at them cautiously, afraid they would catch us looking. It was weakness to show interest. When I had passed, I would glance back over my shoulder. Amalía's dark hair, combed tightly over her head, fell in a thick plait halfway down her back. She had a light step as if she were about to turn slowly, smoothly, stretch out her arms and begin to dance. But she continued down the street. She and her Maroula. Andréas and I chose a pastry shop where we ate sweet cakes and watched the girls walk back and forth.

Andréas was Maroula's cousin but a distant one. We are so isolated here in the sea that everyone is related to everyone else. Shy little Maroula, always in Amalía's shadow, her eyes cast down, her arms full of books. She and Amalía exchanged slow smiles when we went past.

James William Brown

Already Andréas's father the fisherman was ready to speak with Maroula's father the butcher. It would be a good match for Andréas.

"It's no good, Niko," Andréas said. "Fishing is no good anymore. But let's not be so stupid as Ávgustos, eh? May the earth rest lightly on his bones. A good marriage, that's the answer. Maroula will bring the butcher shop with her so one day it will be mine. She has no brothers. Ach, I don't want to be rich but there will be a little money, you know, a house, thanks to God. And Maroula, she knows how to move when she walks, eh?"

He sucked on a soda straw as we watched the girls walk past. We listened to the records on the foreign juke-box. We cracked seeds between our teeth.

Some of us were suspended from school again, for we were caught smoking in the toilets. A teacher, angry, with a red face, shouted, and parents screamed like owls: "What? Again?" So we had a little holiday and I did not mind at all.

I asked my friends, "Do you care? Does it matter at all?" For it was always I who made these plans and they who agreed, who submitted. For they could not define themselves, could not say, Here I begin and here I end. They did not know how to add themselves together. They waited for me. They were broken and separate. But when I came they were complete. This I gave them: this unity, this wholeness. And for this they did not mind a few days' suspension at all.

They would come to my house with their girlfriends (for there are always a few foolish girls who do not care) secretly, through alleyways on Sunday afternoons. My parents went to call on relatives then. So my friends crept into the rooms of my house, couple by couple, and closed the doors. I gave them these hours together. I guarded the door of the house, watching for the school inspector, for angry brothers, for the return of my parents. Sunday after Sunday it was the same. I looked after my friends. They came for my advice. I pulled them together and made them whole.

Ka-boom! The sea exploded all around the island. "Fishing with science, that's what it is," Father said. "Drop the dynamite in the water and—*ka-boom!* Flying fish." After the War, dynamite was suddenly cheap, easy to get. All the fishermen were using it. "Science, my boy, that's what we've got here."

Father was the first victim of the new science. I had not gone out with him in the boat that day. He left with Andréas's father in the black morning and as dawn came I could hear the explosions at sea from my bed. It was later, while Mother and I were drinking cups of sweet coffee, that Mad Manólis pounded on the door. Drooling, not able to speak. We knew. I was first to the harbor, where Father lay unconscious, the stump of his arm wrapped in knotted and bloody rags. He was gray. He looked dead. The other fishermen were packing ice around his side until the helicopter that had been radioed could arrive from the mainland.

I began to shake all over. Andréas's father was beside me, his arm around me. He told me of the fuse that was too short, the stick of dynamite that exploded in the space between my father's hand and the water. The hand was gone and half the forearm. They would cut at the elbow.

"It's your fault," Mother shrieked, coming up behind us, flying at Andréas's father. "You killed Giorgos with the dynamite. You could have stopped him from such foolishness." She scratched his face and would have taken an eye if the other women hadn't pulled her off.

"It was his own fault," they said, "using dynamite. It's a sign. Science, pah!"

"My poor Giorgos, oh, my poor little Giorgos." She bent over him, stroking his face, pushing away the men with the ice. She touched his chest, his good arm; she touched him everywhere. Even between the legs. As they lifted him onto a stretcher she stood up. "It was only an arm, thanks to God. He's still a man."

Days were warm and we lived beside the sea. Andréas and I lay on the sand baking ourselves brown then ran into the water and tried to drown each other. He shoved me backward and I pushed him under. He sat on my shoulders but we laughed and fell over with a splash, then surfaced, shaking the water from our hair, and laughed again.

He nudged me. "Eh, what is this?"

Down the beach walked a foreign girl, tall, with hair the color of wheat. She was wearing no top to her bikini. "Mother of God," Andréas said softly. She was a big girl.

Sometimes they came in summer—the mainland girls on holidays and the Scandinavian tourists full of memories of other summers. We met on the beach in the day, in the olive groves at night. Laughter drifted up through the branches and those were starry nights we spent.

She saw us, then pretended she didn't. The old game. On an isolated beach away from village eyes. She waded into the sea farther up the beach. The water moved up

her legs, around her thighs. "I am the sea," I said to
Andréas—and we both laughed. But wait, this was too
much to stand—she was swinging her arms back and forth,
splashing water, swinging, everything swinging. We sucked
in our breath and started to walk slowly through the water
toward her. She laughed then and ran through the foam
and up onto the beach, her hair shining in the sun, to the
place by the rock where she had left her towel. We ran
after her.

She faced us by the rock drying herself with the towel.
Andréas reached out, pulled the towel from her hands.
She wasn't laughing now and she said something fast in
her language—one of those northern ones that sound like
the speaker has something caught in the throat—and covered herself with her hands.

"Eh, look at this," Andréas said as he gently but firmly
pulled her arms down to her sides. She did not stop him.
She turned her head and looked away from us but she had
begun to breathe heavily. "You watch for me, yes?" Andréas said and began to touch her breasts, to cup them in
his hands feeling their weight, finally to lick them slowly.
Suddenly she threw her head back and laughed while he
pulled down the bottom of her bikini and she slid her
hands inside his swimming trunks. He stepped out of them,
ready.

I looked up and down the beach. There was a family
with a picnic far off. The children were shouting, chasing
each other in and out of the water. They were too far to
hear the noises she made. Foreign women are always noisy.
It's good, this. Not like the mainland girls who lift their
skirts and clench their teeth.

Andréas finished almost as soon as he began. She was

still moaning as I turned her over on her belly. As I covered her she smelled of scented soap and sweat and sea and the body of my friend. I ground my knees into the sand and pushed into her. She clawed at the sand and shouted words that maybe were not words at all but hard flat noises that went higher and higher and ran together like a tuneless song. I had waited all winter for one such as this.

Up and down the street we walked in the evening, arms linked, swaying with the stream of walkers, cracking seeds between our teeth. We spoke to girls with our eyes and laughed and nudged one another, then walked on. Andréas would slip up behind a girl and whisper quickly a single word, a suggestion, then move on with the flow of walkers, leaving as trail only the high color on her cheeks.

This was our evening path, up this worn street and down, the entire village, old ones watching from windows above, from rooftops, as mothers pushed baby carriages and big-bellied fathers with hands folded behind backs talked sports and weather. Now we stopped to peer in the window of the butcher shop where Maroula cleaned her father's block with a rag; now we paused at the pastry shop where children begged parents for ices. We sat in the café on the square watching the faces pass, calling out to friends as we tickled each other with soda straws.

Amalía passed and there was a thread that stretched thinner as she walked away. I pulled the thread. Without it I would drift away—away from my friends talking football, my parents talking money. Each day I pulled the thread tighter and Amalía did not know (there she ate ice cream with friends, there she walked along the sea with poppies in her hand) that I was pulling her close to me.

She pulled away. Even as she strolled the street she would look determined at first, as if she had an important errand to run, then puzzled, as if she had forgotten it. She seemed to swim beneath this moving stream then surface in a place far from where she had dived. And look around herself, startled.

Even when we were children in school, I understood that Amalía was unlike the rest of us. When we looked around the classroom we saw the teacher, the cracked blackboard, the clock, the icon. They were definite. We could touch them. I raced away; I was king of the drowned sailors. But always I came back to these hard objects, for there is comfort in what can be touched. When Amalía's eyes rested on the same objects, she saw something else there in front of the blackboard, in front of the icon. I tried to see what she saw. I gazed, I stared, but I could not find anything to explain the distant, absorbed look that came over her.

Later, after boys were separated from girls in school, a blackboard remained a blackboard. Oh, there were some boys, the weaker ones that I used to kick on the field, who may have seen something else before the blackboard, who can say? But most of us grew up. We made a trade: drowned sailors and crowns were exchanged for card games at the cafés, for stories told by men to the clacking of beads.

Women like Amalía did not make such a trade. They kept their light, their way of seeing. The men in the cafés slid disks back and forth across the board while the women waited at home. Men, taking women into their lives, did not have to worry about the losses manhood brings.

But she pulled away from me. She cared for no one

except Maroula. She grew free like a seed in the earth. She passed me in the street but she did not see me. I was nothing more to her than the blackboard in the schoolroom—there was something between her eyes and my face. And everyone knew. As children shrieked in the street and mothers ran after them, as old women pointed from balconies and rooftops at the objects of their gossip, I felt sure everyone smiled, laughed at me. I pretended to examine other girls. I dreamed of green hills and a night sweet with jasmine, when Amalía and I walked the streets of the village bearing ears of green corn. Pomegranates were smashed at our feet as we passed and the street was slippery with red juice. I became the sun, burning, blazing. She was the sea, hissing among the stones at the shore.

In the square that warm evening, our voices rose up and fell back laughing. Glasses clinked and the eucalyptus trees moved above us. In the distance we could hear the bus rattling toward us from the harbor. Already a crowd had gathered, come to meet those who had crossed from the mainland to the island that night on the weekly ferry. The square was filling with people. The bus carried all we needed of the city, of the world: newspapers, mail, supplies, relatives, good news and bad. It brought death. And life. We gathered to meet both, to watch them get off and jostle for their luggage.

As the bus pulled into the square, hands waved from crowded windows, shrieks of recognition went up from the crowd.

"Welcome, welcome—over this way—look here!"

"The packages, did you bring them?"

"Aunt Panayóta—is she still in hospital?"

Out the passengers poured; hands were clasped, cheeks kissed. The conductor climbed to the top of the bus where he unstrapped the luggage and tossed it down into the crowd. Around the ancient bus the crowd swayed: An old woman carried a live chicken upside down, bound by the legs. Someone had sent a barrel of wine so heavy it took four men to move it. Clothes ordered for a wedding were pulled from their boxes and examined by a young girl's family. The bridal veil, streaming from the headband of false daisies, was passed from hand to hand until an old man put it on and danced as the crowd laughed and clapped.

When the bus was empty, when most of the village had gone home to drink to good fortune or bad fate, then we noticed a foreigner there by himself at the side of the bus. He was tall and wore a large pack on his back. He glanced at us, brushing his long hair out of his face with his hand. Pale and blond, he looked unwashed in his torn jeans.

"Another foreigner? But why?" Andréas asked. "The women, yes, I understand." He laughed. "But foreign men? Why go to a place where no one waits for you at the end of a journey? Where no one claps you on the back and drinks wine to your arrival?"

"He's as young as we are," I said. "How do they have money and freedom to travel this way? Foreign places must be ugly with bad climates. Everyone wants to come here."

He adjusted his pack and glanced at us again. Were we not to welcome him, to know his intent? Strangers are gods, some say. If you have no food for the stranger, as they say, kill your children and cook them. The women tell of a man who turned a stranger away from his door.

When he went back to the meat stew he had left bubbling on the fire, it had been turned to human flesh. The stranger, of course, was Christ.

Looking from side to side, he seemed to take in everything, the houses, the lion fountain. From the other direction came Amalía and her friends. The foreigner stopped them and asked something in a language we could not understand. Norwegian, Swedish? It was Amalía who spoke, answering in English as she pointed up the street. They turned and walked with him, showing him the way.

We paused by the butcher shop to watch and could hear the girls giggling as the foreigner spoke. They were forbidden to speak with us but not forbidden to talk with a foreigner. Because they were being helpful. How unfair it all was. My friends were watching me. I laughed, made an obscene gesture toward the foreigner and casually turned away, friends following. Yet I knew, as I hoped they did not know, that the breeze had somehow turned, that there was a new scent in the night air.

We set out to watch him. It was the kind of game I suggested. When he went into a café, one or two of us sat a few tables away. When he walked over the hills, we followed at a distance. In a shop, in the market, we were always near. Once, late afternoon, in the café in the square, our eyes met. He was at the next table and, as I looked up from my sports magazine, his eyes were on me. Green.

Golden hair, the color of the girl's on the beach. He almost smiled, as I almost did. His was a face like those projected on the white wall behind the village in the summer when moving pictures were sent from the mainland. I knew that shopkeepers came out to look at him as he passed. Women paused in the market and nudged one another, whispering. Even old men in the cafés looked up from their games to see the foreigner. The priest was angry. "How can a foreigner put a tent there so near the chapel in the fortress? Perhaps he is anti-Christ."

"But of course," everyone said, "we must be hospitable."

The old men had the answer, they said. "He's a spy. Sent by the Turks."

"A spy!" Andréas and I laughed at them. "What would he spy out here? Tomato plants? Wheat fields?"

"Our treasures. He has a radio and sends messages to ships at sea. They'll come take our icons, our gold sovereigns and sell them for guns, for knives. To cut our throats, take our women, burn our church."

"But of course," everyone said, "we must be hospitable."

When I looked at him over the top of my sports magazine, his face was lit by the last of the daylight. His hair seemed to glow as the sun sank behind him. A bird called out from a eucalyptus tree across the square.

He stayed many weeks, though foreigners usually do not stay long. Amalía showed him the sunken harbor, translated for him in the shops. They sat on rocks beside the sea and talked.

The men in the cafés talked about them as did the women in the market. They looked at me. They said nothing. They asked without speaking, Will you let him shame you, will you let him shame us? He is a foreigner, yes, but still he is a man.

Andréas and I climbed up to the fortress where we had played as children. In through the archway of great brown stones. We edged our way along the ramparts, up the broken steps to the walls. The wind beat at us and the spring sun burned against our skins. From there we could look down on the whole village. Old women, made tiny by distance, chased chickens in the street, the priest dozed beneath the lemon tree in his garden, and Mad Manólis moved slowly up the street with his donkey, collecting rubbish. The white houses were like steps leading down from the fortress, down to the harbor, where the sea spread out, one great plate of water to the rim of the horizon.

Outside the village stretched the tomato fields. Ever since the War ended and Spyros Galánis returned to the island, wheat had given way to tomato plants and now there were many thousands of them. Men worked among the rows, pulling weeds, irrigating. One of those men was my father, bending and rising with others.

Doing half the work with his one arm that they did, but getting full pay. Mr. Galánis was good to fishermen wounded by dynamite. None of them went out anymore. There were far more tomatoes than fish; there was more money to be made in the fields. How lucky I was to have Mr. Galánis as my godfather, though I was but one of many he had plunged into the font of steaming water in the church, only one of those whose body openings he had sealed from evil with Holy Oil. But I was his favorite. "Ach, Niko," he said when he came to call on the feast day of Saint Nicholas, "when I look at you I see myself as a young man. You and Andréas, you're like Grigóris and me. You are this village. Whatever you need, whatever you want, you come to me." And he led the others in lifting their glasses to me. "Health and many years of life!"

What did I want? Amalía: this was all I knew. And now to know what it meant that this stranger was here, that he was here with Amalía and showed no signs of leaving. When we turned from the ramparts, from the village below us, we saw his tent there in the courtyard of the fortress, near the chapel. The flaps of the tent slapped each other in the breeze. We tossed stones near the tent but no one stirred. Sometimes we came at night and made bird noises from the far corner of the courtyard. He would come out of the tent, flashlight in hand, as we slipped behind piles of rubble to hide. The single eye of the flashlight would move slowly along the ancient walls and, finding nothing, go out.

Other nights we saw him cooking food over a fire in front of the tent. "This is not work for a man," I said to Andréas. "How is it that foreign men do the work of women?" Or he would read inside his tent by the light of a bottled-gas lamp and we could see his shadow on the canvas.

We didn't see Amalía at the tent. But still they said in the village that she came here with him. Often. Whether she did or not, if they believed so, then it was the same.

How tall Amalía's house seemed to me when I was a child. It had grown smaller these past few years and now at night it drew me toward itself. Opening the gate, I ran soundlessly to the left side of the house where there was a giant fig tree. It had always been there. No one knew how old it was but its twisted branches reached up to the second storey of the house. When we were children, we climbed the lower branches, pretending the tree was a mountain.

It was still strong, still a good tree. I pulled myself up through its curling branches; I felt no heavier than a leaf. One of the second-storey windows was partly open.

Inside, a long hall. Here was a frame, a door. I could make out the distant sighing of a sleeper. I turned the handle; the door scraped open. Bedclothes rustled. Inside the room, I closed the door behind me.

"Mother?"

I could make out the bed, a white shape on it. Turn now, rush out the window, down the tree. There would be time for escape before she closed me out as she always had. Run now before words are spoken, before a lamp is lit.

"Mother?"

"Nikos."

"Niko?"

"I want to talk to you."

"Niko! Oh, my God."

"Don't turn on the light."

"Please go away. Please go away now. If anyone saw you come in that window, both our lives are ruined. Oh, Niko, Niko. Are you so crazy?"

There was fear in her voice. But this is the way they behave at first. Everyone said so. At first they pretend to be frightened. They do this to fire your blood.

"No one saw me. The lights are out in all the houses."

"Mother is downstairs. She'll hear you and she'll blame me. She'll say I asked you to come and she'll beat me. Oh, God, Niko, please go away."

"I won't let her," I said, moving nearer the bed. "I won't let anyone hurt you. That's what I came to say. This foreigner, he will harm himself by staying, Amalía, and

harm you more. I don't want this and neither do you."
She said nothing. I could her breathing in the dark. "Why
don't you say something? What are you thinking?"

"I'm thinking that by coming here, you have risked
ruining my life. And yet you say you don't want to hurt
me. Oh, Niko, leave me alone. I don't want to see your
lonely eyes following me anymore. I will be happy to leave
this place."

"Leave? Why? You can't."

"Why not? You have no claim on me. I've given no
promise to you or anyone else."

This is what they do, I thought. This is what women
do. It is a kind of code. They tell you they don't want you,
when all the time they are watching you, waiting. If you
believe their words, if you turn away, they tell everyone
that you are weak and then you are laughed at. I understood the game. I was not to be laughed at. *Go away* meant
Come closer. I reached out to touch her.

"Don't." She jumped out of bed, turning on a bedside
lamp. We stood in the light. The lines of her body under
the long white nightgown—she was nearly as perfect as
the foreign girl on the beach. But younger, firmer.

"You are the other half of me," I said. "If you were
a man you would be me. And I would be you if I were a
woman."

"Oh, Niko, you are no part of me and never will be.
I'm leaving this place."

"With him?"

"Yes."

"No! You'll do what I say."

"Stop it, Niko! Don't bully me. It doesn't work."

I told her they were talking about her, the men in the

fields as they ate their lunches, the old women in the market. What are they doing over there in the cove? they were asking. And they were laughing at her and at me. Yes, even at me. What she did with the foreigner left me open to everyone's laughter. "You are making me out a fool! Every time you walk through the village with him, every time you go to his tent. You do go, don't you?"

"Niko, please leave."

"*Do* you?"

"You have no claim on me."

I wanted to hurt her, to push her into the sea again because she had buttoned her coat, she closed me out. Because somewhere a plate smashed to the floor, cake was smeared on the flowered carpet. The walls moved forward to crush me. I turned and bumped into the bureau where books were stacked.

"Does he like these?" I asked. "Does he like these books you read? Do you read them to him there in the tent?" I raked my arm across the bureau top, knocking all the books to the floor.

"Get out, Niko. Lights are going on in the other houses. Mother may have heard you."

It was not good, the fire. Everyone said it was not good. First, because news of it would spread to nearby islands. Our neighbors in the sea would say we were a mean people who had shamed them all with our lack of hospitality. Second because we had given the *eye* to the stranger. We had admired his beauty, his foreignness and brought bad fortune to him. All this would come back on us someday, the old women said. They crossed themselves three times and watched the sky for omens.

Everyone said I had started it. Or if not, some of my friends had done it for me. I said I hadn't done it but I didn't mind when they told me it was a terrible thing because under their words I could hear respect. They implied I had protected what was mine. Not good, this fire, they said, and looked at me with admiration.

So I said nothing.

The weeds were burned away in a large circle. There was nothing left of his belongings. The petrol can that had been used lay discarded near the wall. The tent must have burned fast for the fire was almost out before anyone could get up to it. No one had seen the stranger. Later we were to learn that Stelios the fisherman had accepted the stranger's radio in exchange for rowing him to a nearby island where he could get a ship to the mainland. But the old men said they were right about his being a spy: Turks had come in a helicopter and taken him away in the night. Pappa Yannis said that the fire only proved that he was right: The stranger was anti-Christ. His evil burned itself out and the stranger sank into the bowels of the earth.

A shepherd was out in the hills one night, our island legend tells, when his sheep were killed by wolves. His flock was the shepherd's only means of support. So he mourned the loss of his livelihood by skinning the dead sheep and wrapping the skins around his body. He took the bells from their necks and fastened them to a harness that he hung from his shoulders. Then he covered his face with a mask made from the skin of a newborn kid.

When he entered the village, he danced from café to café with the bells clanking and banging. At each café the men gave him something to drink and soon he was drunk.

His dance became more frantic as he whirled through the streets of the village. Up the steps he danced to the great rock where the old fortress now stands. From this, the highest point on the island, he threw himself into the sea below. Today the priest says that he danced to the chapel within the walls of the fortress and there collapsed before the icons. But we know there was no chapel so long ago, nor even a fortress.

Each year the priest waits in the chapel to bless the goat dancers and to ask the saints to smile on our poor island, lost in the great sea. To strengthen us for the sacrifices of Lent that we might celebrate the more in forty days when our dead God lives again.

The goatskin mask and the sheepskins are the most important of all the masks and costumes. We all wanted to wear them, all the young men of the village. Even those who had left the island came back for Carnival. We watched them get off the bus, our cousins in their city clothes eager to dance the ancient Carnival dance.

On the last day of Carnival, I pulled on the heavy shepherd trousers and wool socks. My feet were bound in strips of leather and my mother wrapped my body with the heavy skins.

"How tall you are, my son."

Together Father and Mother put the harness of bells on my shoulders, a duty that was once his alone—but since the accident, one they shared. Twenty kilos of bells there were, and I staggered under their weight.

"How strong you are, my son."

They straightened the costume and I covered my face with the mask. It was a new one from a stillborn kid of last December. Its skin was smooth against my skin. The fur had few markings. Albino. No one else in the village would have one like it. Inside, my mother had sprinkled cologne to lessen the bad odor if the sweat of my face caused the quickly tanned skin to rot. The mask closed me in. Through the two eyeholes I made out the kitchen table, the wood pile in the corner. "Can you breathe?" they asked. "Can you see?" With a great clanking of sheep bells, I was guided out the door.

The night was full of bleating Carnival horns. I made my way down the steps carefully as my parents watched from the door of the house. I walked slowly, easing one foot out, then the other, searching for the edges to the steps. Shutters flew open as people heard the clanking bells. Voices called out, "Come look—a white mask."

"How tall he is," women said. "Who is so tall, with such a mask?"

I passed slowly down the steps, clanging. The last was level with the main street. I paused there in the darkness and then moved into the street, beginning the first of the ritual gaits to make the bells clash and clang in definite rhythm: a loping walk with a bucking movement after each step. As a boy I had watched the men do it year after year, had studied them, had awaited my turn. I had practiced with my father, for he still remembered well the steps from his youth. I moved in a circle then, shaking so that the bells of different pitches would ring, jingle, clank. The circle tightened as the interest of the crowd tightened. Children shrieked and were pulled back by their mothers.

Do not forget me, the dance seemed to say. Do not forget my sheep eaten by wolves. Each bell rings out a life devoured. Do not forget me lest you be forgotten also when wolves call out on midwinter nights.

I moved down the street with difficulty, jumping into a stride, a heavy two-beat rhythm, lunging now right, now left. Old women screamed and called out to one another, "Who is it? Who's the white-masked dancer?" I paused at cafés where men passed me tiny glasses of raki that I slipped under the mask and gulped. Then water. Long glasses of water.

I had danced far up the street when I saw Andréas in his spotted mask and some of the others. Their bells together with mine were deafening. We whirled and crashed into one another as the crowd cheered. The four of us formed a circle. Leaning on our crooks, we shook our bodies as hard as we could for over five minutes, driving the people back with the noise. Then we turned again and moved off in different directions. The raki and the heat inside the costume had made me dizzy. I was afraid of losing my balance, falling. I jumped through a parting in the crowd into a narrow lane between houses where I hoped I could just stand for a minute to steady myself.

But suddenly something was thrown against me. Someone pushed and shrieked. My mask was pulled sideways and I could not see. As I fell back against the wall, a man's voice swore and then a woman said, "It's a goat dancer. He's run into us in the dark." I pulled at my mask and slid it into place in time to see through the eyeholes a couple dressed as pirates rushing away out the other end of the lane. The woman cried, "He saw me! He saw me!"

Who was she? All was clouded by exhaustion, by the raki. I felt behind me to see if all the bells were in place. Who was she? I wondered again. Anything was possible on the last night of Carnival; anyone could dance. Perhaps even good fortune was in our village, dancing behind a mask. And death. I would dance to them both.

I walked back into the street and began another gait, crossing one foot in front of the other, then stepping behind, one long beat and a short. I was no longer Nikos, no longer the son of the fisherman. Nor was I the poor boy turned rich nor the leader of his friends nor the child of his mother nor the descendant of his ancestors framed on the wall. That night I was not to be divided among those who needed me. I was the goat-faced creature with the clanking bells. I prowled the hills and slept in olive trees. I mourned the murdered sheep and ran against the wind faster than wolves. I knew secret caves and the hearts of boulders buried deep in mountains. The hair on my skin glistened as I danced and the bells cried out. I turned and again turned. Each step led me higher with the other dancers and the crowd following. The street went past lighted houses. I spun; I leapt. I could not hear for the noise of the bells. The mask was damp and stuck to my face. I breathed the odor of goatskin and eau de cologne. Children pushed me from behind.

The crowds had pulled back so I knew we had reached the entrance of the fortress. Guided by the light from the chapel, we raced across the courtyard. I was first to grab the rope and pull so the chapel bells rang down across the village and the crowd cheered me. Other hands seized the rope from me and the bells rang out as I danced into the chapel and turned and turned one last time. The others danced in behind me after each had rung the bells which resounded in the dome of the chapel along with the noise of our sheep bells. We ended our dance there in front of the gleaming icons. Hands removed my mask and I saw the Holy Lights, the white-bearded priest. We prayed then, repeating the old words made smooth from our tongues. But few heads were bowed as people stared at the face that had been beneath the albino mask. "Nikos," they said. "Nikos," they repeated. My name was woven in with the prayers.

Garlands of lights were strung among the eucalyptus trees. The sea breeze rocked them and the branches cast crazy shadows across the square as if arms were reaching out, then back. Children chased one another, blowing Carnival whistles and horns, flinging fistfuls of confetti into the crowd that had gathered. There were princes and bears, slaves and gods, clowns. We had come down from the fortress to watch the dance of the young women. It was the most beautiful of all the Carnival and Amalía would lead the dancers, as she had each year for so many. I had changed out of my costume and stood with the crowd around the square.

The music was beginning. At the edge of the square next to the microphone, Mad Manólis was making a few squeaks on his clarinet. His cousin Dimitrios forced a fiddle to cry out in pain. And Rondélis, Maroula's father, plucked drunkenly at the strings of the bouzouki. The professors, we called them. They had played at every Carnival as long as I could remember. Their tuning-up notes came and went as the speakers, hung along with the lights from the lower branches of the trees, swayed in the breeze.

Old men came up to me to shake my hand, to embrace me, to tell me that my dancing was the best in many years. "Better even," one whispered to me, "than in my youth.

All were good, but you," he said, "you, my child, were best of all. Health to you." He touched the side of my face with a hand like well-tanned leather, this elder of one of our oldest Houses. And moved off through the crowd which parted in front of him and greeted him silently with respectful nods of heads.

At last the professors attacked the music. The fiddle fought the shrieking clarinet for the lead and the bouzouki strummed in the background. They were too near the microphone, which sent ear-piercing sounds and distorted music out through the swaying speakers. We held our ears and shouted, "Ugly! Ugly! Ugly!" The music died out. The professors looked at us, surprised.

"Why do you shout?" Mad Manólis shouted.

"This is music?" a voice cried out.

"You want Beethoven?"

"If he plays better than you do," the voice returned. Everyone laughed.

The professors talked among themselves angrily while the crowd argued—some in favor of phonograph and records, others wanting to disconnect the speakers. From the way the professors were packing their instruments into their cases, we understood that they had been insulted. Mayor Kontópoulos rushed over to them, his big belly bouncing, and explained that they should stand farther back from the microphone. They did not agree. Much hand waving, shouting. If something was wrong with the microphone, Mad Manólis announced, it was not *their* fault. They would go to the café. If God willed, someone would repair the broken microphone. Then they would play again, *if* they were asked to.

We jeered and sent them to the Devil. The professors

turned their backs and left the square. The mayor tested the microphone, counting into it, and even sang a few bars of the national anthem. Everyone applauded. Nothing was wrong with the microphone. He waited a few minutes before going to tell the professors that the equipment had been repaired. We stood without sound as he walked down the street. We could hear him apologizing on behalf of the microphone, the crowd, the speakers, the wind, fate. If only they would reconsider.

They reconsidered. Once again the music swayed into the crowd, still unclear but perhaps not as loud.

From the back of the square came two lines of girls. They wore the long gowns of our island. Each deep red with a gold-embroidered panel down the front of the skirt. Their hair was bound up in red village scarves. When they reached the middle of the square, the two lines stopped and turned to face each other. They joined hands, waiting for a pause in the music. Perhaps it was the beauty of the girls, the way the breeze fingered their head scarves and stroked the folds of their gowns, the way the light rested on their faces, this and more that moved the professors. For when the music began again, it flowed evenly.

The girls stepped into the music as if it were a stream in which they dipped and bowed. Amalía moved between the two lines. Chains of coins were strung across the top of her dress in imitation of the old way of displaying dowries. They glinted in the lights from the trees and in her hand she carried a long scarf. Passing quickly between the lines, she raised the scarf to cover her face, then lowered it. She paused at the far end of the two lines with her arms held out. The first girl in each line took hold of one of

Amalía's arms, the two lines became one, united by Amalía, and the girls began to sing:

> "This black earth we tread,
>   Tread it all together;
>
> "This black earth we tread,
>   Tread it all together."

The single line of dancers curled into a great half circle that flowed around the square. The shadows of the trees moved over them as if in time to the song. The breeze whipped the skirts around their legs. They passed by me one by one, girls I had known all my life, turning now into women. Amalía was far down the line, moving this way, Amalía, with whom I had run foot races as a child, played war games and climbed trees. Amalía, who buttoned her coat and closed me out one day beside the sea. The Amalía I pushed into the water now moved toward me, then as the line paused and reversed direction, moved away.

> "This green earth with its flowers
>   Eats away the endless hours."

The dancers faced out toward us. Relatives called out names as daughters, cousins, nieces passed by and then paused and passed the other way. People behind me pushed forward, admiring the girls, comparing this one to that, Chrysoúla to Maria. I told them to shut up, for once again I saw Amalía's section of the line coming closer.

Suddenly it stopped just there in front of me. Amalía and I, face-to-face.

> "This old earth with its grasses
> Eats brave lads and the lasses.

> "This old earth will eat me too;
> What will my poor children do?"

The village turned around *us*. It was for *us* the lights cast patterns on the square, for *us* the shadows of the trees reached out, then back. We will come together and exchange wreaths, we said with our eyes. Pomegranates will be smashed at our feet. Our daughters will dance in this square and our sons will wear the albino mask. The village will turn and again turn and at its center will be my line.

The dancers reversed direction; she was gone. The crowd applauded and cheered as the line neared the edge of the square. Everyone took up the song, the voice of the village ringing out:

> "This black earth we tread,
> Tread it all together."

As soon as the village quieted that night, as soon as the Carnival horns died down for another year, I opened my bedroom window and said, "I am the hunter."

The houses were sleeping. I walked the lanes among them and from a window, a door heard the last goodnights, the last wishes for health exchanged. Hyacinths in courtyards sweetened the night but from the hills the wind brought the wilder scents of wet earth, of thyme and sage.

Someone had forgotten to turn off the lights in the square and the shadows did their own dance now, rocking drunkenly across the pavement.

In a downstairs window of Amalía's house, two figures cast shadows against the curtain. But I didn't pause before climbing the tree, slipping in the open window again. Scraping open Amalía's door.

The light was on. Her Carnival gown was thrown across the chair, its gold coins tumbled amid the embroidery. Amalía was in bed reading. She dropped the book, cried out.

"Niko! Oh, God, no, not again."

"I had to come."

"I asked you not to. Oh, Niko."

"You know why."

"No, I don't. What I know is that you're determined to ruin us. Already the women have seen you, I'm sure."

"It doesn't matter anymore. I have to tell you about the dance, how when you stopped on front of me, I understood. My Amalía. Your eyes. I saw the promise in them. I will never be able to get beyond you." My words came faster and easier. At last it was taking place. She was breathing rapidly. "Now we must tell the village, speak of this bond between us. Ach, how beautiful you were tonight."

"What are you saying, Niko? The dance moves and stops. You know that. You know the dance. It was just chance that I stopped in front of you. It didn't mean anything. It was only the dance. Are you saying that I made some signal to you there in front of the whole village?"

"Yes! You know you did. Don't play with me, Amalía. I understand these games, but we don't need them anymore. We *are* the village. Don't you understand? We can do anything we want. They need us. They wait for us." I came close to the bed and reached out to lay my hands on her shoulders, to hold her.

Suddenly her mouth was on my arm and she bit down hard. The fold of flesh between her teeth, the skin tearing, the blood. I could not cry out so it seemed to go on forever, as if I had always been there, in that room, watching her down-turned head, the collar of her gown. I slapped her hard with my other hand and jumped back free. My arm was bleeding. I would carry the mark of her mouth on my body the rest of my life, there near the imprint of the medusa that had grazed me, stinging me with its many sharp mouths, the previous summer in the sea. Amalía seemed far away, tiny, on the other side of a vast bed, her hand over her mouth.

The lamb turned on a motorized spit over the bed of charcoal and I watched its single eye go round and round. The other had fallen out already and the delicacy had burned away unnoticed in the charcoal. Across the garden, neighbors and relatives were dancing drunkenly in a line to music from the radio inside our house.

"Happy Easter, Niko," my godfather said.

"Happy Easter."

"Can I take this chair here beside you? Ach, my bones are tired." He sat on the old cane chair.

"But let me get you a better one . . ."

"Don't trouble yourself, Niko. This will do. So another Easter is here. Christ is risen, as they say."

"Truly risen."

"I like the old customs, you know. Come, let's crack eggs and see who's the strongest." He reached to the table under the lemon tree and took two red eggs from the bowl. He held his over mine and brought it down hard. His cracked; mine did not.

"Bravo," he said. "Such are our lives. Strong young men take over from the old ones."

"Old? You? I saw you dancing over there. You were the best of them all."

"It's good of you to say so. But I have my years, you know. Not like you young warriors." He laughed, and then said quickly, "I suppose it won't be long now until you're telling us all you want to marry, eh?"

For the first time in years, I could feel my cheeks burn. "Pah! Who says this?"

"Oh, people here and there. You know."

"It isn't true."

"Isn't it?"

With a burst of drums, the dance ended and the dancers fell into one another, laughing, shouting, calling out, "Niko, Spyro, come dance with us. So serious today? Bring the wine."

"Later, later!" he shouted. Then he continued to me, "Now the best dancer I ever saw was the father of Amalía—Grigóris. We used to call him the president of all dancers, he was so good. Amalía, now she's a good dancer too, eh?"

"Very good."

"As good as you?"

"Better."

"I see." He turned to watch the lamb on the spit. "Doesn't that smell wonderful! And now they have those little motors to do all the turning. In my time I turned the spit by hand until my arm was as roasted as the lamb. But everything changes. In my time when a man liked the way a girl danced, he didn't wait long after he'd climbed her fig tree. It's been a while since Carnival, Niko. Lent is over."

I looked across the garden at the dancers who were lining up and laughing, getting ready to begin again. I said quietly, "She doesn't want me."

"Ach, they all say that. That's no problem. There isn't anything else, is there?"

"What do you mean?"

"I mean, you're all right, aren't you? You know what you want, don't you?"

"Yes."

"Then take it."

"How?"

He laughed. "As they say in one of those countries where I sell a lot of tomato paste—I don't remember which one—if you have to ask, then you wouldn't understand the answer."

I stood up, started to walk away.

"Come, Niko, sit down. Now I've insulted you; I'm sorry, forgive me. Please. Sit down." He took my arm and pulled me gently back to the chair. Another dance had begun. They were all shouting "Oh-pah!" and whistling as they turned around a mulberry tree.

"What I want to tell you is just this: Froso and I had no children, you know, and I've always wanted a son like you. Oh I have other godsons—who knows how many? But you, Niko, I could help you." He paused, brushed off one of his cuffs, sighed. "I'm alone. I need someone to learn the business, maybe take over after I'm gone. But I need a man, a man who'll make strong sons, a man who

knows what he wants and takes it, eh? No, don't say anything. But remember, a man dishonors his family and
friends when he fails to act. The world turns around, eh?
And there are always . . ."

"Come!" shouted the dancers who had stumbled in
our direction, led by my father. "It's Easter. On your feet!"
Hands grabbed ours and pulled us up, dragged us past
the lamb hissing over the charcoal.

"There are always others," my godfather shouted at
me over the music, "to dance the dance. Right, Niko?"
The line stumbled on, pulling us with it.

"Oh-pah!" they shouted. "Oh-pah!"

I would not fail to act. When I next saw Amalía, she was
standing on the seawall, looking down at me in fear and
disgust. Our eyes met just as I hefted a great stone over
my head, ready to bring it down on the huge shell of the
female sea turtle, the biggest one to come ashore that year.

"Break her, Niko!" the men shouted.

Amalía mouthed *no* to me. But I could not turn away
from what I had to do. All men want the sea turtles to die.
And this one was full of eggs. Out of her could come many
more to shred our nets, our flesh.

The turtles had risen through the water off the south
coast as if the sun were pulling them. Faster than my
father's boat, their shadows passed over stones on the sea
floor below. This one was bigger than the others for she
had whorls on her shell that were perhaps a hundred years
old. She glided through the water as bands of light broke
over her. It was strange that she could be so huge, so old
and still so graceful. She was also frightening. I could see
the great claws on her feet.

"Niko! Break her!"

Down I hurled the stone with all my weight. The men cheered and closed in. When I looked up, there was no one on the wall where Amalía had been. I pushed through the men and leapt onto it. I could see Amalía running along the seashore. She glanced back at me, then turned into a narrow street. And I after her, strong with the turtle's strength. Amalía ahead ran wildly with arms outstretched as if she would fly. The streets were deserted, the women inside behind closed shutters. Blue, green, red—the colors of the doors beat a rhythm as we ran past, rounded corners, up steps and more steps, under the fig tree by the lion fountain. She kicked off her shoes and ran barefoot, her feet slapping the cobblestones. Somewhere a girl's arm was lying on a window ledge; somewhere a door was being opened by someone who could not be seen. Up we went to the fortress, through the great archway, across the court-yard and the burned place where the stranger's tent had been. There was no place to go from there, no place but down to the rocks and sea below. Against the wall Amalía stopped, her hands behind her back, grasping the stones to support herself, heaving for air. We stood facing each other, trying to breathe, a stinging in my head as if I had dived too far beneath the sea with too little air. We did not move and there was only the sound of the wind singing in the ramparts. I stepped closer.

She spoke.

AMALÍA

Listen to us. Listen! whispered the *Tse-lapétina*, the great feathered one.

I'm falling! the dragonfly screamed. *Save me!*

Then Poseidon roared, one long bellow that drowned the voices of the others. Two places collided within me. In one, the old place where I had lived so long, I felt myself explode. In the other, the place of day spirits, Nikos came closer, his chest rising and falling under the blue shirt stained black with sweat and the blood of the turtle. His eyes were huge and crazy as he backed me against the wall of the fortress in that kind of silence that comes before trouble—the silence that filled the room where Papa lay before the women came in to mourn and the gods to scream, the silence I had to break.

"It's all right, Niko," I said. "I will, I swear I will."

Done! called Poseidon in the boom of the waves far below. *Done.*

Then Nikos's hands were on me, pulling at me. I hit out at him. It was not for this that I had run up from the beach, knowing he would follow, leading him here for all the village to see so it would be final, decided, with only details for the families to work out. But if the life in me were taken, I would be worth no more than a turtle broken on a beach. I screamed.

"Do that again," he said. "It's what they've all been waiting to hear. It's what they all want."

"I'll marry you. Understand that. You don't have to do this so stop now before something stupid happens and everything is ruined." But he went on pushing me into the wall, pushing himself up against me. As he took one hand off me to pull at his clothes, I was able to tear free, turn and get a foothold on the lower stones of the wall. Before I could pull myself up, his arms came quickly from behind, dragging me down, my hands scraping stone. "You'll marry my death, Niko, I swear it."

"Amalía!" Mother's voice. "Amalía!"

Nikos stood back. A cool breeze ran along the ramparts pressing our damp clothes against us and throwing dust in our mouths as we gulped air. Mother came through the archway, hurried over to us, her eyes full of anger and questions. I met her stare calmly: Ask what you will, I told her with my eyes, I have nothing for you now. But there are years ahead to bring you such answers as you want.

The women who watched from rooftops as she led me home are the same who watch with their families now when the wreaths lie before us and the eyes of the priest slide over the people packed into the church as he calculates his fee. He takes his hands from under the vestments of gold cloth, looks at us wearily, holds his right hand up in blessing and a single chord, rich and full, is sung by the choir. It fills the church, swells into the dome, where it hovers for a minute, then dies away.

Turn, run! says the *Tselapétina*, hanging upside down in the dome, its feathers fluttering in the coils of incense rising.

No, never again.

The dragonfly lights on the shoulder of the priest. His wings glisten. *Take me*, he says. *Eat me.*

But the old longing is gone, the need to swallow Papa's death, honor Maroula, punish myself.

The choir sings:

> "The watchman says
> the morning comes,
> and also the night."

"Look! Hair the color of sovereigns!"

"And he's tall as a tree."

"Why is he here?"

"Say something to him, Amalía; you'll know what to say."

"Don't be stupid," I told my classmates. "I don't even know what language he speaks." Few of us had seen a foreigner before last winter but that was no reason to act like a fool. We had been walking near the square late that afternoon when the bus bringing the ferry passengers from the harbor arrived. Nels was the last off—though I didn't know his name then—tall and thin, carrying a guitar. With his hand he brushed the long blond hair off his forehead and stepped to one side while the conductor threw the luggage down from the roof of the bus. When his big pack hit the ground, Nels stepped forward, put down his guitar and lifted the pack lightly, almost delicately to his shoulders. He slipped his arms easily through the straps, though we knew from the way the pack had fallen that it was very heavy. He looked over at us watching him and smiled happily as if to say that the journey here on the old ferry (its overflowing toilets, its cracked plastic seats) and the bus trip up from the harbor (everyone standing in the aisle, the smells of garlic and sweat) had been wonderful. He came over to us and spoke in halting English.

"Is here someplace cheap? Goot but cheap? Hotel, pensione, maybe?"

The girls all giggled at the foreign words. Only I knew any of this go-between language but I had learned the pronunciation from the radio and from lessons on records so his accent was hard for me to understand. English was no more his language than mine, but I had passed first certificate in it and I was better at it than he was.

"Here? Now?" I asked. "In summer, yes, there are places for visitors, but not now." He laughed. It was a big laugh, one that went on and on, a good long laugh, as if it were funny that he had come here to this place in the stormy sea where there was nowhere to stay when nights were cold and the sea wind had bite to it. It was the kind of laugh that makes you laugh also and soon we were all laughing with him, though the other girls hadn't understood anything he'd said. Passengers from the bus, hurrying home with jugs of wine and baskets of onions and suitcases tied with rope, turned and looked at the tall stranger laughing with us in the street.

"Is a place for a tent here?" he asked us. "A high place? I have a tent."

"Yes." I pointed up the winding street. "Go up all the way. Inside the old walls is the highest place."

"Goot. I can see the stars from there."

"What is he saying?" the others asked. "What? What?"

"Stars. He says he can look at stars."

"Stars." They giggled. "This is what foreigners do?"

"Am I to know?"

"Ask him! Ask him!"

"No, it's stupid. Don't be foolish."

"Oh, ask him, please, make him talk some more," they begged, giggling. But by this time he was up the street, waving to us as he went, probably thinking us all idiots. How light he was, how lightly he went, not like our men at all but hollow-boned, it seemed, laughing, with hair in his face. Before I could even think about it, I was running up the street after him.

"Wait!" I called out. He stopped and turned.

"Yes?"

Beware, the *Tselapétina* whispered. *Treachery, all is treachery.*

"Yes?" he said again, smiling. He had green eyes. I had never seen them except in foreign film magazines and I thought most of those were just colored on the photographs. I backed away from him stupidly, my heart pounding.

Run! the dragonfly screamed. *Turn, run!*

I flew down a side lane, looking neither left nor right, cutting through courtyards, across the village, up the long steps toward home. *Trust us*, the *Tselapétina* said. I finally reached our back garden and stood panting beside the lemon tree, holding on to a branch for support.

How bad the whole winter had been. Everything was my fault, everything was always my fault. I had to punish myself before the world could punish me. But I knew that wouldn't stop the world. You can't ever stop it. But at least I could control my own punishment and get ready for the world. When I thought of poor Maroula and blamed myself, the dragonfly god said, *Eat me, eat me,* and I tasted again the secret taste. I found my pockets full of crawling things and I was sick for a long time until I decided to go away. I packed an old laundry bag, then unpacked it and packed again. I didn't know where to go or how to get there or what to use for money. Only once had I ever been off the island and that was just to Athens with Papa for a day, years ago. I wanted to burn up the island and myself with it. I walked in the hills with them, the *Tselapétina,* the dragonfly, and looked for the bones of donkeys fallen into ditches. One day I brought home a skull. I put on a dressing gown back to front, set the skull on top my head and wrapped a purple shawl around it covering most of my face below, except for one eye. Then I walked down the staircase singing the national anthem as loudly as I could. The housegirls were cleaning out the fireplace in the sitting room when they saw me. They both screamed, dropped the bag of ashes on the antique carpet and ran out of the house.

"Why do you do these awful, crazy things?" Mother shouted after she had slapped me across the room.

"I don't know. It was just something to do. I don't know."

I felt as dull and tired as this island, sitting here in the old sea with the world passing it by. Everything seemed to hurt; even the wild narcissi opening by the thousands on the hillsides made me sick with the sweet smell I'd always loved. And the lighted windows of ships passing at night made me want to cry.

There was no one to talk to in this place of day spirits after Maroula married and worked full-time in her father's butcher shop. There were my schoolmates, but even though we were together in the last year of school, we were not friends. I was caught between them and Mother. I've been alone with Mother all these years and I suppose I've picked up a little of her way of speaking and behaving. I can't help that, even though Mother says, "You'd think you were the daughter of a goatherd, the way you talk and run around." But to the other girls, I had a more adult way of speaking that they made fun of. Once I said that the cold weather was *astonishing* and they looked at me, amazed. Words like that always got me in trouble with them.

"What an *astonishing* dress, Amalía," one of them would say of my school uniform.

"I just feel so, well, *astonishing* today, don't you?" another would laugh.

I never used the word again. It wasn't my fault that my mother talked differently than theirs. It certainly had done me no good for I hadn't inherited her cleverness at all; many of the girls were better students than I was and I admired them. I was of this place, after all, just as they were, just as Papa was. But still I was the daughter of the foreigner. And they, who couldn't ever stand to be outside a group, sometimes liked me but often kept their distance. I have always been caught between Mother and the island.

It was a lonely winter and a cold one. Great storms threw themselves at the island and took bites out of the

shore. We couldn't seem to stay warm and dry. The walls
of the schoolroom and of the house were damp and you
could see the mold spreading up near the ceiling. There
was a skin of ice on the puddles in the street and in the
harbor standing water was frozen hard as glass one morning. I thought that if I held myself as stiff and straight as
I could, I'd feel warmer, better. All day I tried to do that
and even lying in bed at night until it seemed to me that
there was a fist inside my chest, a tight fist with my heart
caught in it. Winter seemed to last years, though now when
it is almost summer and I think of myself standing under
the lemon tree in the back garden the night Nels arrived,
it seems winter passed in only a few minutes, but long ago.

After I had caught my breath under the tree, I began
to wander back toward the square. There was no sign of
the new arrival to the island and my classmates had gone
home as had the passengers from the bus who probably
were then in their houses chewing over the news from the
mainland. Children had taken over the square, chasing
each other around the eucalyptus trees, screaming and
shouting, throwing balls in the clear, cold evening.

"Come dance with us, Amalía, come!" the girls
shouted at me. They were practicing some new steps they
had learned at school and they wanted me to help them.
When I was their age, there had never been enough time
to play as long and hard as I'd wanted to. Mother was
always calling me home because, she said, the other girls
were "dirty." Suddenly, when the children shouted to me,
I wanted nothing more than to play and play. The girls
pulled me into their circle but we had only begun to dance
when the boys started throwing balls at us. The girls
screamed and ran after them, I out in front, catching the

leader and lifting him high as he shouted, "Swing me, Amalía, swing me!"

"And what if I let go?"

"God will punish you."

"That won't help you, will it?"

We both fell to the ground, dizzy. The girls ran over and pulled me up, then took me behind the trees to tell me secrets about their new teacher.

"She takes her teeth out and washes them in the toilet."

"She doesn't wear anything under her skirt. You can see everything when she bends over."

"If you tell, Amalía, we'll cut off your ears!"

"And your nose."

"And make you eat them."

After a while the voices of the mothers called, but we ignored them and played even more wildly, throwing balls higher and higher into the branches of trees in the hope that one would catch or burst, any small crisis to draw out the evening.

"Andóni!"

"Kosta!"

"Maria!"

The mothers continued to call and the girls began to answer, to trail away and the boys too wandered off. I didn't want to go home but the square was lonely and deserted after they had gone and I stood a minute under the stars that were beginning to appear in the night sky. They made me remember Nels—he had said something about stars. I saw again the graceful way he had slipped his arms through the straps of the pack.

The night, the trees, the departing children, all seemed strangely filled with his presence. I thought of the light way he moved and suddenly the fist inside me loosened, the hand freed my heart. I knew what it was I had wanted to say to him in the street: Take me with you when you leave.

Peering under the entrance flap of the small tent, I could make out dark shapes: some books, the guitar. I crawled inside. The wind in the fortress slapped the sides of the tent hard so that I felt as if I were inside some living thing that breathed and wheezed. What a wonderful way to live—in a house you could roll up and carry on your back! There was a little kerosene burner where I suppose he made the tea that was in a box beside it, a big flashlight, and a kind of long sack with a zipper, big enough for a person to wrap himself in. Everything was neat and carefully arranged, as in a toy house.

I'd gone home from the square the night before feeling happier and more excited than I'd felt in a long time. I'd get him to take me with him when he left, yes, he'd know where to go, what to do, yes. I thought of his wonderful hair, the way he moved. Well, I was stupid, of course, but I knew nothing of men other than Nikos and his friends who'd always been pests, following Maroula and me, staring at us with their shiny eyes. We'd all known each other always, played together as children, but never had I felt anything for any of these village boys. Nothing had ever happened to me. And once the idea of leaving with this foreigner came into my mind, I wanted it so badly, wanted it more than I had ever wanted any one thing. My head was singing with it all and everything seemed so clear, so simple. Before I knew what I was doing I had begun to repack the laundry bag and was sitting in the middle of my bedroom floor surrounded by clothes. What did people in the world wear? Not school uniforms, certainly, but that was all I'd ever needed. Oh, what did it matter? I would wear bedsheets, I would dress in leaves.

And then a strange thing happened: Though I had seen him only that once and didn't know why he was here or where he was going, my mind just jumped over all that and I knew, I really *knew* that he would take me away with him. Anything you wanted that badly would come to pass. But then the old fist grabbed my heart again.

Never leave, the dragonfly said.

Trust only us, whispered the *Tselapétina*.

I disobeyed though I knew they would punish me. The next day I went out and picked a huge bunch of narcissi to welcome the foreigner to our island. Their sweetness no longer bothered me; in fact I liked it again, now that I knew I was leaving. But he was away somewhere and I sat in his tent, smelling that faint aroma of man, of soap, of tobacco that gave me a sense of comfort I hadn't felt since Papa died. I lay back on the sleeping bag and plucked one of the strings of the guitar as some petals from my huge bunch of narcissi fell to the ground. I was going to throw them outside but I reached for the stack of books, took a notebook from the top and, opening its pages, I scattered the petals here and there, shaking more from the bouquet as I flipped through. The notebook was bulging when I closed it and put it in its place with the others. When he opened it, the petals would snow down into his lap. I left the tent quickly before he could return.

"How beautiful he is," said the girls in the schoolyard the next day.

"So fair and tall. We saw him in the marketplace."

"He was taking photographs with a camera."

"Photographs of old Markos selling his oranges. Think of wanting a photograph of that!"

"Have you talked to him, Amalía? Have you?"

"No, why should I?"

"Because you're the only one of us who can."

"Ach, what is that to me?" No one was to know of the leaving and especially not these girls who would have my secret in everyone's mouth before the hour was out. I yawned widely. "Foreigners are not interesting."

"Po-po-po. As if you have known so many. And if they're so uninteresting, why did you run after him when he got off the bus?"

"Yes, why?" they all demanded. "Why?"

"I was just going to warn him about the little scorpions that live in the old walls. But I decided not to bother. What does it matter—foreigners, scorpions, they're all the same to me."

They laughed. "How great-hearted you are, Amalía," one said as the bell rang, calling us back to the building.

It was night when I went back to the fortress and stood in the archway looking at the dark tent, trying to get the courage to go over and see if the petals were still in the notebook.

"Hallo," came the voice behind me. I jumped and nearly ran.

"I'm sorry I frightened you. I called from back there, but the wind is strong today."

"Yes." I could barely see him in the dark and for a

moment I forgot all my English. It was almost as if I had never studied it beyond the beginning level. A memorized sentence from some early lesson came to mind and I said brightly, "One feels that the weather is always subject to change."

"Subject?" he said in the dark. "What means 'subject'?"

"Nothing . . . Never mind." I could see him a little better now. He was looking hard at me.

"Was you? So many flowers in my book?"

"What flowers?" Mother always said it was best not to admit at first that you wanted a man's attention.

"Ah, don't do that." He brushed the hair out of his face but the wind blew it back at once.

"I'm sorry."

"Is bad for you to go in the tent when I am not there."

"Yes, I know. I'm sorry."

"But I like flowers. Pretty, these."

"The old women say that flowers of the field grow from hearts of the dead."

"But there are so many. If true, your island is a cemetery."

"Sometimes I think it is."

"Why?"

"Because everyone who lives here is dead."

"They look very alive to me." He laughed.

"Will you stay long?"

"Maybe yes, maybe no." He laughed again as though it were all the same. "My name is Nels."

"Amalía, I'm Amalía." We shook hands and then had nothing to say so I began to ask him about his country, his travels. He told me that he visited warm places at this time of year because it was so cold where he came from, ice and snow everywhere.

"You walk through tunnels under snow from house to house?" I couldn't imagine so much snow. Here on the island we once had a little a few years ago and school was let out so everyone could watch it fall. But it melted at once. "For me," Nels said, "your winter is my summer." Every winter he left his frozen country and traveled. He seemed to have been everywhere, to have seen everything.

"And everywhere you watch stars?"

"Ah yes. Here your sky is clear. You can see all . . . the star pictures—what is the word?"

"I can't remember it either but I know what you mean."

"These here are not so different than in the North, but much clearer."

"Aren't stars the same everywhere?"

"No, no. In Africa you can see Acrux, the bright star of the cross in the South. This you cannot see in the North."

"What is it like?"

"Is really two stars, with more light than the sun."

"But the sun is brighter."

"Because is closer. The light of Acrux is very old light. Started to travel to us thousands of years ago."

"I never think of light as young or old."

"Now always you will think so."

Look at me, the dragonfly said, *I am prettier than two stars. My wings, how they glisten.* He turned his wings against the light behind my eyes. *You see?*

Not as beautiful as my feathers, whispered the *Tsela-pétina. Green and amber and red.* He preened.

Nels asked me many questions about the island and I told him what I knew of its history, of the story of the fortress where we stood, of the wild boy and the sacred word.

"And what this word was?" he asked.

"Listen, perhaps you will hear . . ." The wind was moaning around the fortress, whistling through what once were windows or archers' holes.

"Is only the wind," he said.

"Yes, but they say you hear the word the boy said in the sound it makes." We listened but there was only the whine of it, prowling among the old stones. *Shreeee*, it said, or, *Wheeeeeer*. Whatever the word was, *love, courage, wisdom* (as the old ones say), it all came to the same thing now in the fortress—just so much sea wind.

Nels was especially interested in the coves that he could see from the fortress, in the history of pirates and ancient shipwrecks here. He always tried to learn the history of places he visited, he said. He had looked at the ancient things in the museum on the mainland and was interested in visiting the sites where they had been found. I told him that Mother used to work at the museum and had come here on an excavation, had met Papa and decided to stay.

"Ah, then you know all the ancient places here. You will show me?"

"I'll show you everything."

Now that I would be leaving the island, it seemed a different place. It was if I had left already and had been away many years and returned to look at it afresh, thinking, How sweet those hills are and what a pretty village. But at night, I went to the other place, the place of punishment.

They flew at me to bite and scratch. I saw her down below me, Amalía, beneath the wings of the *Tselapétina* and dragonfly as when Papa died.

Still exhausted I rushed to the fortress after school or during the afternoon when everyone was sleeping. I memorized sentences from Mother's foreign archaeology books so I would know the right way to talk about history.

"We are doubtless aware," I said, pointing to the few stones left at the temple excavation where Mother had spent her first days here so many years ago, "that ancient temples were painted all the hues of the sky and earth and were not the simple color of the stones remaining today." Nels wasn't listening.

"But where the rest is?"

"The rest?"

"Columns, statues, small things. Is here only some big stone blocks in the ground."

"The good things are what you saw in the museum. Everything else has been lost or stolen."

"Stolen? Is terrible, this."

We wandered the island every day. When it rained we ran into caves or sat under old trees in the olive groves. Nels told me about his work. He was a printer's helper in his small town. "Printing advertisements for newspapers, cards for visiting, invitations for weddings, things like that. But is stupid, this town. Everyone pays bills, goes to bed at nine o'clock all their lives. They never cross the street against a red light even if no cars come for hours."

"People are like that here too, but there are no red lights, no cars, just our one bus from the harbor and back." I still didn't understand how he could manage to travel to other parts of the world every winter. Was printing such good work?

"Is only part-time, the printing. Other times I am working in the marketplace where are many shops. I buy from one man, sell for a higher price to another."

"Buy what?"

"Anything that makes money. Is interesting, this. When I was a boy, I caught wild birds to sell. That was only a little money. Now I make much money."

"So you work part of the year, travel the other part. What a wonderful way to live. I have never heard of such a way."

"Is important to be free; and for a short time again, not to be free."

One day I took Nels to the place of Poseidon, the cove on the other side of the island where Maroula and I used to swim. Even when I was a child, I liked this place. There were many small stones along the shore that all knocked against each other and rattled when the waves rushed in. When I was small, I thought I heard silly words without meaning: *clock clock* or *cloth coat* or *lost boat*. Later I knew it was a kind of code from the sea, from Poseidon.

"You find gods everywhere, Amalía," Maroula would say. "It's just water washing over stones or the current that pulls you out."

But I knew she was wrong. *Doomed, doomed*, Poseidon said when Maroula was with me. *Doomed, doomed*. And he was right. When I swam out, it seemed that a hand took hold of my ankle and pulled me out farther, took me under then let me go, teaching me, showing me his strength.

I had copied pictures of him from Mother's art books and hung them in my room. They were alongside the old piece of island embroidery Mother had given me, the *Tselapétina*, bird of our island folktales. It was later, after Papa's death that I came to believe the *Tselapétina* was one of the true gods, he and Poseidon and the dragonfly. He would not die, even after he was eaten.

"Is here a place where pirates come?" Nels asked.

"I suppose. Mother says so."

"Is treasure here?"

"I don't know." I wasn't really listening to him.

Soon, said Poseidon. *Soon*.

"Let's go, Nels. Let's go back to the fortress."

Once we were there, he cheered me up by playing a song on his guitar. He sang it in his own language so I couldn't really understand but I was sure it was interesting. He said it was about freedom. He had read lots of books, he told me, "books about freedom and life and death. Philosophy books, these I read." His voice, when he sang, wasn't the best, but I told myself that it was the strength in his songs that mattered. They were so, well, free.

"But how can people be free?" I asked him. "I don't understand."

He stared off into the night sky for a long time and said nothing. I was beginning to think perhaps he hadn't heard me, though that didn't seem possible when we were standing so close together. But then he turned and put the palm of his hand on my forehead and said slowly, "You have to let yourself go." There was a long silence that was full of meaning, though I wasn't sure what it meant. To be free of blame, to be free of punishment? Was this possible?

I decided that I would practice making myself free. He would expect me to be a free person when we left together, I was certain. But I wasn't sure what to do.

That evening Mother came into my room and found me standing at the open window with my arms stretched out in the direction of Africa, imagining the twin star Acrux.

"And what are you doing?" she asked.

"I'm letting myself go."

"What? Tell me that again."

"I'm becoming free."

"Amalía, close the window before you catch a chill. Sometimes I think you're losing your mind."

One night Nels pointed out the star picture of a peacock's tail in the sky and told me that when he was a child his father had been caretaker of the town park where there was a pair of peacocks. The pair had been given to the town by the royal family and was kept in a small birdhouse in the middle of the park. "I loved these birds more than anything since. Long hours each day I was looking at them because they were all I knew of beauty. My father took best care of them." But in the time of the occupation, Nels's father disappeared, leaving Nels to care for the park and the peacocks. He never returned. "In those times was not even enough food for people so how I could give bread to birds?" He had his mother to look after and four younger brothers. They knew that someone would steal the birds and eat them so finally Nels was forced to kill them himself to provide food for his family before someone else could get them. "I cut the head off the female first. At that moment, the male screamed and opened his tail.

Then I killed him too." He refused to eat either bird after his mother had cooked them, though he had had nothing but bread and water for days.

Because of this, Nels refused to eat meat now. He seemed to live on only raw vegetables and tea. "Is bad thing, eating animals; they must be free too," he said. But he had difficulty making the shop owners understand what he wanted and what price he was willing to pay. I took him to Papa's shop to meet Pavlos, the manager Mother had hired. I had never liked him much, that little fish mouth of his, always moist under the pencil mustache.

"Tomatoes?" he asked, repeating my order while looking Nels over head to toe and back. "This is what foreigners eat?"

"Just give him three good tomatoes, please, Pavlo."

"Yes, yes. I just wondered." The women stared at us, too, as they poked through the flour, looking for bugs so they could demand a lower price.

"Health to your mother, Amalía," one said.

"And many years." They didn't take their eyes off Nels.

"Welcome, welcome to our island," they said. I translated for him.

"Thank them for me." He laughed.

"He thanks you."

"Who is he?"

"He's a visitor. His name is Nels."

"What kind of name is that?"

"It's his name. You have names, he has a name."

"Why has he come?"

"He's a tourist. He's interested in ancient things."

"Ach, like your mother was."

"In a way."

"What they are saying?" Nels asked.

"They're curious. They want to know about you and why you've come here." Just then I saw Pavlos putting three half-green tomatoes in a bag.

"Not those, Pavlo! Give him three good ones."

"Ach, these are not for him, Amalía," he said nervously. "I was just going to throw them out." He put the bag aside. Nels saw what was happening and laughed.

"Why does he laugh so much?" one of the women asked.

"And why does he take photographs of only some of us?" Another pouted. "It's not fair. He should take them of all of us."

Before I could answer, someone called out from the other side of the shop, "How is it that your mother allows you go about with him if there is no agreement between your families?"

"Let's go, Nels," I said.

"But my tomatoes? And the other things? Is your father's shop this, yes?"

"Let's go!"

Poor Papa. Thanks to God he couldn't see me buying from someone else in the company of a man or see the kind of manager Mother had hired for the shop. She has always been hopeless at business, hopeless in dealing with people in the shop.

"Peasants, fools!" she still mumbles behind closed shutters. "Your grandfather was a museum curator, a respected, educated man, Amalía; never forget that." As if I could. We have been closest at times when she has talked to me of my grandfather and the City, its roses, its museum, its beauty, in fact the beauty of anyone or anything not of this island. She has always wanted me to dislike people here as much as she does. But I am of this place and she is not. It is different for me, though she would have it the same.

"They're not very clean, these people," I remember her saying at the dining-room table one day in the last months before Papa died.

"Don't talk stupidities, Katína," Papa said. "They're as clean as you or I. They may be poor, but they're clean."

Mother sipped her wine thoughtfully, then lowered her voice so the girls working in the kitchen could not hear and asked, "Then why does little Maroula often smell of kerosene?"

"Kerosene?" Papa asked. "Does Maroula smell of kerosene?"

"Sometimes," I said. "I don't care." It was true that Maroula's mother poured kerosene on Maroula's hair, saying that it kept away fleas and lice. No one here had such things. Maroula's mother was crazy and always embarrassed Maroula. Everyone at school made fun of Maroula and held their noses when she was near. Or at least they did until I became her friend, for I was as strong as any boy and fought as hard. Someone had to protect Maroula for she trusted everyone and took no care of herself.

"She came in here with Amalía the other day," Mother said. "And I rushed to put out the fire in the parlor fireplace before the poor child could get too close and turn into a torch."

"That doesn't mean she's dirty," Papa said.

"Fleas may not mean dirt here but they do anywhere else. I'm surprised you don't get them from customers in

the shop." She leaned forward, staring at his hairline.
"What's that black spot there? I think it's moving."

"What spot? Where?" He grabbed at his hair.

"How can I tell when you've got your hand on it?"
She couldn't keep a tiny grin off her face. Papa saw it and
brought his fist down on the table.

"Enough, Katína, enough! It's not funny. There are
no fleas on my head or on any other in this village and
you know it. These are my people and they're clean!"

Poor Papa. When I was very small, I would stand in
the bathroom doorway and watch him shave in the morning. He'd flick a bit of lather onto my nose, put one hand
on his bare chest, wave the shaving brush in the air with
the other and sing:

> "Come, my sweet basil,
>   My glass of mint tea,
>   Come over the ocean,
>   Please come marry me."

"I will, I will!" I'd shout.

"Oh no, you won't," Mother would call from the
kitchen. "I already have."

At Carnival time he once dressed like a woman but
tied a long cucumber under his skirt. When the old women
passed in the street, he'd pull up his skirt and wave the
cucumber at them. They screamed with laughter and tried
to tear off his mask. Mother too laughed as she watched
from the window but I didn't understand. "It's just a way
he has that makes women silly," she said.

But then everything changed. He seldom came home until late at night. "Where is he?" I'd ask Mother.

"At the taverna," she'd say in a voice calm and sweet and full of despair. "Go to bed."

But I wanted nothing more than to be with him, to try to take away that look of hunger and sadness that he wore to the taverna each night. I hid around the side of the staircase to watch him come home late, drunk, still humming to himself as he climbed the stairs. I loved the scent of cigarette smoke and wine and pine cologne that came from him. Sometimes he picked a flower from someone's courtyard—a bit of jasmine or a wild rose—and tucked it comically behind his ear so that its scent mixed with the others. He leaned sharply to the right going up the stairs, as he always did when he had been drinking. He was my handsome, good-smelling papa, the best dancer, the best singer and the loneliest man in the world.

I didn't understand why he was so unhappy, but he no longer sang to me or played with me so it had to be *my fault*, I thought. I quickly found reasons. Nothing about me was right; I was untidy and ugly, I dropped things and talked too loudly. I was sure that Mother had told Papa how terrible I was for she knew much that he didn't. She had turned him against me. It wasn't until after he was dead that I understood: I was a girl and because of my difficult birth, there were no sons.

"If he'd had a son to put his dreams into," I overheard Mother telling Lilliána, "perhaps he wouldn't have gone off trying to solve the problems of some foolish boys on the beach." So it was my fault, his death was my fault, I reasoned. If I had been a boy, perhaps he would have lived.

I no longer think this but at the time I believed it completely. It did not come into my mind that if Mother had been able to bear other children, they might well have been other daughters, not sons. And I did not see that Papa had turned away from her also. So I blamed myself and resented her.

The neighbor women came to school that morning and brought me home. He lay there on the bed upstairs, looking much as he had on the days when he took the ferry to the mainland to get supplies for the shop. He had not lost his color yet and looked lightly asleep except for the huge bruise at the side of his head. There was a pounding on the front door downstairs and I could hear Mother letting the coffin maker in and the neighbor women who had come to mourn. But in the room there was only deep, thick silence. I touched his hair. It was coarse and black as ever. He looked young and handsome and well cared-for, not dead at all. His hands were carefully folded over each other, hands that had measured cloth, stroked my hair, lifted countless glasses of wine to his lips. As I stared at them, dazed, a dragonfly coasted in through the window. It lit on Papa's right hand and for a second I waited for the hand to move, to brush the dragonfly away. I knew the hand wouldn't move but still I waited and the full horror of it broke over me. He was dead. He belonged to the kingdom of insects and other things in the soil.

The door banged open, pushing me back against the wall, as the coffin maker came in noisily, followed by the women who were already wailing and shrieking. One clutched her hair; another scratched her face with her fingernails. No one noticed me in the noise and confusion. I stared around the door as the coffin maker measured

Papa and one of the women began to stuff his pockets
with slips of paper—messages for her dead relatives whom
Papa might meet on the other side. Two other women
stood right in front of me, crossing themselves repeatedly
and talking.

"Poor Widow Katína. Some have no luck with their
husbands and lose them young."

"Won't take her long to find another now that she's
got the shop."

"And the house and land."

"Poor Grigóris, last of his line. Now there is only the
daughter."

"Poor is the man who has no sons."

"Yes, it's a world full of troubles."

I had begun to sob. I pressed myself against the wall
but they noticed me.

"It's Amalía!" they shrieked. "What are you doing
there?"

"Come out here. Don't you want to say good-bye to
your father?"

"Yes, you should kiss him good-bye. If you kiss the
dead it makes it easier for you later."

"No," I said and tried to get past them, out the door.
But their hands were on me.

"You'd better do it now. Soon they'll put him in the
box. Come, now!"

I trembled all over and tried to get past them but their
hands were on me, all over me, lifting, carrying me near
the bed. I shut my eyes and screamed as they lowered me
closer until I fell into a place of noises and nameless terrors,
unintelligible shouts and moans.

I felt something dark rush through me and I sat up in

my own bed in the night, not knowing how I came to be there as if I were a wind rushing over the earth or a black river deep beneath it. A force that had dropped suddenly into the body of a girl in bed. I watched her from across the room, this girl; watched the dragonfly come and say, *Find me, take me.* And the *Tselapétina* was there, flying out of the embroidery and around the room, whispering, *Now, hurry, run.* I watched her get out of bed, steal down the stairs and into the garden. She stood beneath the lemon tree, there where a spider had hung a great web between two of the lower branches. The moon was bright and its light through the web cast fine lines across her face as she plucked, carefully and slowly, the husks of flies and other insects from the web and put them into her mouth. She choked once and spat out what she had half eaten, then began again to pick things from the web, tearing the fine threads of it, pulling it to pieces now with both hands, then turning, walking back into the house.

When I came to myself again in bed, I had no idea of what day it was; I was outside time, beyond exhaustion, feverish. Lilliána was there, holding me. "I know, I know, you see things, yes? I know how it is, you can't stop them until they stop themselves. But they will, they will. Thanks to God, they will." The house was quiet; the shutters were closed, so I supposed Papa had been taken to the church. There was something comforting in Lilliána's ragged clothes, her musty odor. She made the sign of the cross on my forehead, then took a glass of Holy Oil and poured it into a carafe of water, staring at it and muttering. "Lie still now, clear your mind of everything. Let your mind grow as clear and calm as a glass of water." She set an incense burner with three live coals on the table next to

the bed and sprinkled gunpowder out of an envelope.
There was a flash, smoke. I felt dizzy and weak, as if there
were no blood in me. Lilliána began to chant:

> "There are three plates,
>   Honey in one, milk in another,
>   Man's intestines in the third.
>   Eat the honey, drink the milk,
>   Leave the intestines.
>   A wind brings them, a wind takes them,
>   to the forest under the cold waters.
>   The bent old man follows a bent road,
>   Twists willows in a basket by the stream.
>   How much water stays in the basket,
>   Let so much pain stay in your heart."

She went through this twice and then sang some words
I could not understand. My head did seem to clear a little.
She made the sign of the cross on my forehead three times.

"You are light-shadowed, you know, that's what it is.
I've long thought you were but now I know. It's a gift.
Others make fun of it but you must pay no attention. What
are they to you? Most people are either fools or demons.
Pass them by."

She explained that light-shadowed people are those
who grow into themselves more than others and so they
attract bad feelings and spirits. They are trusting and slow
to become adults and some can talk to animals and trees;
others know how to heal or can take the pictures that come
into their minds and put them on paper. Sometimes they
become monks or nuns. All are close to the powers of the

earth; all can look into themselves and others more deeply than most.

"Now come," she said, "you must tell me what you have seen in this place you have been so long."

"So long . . . ?"

"Since yesterday morning. One whole day."

But I remembered nothing except the girl and the web. My stomach turned over; I was going to be sick.

"I can't."

"I suppose not. The light-shadowed seldom can."

"I'm not light-shadowed. I'm just sick to my stomach."

"It will pass, don't worry. Your father was light-shadowed too but he always fought against it and the fight killed him. He went to help those fighting boys. Only a light-shadowed person would be so foolish as to try to bring justice to that little corner of the beach. But he gave himself up to it; he swallowed his fate. Do you believe these were boys? Pah! Who knows what they were. Devils, I say. He should have understood this."

"But it was just some of the boys from school."

"Don't believe it! He-Who-Threw-the-Stone was not just a boy. Don't be as foolish as your father. He was full of longing for things that could not be. Such are the men of this island. It is their curse. And it is the curse of the women here to love them."

That night I fell into another troubled sleep. My head seemed full of blood and it pounded as if it were a heart.

Wicked! screamed the dragonfly. *Wicked girl!*

Come with us, stay with us, whispered the *Tselapétina*. Again I saw the girl go into the garden. Again she shook the branches of the lemon tree and things crawled into her mouth. This went on for many nights. In the days I was

feverish and wild, they told me later, tossing and screaming
in bed. At some point, I remember Mother forcing the girl
to drink something hideous. It is poison, I thought; now
they will poison her because she is so wicked. Then I was
back inside her, inside myself, coming back from the other
place. Mother and Lilliána seemed ghostly, indistinct.

Day spirits, the *Tselapétina* said. *They will betray you.*

"It has broken the fever," Mother said. "This liquid
Lilliána told me to give you." I was wet and shivering.
"She says you tried to swallow your father's death."

I didn't know what she meant. I only knew that they
were there, part of me, these strange gods for a long time
after that. I would not see them or hear their voices for
days, sometimes weeks. And then they would come, saying
they were my friends.

*Only we love you. Listen to us. We will protect you.
Never trust the day spirits.*

They were vain and sometimes they bickered.

See me shimmer for you, Amalía, said the dragonfly,
and light seemed to come out of the bulging eyes that
covered its head. Beautiful light, full of colors as if it had
poured through jewels inside the great head.

Not as nice as my comb, whispered the *Tselapétina*.
And this was true for it had a crimson comb and wattles
that were iridescent with hues of purple and deep blue.
But more often they were hateful, punishing. For feet the
Tselapétina had the dangerous, ripping fins of fish. The
dragonfly boasted it could sew up the eyes, ears and mouth
of a sleeping person.

"Who are they?" Nels asked. "I see them everywhere I
go." He was standing against the west wall of the fortress,

looking hard at me. I had just come up the hill, nearly running into Mad Manólis who was standing there in the weeds looking down the lane as I came up, as if he were waiting for someone.

"To your health," Manólis had said to me.

"And to yours," I answered. He smiled, moistening his lips with his tongue.

"How goes your life?"

"It goes."

"And that of your friend?" He nodded toward the walls. "Does he pass his time well here?"

"Yes, he likes it here." Manólis smiled more widely then. His right hand was inside his trouser pocket and he rubbed it there, looking me over, still smiling. The village men were talking as much as the women, I was sure: "She is unmarried and goes around with the foreigner so she must no longer be a maid." But I was still the daughter of Grigóris, still of the best family, and only someone as stupid as Manólis would have waited for me by the side of the lane. I hurried past him and through the archway of the fortress.

"Who are *who?*" I asked Nels. "What do you mean?"

"Are two of them. One tall and dark with lots of hair. Is shorter the other, more heavy, with small eyes. In the café, they come and sit at the next table. If I walk away, they walk too after me. They watch when I swim in that cove. I can't do anything. They are everywhere." His voice went up as he spoke. "Who are they? What do they want?"

"Nikos and Andréas." I was certain it was they. Nikos had climbed into the house through a window a few nights before to warn me against seeing Nels. "They're just village boys who don't have much to do with their time. They're curious because you're foreign and because they can't talk to you. Pay no attention."

"How I cannot pay attention? They come here at night also."

"Here? To your tent?"

"Yes. I don't see them but I can hear voices by the walls. Sometimes the call of a bird I hear. But is not a bird. With the flashlight I go out of the tent but I see no one."

"The dark one is Nikos. He thinks he has the right to tell me what to do, as if I were promised to him but I'm not. It has been this way ever since we were children and played together."

I remember how we once dressed up a little pig so it looked like a baby and walked around pretending we were man, wife and child. It seemed that Nikos had never grown away from the idea that one day we would be man and wife in fact. He had stood in my room only a few nights before, his face red from anger or from the effort of climbing the fig tree to get in the window, and said, "You're making a fool of me, a fool!" He tried to warn me about Nels, but all I could hear was the son of the fisherman speaking, afraid the village was laughing at him, afraid he might lose the respect he needed so badly. Poor Nikos. What frightened me most about him was that something in me felt for him, wanted to reach out and soothe him, as I had wanted to reach out to Papa. To tell him that what he wanted wasn't that important, didn't really matter. "Full of longing for things not to be," Lilliána had said of the men of the island. I had to fight against this urge to soothe, because the violence of his feelings stirred me, awakened me to him in ways that might not be in my control if I even once reached out to help him. So I fought him and hoped for what seemed impossible: that he would turn to someone else, or that Nels and I would soon be gone.

"The other one is Andréas," I told Nels. "He's a kind of shadow to Nikos. He just got married not long ago and ought to be at home. But they're both the kind of boys who'll push you only if they think you won't push back. If they try to bother you again, just tell them to go to the Devil."

"But I can't speak their language."

"You don't need to. Say it in any language you want. That's one thing no one misunderstands, my mother always says. It's the tone of voice that matters."

"But is the same with everyone here."

"What do you mean?"

"Everyone, except you. They stare at me and all talk stops when I go past. Is not so in other countries I've visited."

"Look, Nels, these are simple people who don't see so many foreigners. What can you expect? If I came to your country probably the people of your town would act the same to me."

"No, is not true. We are more, how do you say?— civilized."

"Civilized?" I heard my voice go up. He seemed so foreign standing there, so tall and blond and cold. I could never really get past what he looked like to see who he was. I had been raised by Mother to think all things foreign were good. But when he criticized the island, suddenly I was Papa's daughter and hated in Nels what I had most liked: his very foreignness, his pointless laughter and bland good humor, his eyes, his hair.

"Civilized?" I said again. "You talk of civilization. You, whose people probably wore the skins of animals and lived in caves when there were marble temples here on this island!"

He looked startled. His eyes had never seemed wider, greener. And instantly, as though a light had been turned on, his expression turned into a good-humored grin. "I'm sorry," he said sheepishly. "Was a bad thing to say. I'm sorry." He smiled shyly, laughed, brushed the hair from his face.

I hate myself now for how quickly my anger drained away. He had turned back into a film magazine photo that promised everything. The wind blew his hair into his face and I had to keep myself from reaching out to push it away for him. Here it was again, the face that woke me in the night, came to me in my schoolbooks, on the blackboard, in the street. The eyes that I was sure saw me only as a stupid island girl, not at all free, whatever that meant. I still didn't understand. Whenever I practiced letting go, I dropped things and bumped into walls. I just couldn't seem to get it right. Once I had nearly fallen down the front stairs because my legs were freer than the rest of me.

"It's my fault that they all stare at you," I told him. "My friend Maroula married Andréas and it is expected that I will marry Nikos. Most people here do what is expected of them."

"And will you do what is expected?"

I wanted to tell him that all I cared about was leaving the island with him but instead I blurted out, "I just want to be free."

"Are you sure?"

"I'm sure." He smiled, pushed the hair out of his face

and suddenly we were holding each other and laughing as we walked slowly toward the tent. Once inside he began to touch me everywhere and it was very nice but I still kept waiting for him to show me more about freedom and letting go until, with a shock, I realized that he was doing exactly that.

I let him. I let him do some things but not everything. I didn't let him do *that*, but just about everything else. Mother always said that you should never give a man everything he wants all the time. I hadn't known how many other things there were to give. But Nels showed me. He was gentle, kind. I thought he might be able to free me from the other place. Now I was ready to live the way he did. I imagined us on the ferry as it pulled away, the island growing smaller. The thought of leaving and my feelings for Nels were mixed together. I was in love with the idea of leaving but it seemed to me then that it was Nels I loved.

Traitor, whore! You can never leave, the dragonfly said.

Feel these fins, whispered the *Tselapétina* in the night. And I did.

I deserve this! I screamed. *Do as you like*. But my happiness was so strong that I began to accept suffering, to think there was a balance between it and happiness. So much of one paid for the other.

In school, I composed postcards I would write back to my classmates, to Mother, views of cities and places along the way. I had asked Nels where he would go when he left the island. Home, he'd said, to make some money. I thought of myself in tunnels under the snow. What would I do there? Oh, it didn't matter, it would work out somehow, it would have to. I knew so little of the world beyond the island that whatever I imagined was sure to be wrong. I looked around the classroom and thought, You'll all still be here when I am gone.

"The three major exports of our country, blessed by God," recited someone in the back of the room, "are tobacco, tomato paste and olive oil. Tobacco is grown in the plains of the north and harvested by workers who come from all parts of the country . . ."

The clock ticked and Jesus hung on the cross in the icon above the blackboard, eyes closed, for he was tired of tobacco and tomatoes and olive oil. Who could blame him? The teacher was tired too, I thought, tired of this post she had been assigned to because she probably did not have a relative in the Ministry of Education who could push one of the choice mainland vacancies her way. She tapped her pencil on the desk and stared out the window. "Good, Maria," she said. "Continue, Chrysoúla."

"Our third major export, olive oil, is pressed . . ."

Each of my teachers had said to me, "If only you would work harder, Amalía, you could go to university." But I was an uneven student, at the top of my class in a subject that interested me—languages or history—at the bottom in one that didn't—mathematics. And I did not want to sit in more classrooms and then someday become a teacher who would stare blankly out the window while someone talked about tomatoes.

It was Maroula who had the bad luck to be a good student. I looked over to where her place was still empty. The teachers had been afraid she'd spend her whole life helping out in her father's butcher shop, cleaning the block with bloody rags. "I don't mind," she said. "It's my duty." So the teachers had given her a dream: There was a special

boarding school for girls on the mainland, private, selective, expensive. Our headmaster knew people there.

"He'll write letters about me, Amalía, and maybe they'll let me go there spring term," she had told me happily last autumn. "Just imagine! It's a school for rich girls but they let some others who are good students go there free. And he says it's all modern with a theater for plays and there are classes in music and painting. Just think, Amalía, they let you draw and paint and sing *in school!*"

"Mother went to a school like that when she lived in Smyrna," I told her.

"Oh, it must be wonderful. The most wonderful thing in the world. If I do well there, I'll have a good chance of going to university."

My sweet Maroula. It had been a long time since she had gone meekly about, smelling of kerosene. She had grown into a plump young woman, no longer so tiny or shy. We drew around our eyes with burned matchsticks, hoping to look like the women in the foreign film magazines. We cut out pictures of royalty and movie stars to hang in her room and ordered novels about love affairs and divorces and adulteries in the world beyond the island. The boys who walked around the square in the evening in their tight trousers with their shirts unbuttoned to show their hard chests only made us giggle. They were very silly, we said, and we didn't see why everyone was so secretive about sex. After all, we'd seen cats and dogs and birds at it and once even donkeys, with lots of braying, as if a door on rusty hinges opened and closed many times and finally with terrific noise, fell off its frame. "But what is it like?" Maroula asked. "In books, just when everything gets thrilling, there is always that white space. And then the next chapter begins, 'Later . . .' or 'Afterward . . .' What happens in the white space?" She was to find out before I did.

Her parents didn't like the idea of the new school. "Foolishness!" said her father.

"Why should a girl study?" her mother asked. "I've taught you to weave and clean and be modest. What more do you need to know?" It's a woman's duty to marry and raise children, Maroula's parents told her, and to protect the honor of her husband's home. Already Andréas's father had spoken to them about an agreement between the two families. Andréas was strong and healthy, Maroula's father said, and would be a good worker in the butcher shop. He could give Maroula sons and continue the line of the two families. Maroula had no brothers so her father was eager to have a young man in the family. Someone he could train to run the business he had spent so many years building. "They'll never accept you at such a school," her mother said. "They'll just laugh at you for trying—a butcher's daughter from a village they've never heard of!"

Maroula knew they were wrong. She wrote the school and filled out the forms, asked the headmaster to recommend her and waited. "Once I'm accepted," she told me, "and have the letter in my hands, my parents will understand that it is an honor to our family for me to go to such a school. A much greater honor than to marry Andréas."

Ach, Maroula! She always tried to think the best of her parents. The acceptance arrived a month later but by that time her parents had hurried along the marriage agreement with the family of Andréas. The shop was to be Maroula's dowry. When her parents saw the acceptance letter, they were furious. Maroula had sneaked around, they said, had tried to shame them in front of the whole

village. Everyone would laugh at them if the agreement
were broken; their good name would be ruined and they'd
never find her another husband. You could hear the shouting all over that part of the village. The headmaster went
to talk to them but they threw him out of the house. The
next day I stood below Maroula's window and called her
name. She came to the window, crying, and told me all
that had happened.

"I have to get away, Amalía, I have to. Oh, God, I
don't want to shame my parents, I really don't. But if I
marry Andréas I will spend my whole life washing the
blood out of aprons and cooking the bits of mutton that
are too old to sell in the shop. That's what my mother's
life has been."

What could I tell her? If I had told *my* mother that I
wanted to go away to study, she probably would have been
pleased. She had always wanted me to have that life she
might have had if she hadn't come here and married Papa.
But I didn't want to live her life for her. She pushed me
to go; Maroula's parents wanted her to stay. "Leave," I
told Maroula. "Go as soon as you can, straight to the school
on the mainland. Tell your parents nothing. If you need
money for a ticket, I can get some."

"I don't know, I don't know."

"Don't let this chance pass by like one of those ships
whose windows we see at night, the ones that never stop
here. Get on the ferry tomorrow morning. Oh, but I don't
want you to go, you know! I'll miss you so much . . ."

"And I'll miss you . . ." Tears were running down her
face and from another part of the house we heard her
mother's voice call out.

"Maroula!"

She closed the window and I went home to take some money from Papa's old box of sovereigns which Mother still kept under the bed. She must have found the money missing, for the box was moved after that and I never saw it again. Perhaps she suspected the housegirls, for she said nothing to me about it. When I came back to Maroula's house later, the window was still closed so I left the money in an envelope on the ledge. The next day she was gone. Her parents searched everywhere and it wasn't long before the whole village knew the story. The ticket taker on the ferry said she had gone to the mainland with a suitcase. So her father closed the shop and, with her mother, went after Maroula. The teachers at the school on the mainland couldn't do anything to keep Maroula there. These were her parents.

On the ferry back to the island they bought first-class tickets and took Maroula to the lounge where no one ever sat. They closed the door. The ticket taker told everyone in the village that the noise was terrible to hear. Even in third class, where everyone else sat, they could hear the beating and her screams. They beat her so badly that when the ferry docked here, she had to be carried off with everyone watching. Her father said she'd had an accident. But the village knew; it always knows.

Maroula was never the same. Everyone said her father had hit her too hard too many times on the head. Sometimes she falls on the ground in a frenzy of trembling, her eyes roll back and once she bit off part of her tongue. When she is all right she is never really all right.

"Hello, Amalía," she said calmly, the next time I saw her, cleaning the counter in her father's shop. "How are you?"

"How are *you?*"

"All right. I feel better today, I think. I've been ill."

"Ill?"

"Yes. I should not have left. It worried Mama and Papa so and made me ill. That's why I came back. It's best this way."

Best? I started to say. *Best?* But I didn't say it. When you looked in her eyes, they were dead. I embraced Maroula quickly and left the shop.

When Andréas understood that Maroula was not "right," he tried to break the marriage agreement. But her parents increased the dowry, saying that he could have their house when they were dead and the gold sovereigns they had hoarded for years. When they had offered everything they had, he agreed.

I couldn't stand to see Maroula or to think about my role in all that had happened. But a few days before the wedding, I was walking alongside the stream outside the village when I heard music—the scratchy recording of an old dance, all frantic bouzouki, clarinet and drums. It came from a garden beside the stream, where some old women had set up a record player next to the wooden troughs where they sifted flour and kneaded dough. They were laughing and talking, gold teeth glinting in gummy mouths as they told wedding-bed stories about grooms who couldn't or brides who wouldn't and sheets hung out the next morning stained with the blood of a chicken. It was the Day of the Leaven for Maroula, the day they baked her wedding bread.

They called out to me as I passed, and they pulled me into the garden with hands sticky from the dough. Their fingers pointed between my legs.

"Soon we'll bake your bread too."

"You'll see, you'll see."

"The bread is for Maroula?" I asked.

"For you, for you. We bake the bread for you."

But I knew it was for Maroula's ill-fated wedding that weekend. "For you, for you," they continued to insist, hopping around to the music, dragging me with them, laughing and wheezing. The same women who all year long complained of arthritis, of rheumatism. They smelled of yeast and wine. They squeezed my hands until I thought the bones would crack, as we went from trough to trough to see the dough pressed into the wreath molds that would mark the bread with crusty doves, chains of flowers, linked wedding bands. One of the women came toward me with hands full of unbaked dough and before I could stop her she reached up my skirt and rubbed the dough there between my legs. Women seemed to come from all sides with more dough in hands outstretched. It was said that the yeasty dough of wedding bread makes a young woman fertile, brings her a man to give her sons. "For you! For you! Health and children for you."

Somehow I pulled free and ran through the lanes between houses where no one could see, trying to pull off the sticky dough. I started to cry, just a little at first but soon great, ugly sobs were tearing through me. "Maroula!" I cried out. "Maroula!" It was all my fault for telling her to go away, for giving her the money. *My fault, my fault.* Just as Papa's death still seemed my fault. I had loved them both but how little good my love did either of them! Papa lay among the roots of the cypress trees and Maroula had found another kind of fate in her father's shop. Mother said you should never blame yourself for loving, for trying to help others.

Lies! shrieked the dragonfly. *Swallow me!*

For you, all for you, said the *Tselapétina*, brushing its wing along the wall where a line of ants were crawling. I saw my hand reach out, as if in a dream, and scrape them off. All the way home I stopped here and there to collect spiders and moths, beetles and others. I kept them in my pockets and ate them secretly over the next few days. By the day of the wedding, I was so ill there was no question of my going to the church. The rains had started, and with them came the cold weather. A few days after the wedding, I found myself wandering the beach in the cove where Maroula and I used to swim. The water was calm and there was no wind. Small waves rippled over the stones and Poseidon said, *Lost*, then sighed and said again, *Lost, lost*. I went home and began to pack the laundry bag. A few days after that, Nels arrived on the island.

"That's my friend Maroula," I said to Nels as we walked down the street one day. We were passing the butcher shop where I could see her through the window as she stood behind the counter watching her father carry a side of lamb out of the cooler. She and I seldom saw each other now that she was not in school and when I did go in to say hello or to pick up something for Mother, she was pleasant but asked after my health and that of Mother as if I were just anyone else in the village. I avoided going there.

"I mentioned her to you," I told Nels. "She's the one who married Andréas." But Nels did not catch the direction of my glance and looked instead to the other side of the street into the shop of Panos the potter. Panos was firing his great oven but Nels did not seem to notice that the sweaty potter couldn't possibly be someone named Maroula who had married an Andréas.

"Uhm," he said, nodding, and continued down the street beside me. I was going to say, No, look the other way. But we were past the shop then and what did it matter? I could hear Mother telling me that we were all equally picturesque to foreigners, but no, that wasn't true, I thought. Nels was just distracted. But then he was always distracted. He was never at his tent and seemed to care for nothing but swimming in the cove on the other side of the island. I brought food to the tent and left it there for him because Nels didn't like going into the shops where everyone stared and frowned. He was my guest here so why should he be treated this way? I just went into the storeroom in the back of Papa's shop and told Pavlos that we needed a few things at home, and I helped myself. If Mother noticed things missing from the storeroom, it would not happen until we were gone and then she'd blame it on old fish-mouthed Pavlos.

The village was turning uglier each day. The old priest had come up to Nels one day in the street and begun to shout at him. I was in school at the time and Nels was alone. "He made the sign of the cross many times," Nels said. "Was very angry." Our priest had always been stupid. Even when Maroula and Nikos and the rest of us were children, it was easy to trick the priest and we often did. Now he was old and superstitious and probably thought that Nels was a bad spirit of some kind. Another day some children threw stones at Nels. And men in the cafés along the waterfront pointed at him as he went past and made hissing noises. Nikos and Andréas were still prowling the fortress at night. It was time to leave.

But Nels did not mention leaving. Each day he swam in the cold water that he insisted was warm for him. And I sat in the classroom while the lessons droned on and told myself every day, Tomorrow I will not be here.

"It worked for your mother; it will work for you," Lilliána said when I went up to her as she was gathering stones on the beach. I had seen her from a distance as she walked along the water's edge, the hem of her old dress dragging wetly across the sand. She stooped to pick up stones, muttering.

"What will work?" I asked.

"A thread. Bring me a thread from his collar or his cuff. And I will use it to bind him to you."

"You did this for Mother?"

"Of course. Why do you think Grigóris married her? Now hurry up because the stones tell me I will die soon." I did as she said and unraveled a bit of the sleeve of an old sweater while Nels was away swimming. But when I brought it to her house she said, "And what is this?"

"You told me to bring it."

"Ach, did I? Whose is it?" I told her. "It probably won't work on a foreigner," she said. "Men of the island, hopeless seekers, it works on them. Oh give it to me, who knows?" I held out the thread. She snatched it from my hand, saying, "You still think you're not light-shadowed, don't you?"

"I don't ever think about it."

"Fool!" She slammed the door.

Leaving was all I thought about, that and the clatter of the voices.

I'm dying! screamed the dragonfly. *Don't leave me.*

You're always dying, I said. I had started to talk back. And it was true. Whenever things didn't go his way he said he was dying. He made his wings appear shredded.

I can't leave the island, said the *Tselapétina. Have pity. I am of this place. My wings melt over water, near the sun.*

You're not Icarus.

You do not know who I am.

Somewhere else in my mind, like a low buzz, was the fear that Nels wouldn't want me to go away with him. I couldn't stand to think about it and drove the idea out but it always crept back. I tried to talk to Nels to say, Take me with you. But each time I came close to saying it, my tongue seemed to become paralyzed and then my mind just jumped over the words again and I was in the other side of them where everything was decided and need not be talked about.

Then, walking home from school through the marketplace one afternoon, as I was passing a group of women, someone spat at me. It went on the ground in front of me, just where I was about to step. When I looked at them, stunned, the women turned their backs.

From the time I crept down the staircase that same night with the laundry bag on my shoulder until I returned (my fist in my mouth so Mother wouldn't hear me on the other side of the door) everything seemed to happen quickly. By eight the next morning when Mother unlocked the door, it was all finished. Nels had gone. The thread hadn't worked.

No one would ever read on my face what had happened, this I resolved. No one would know how I came home from the marketplace, thinking, *Now, leave now*, and waited until dark, until the house was empty. But Mother had come back and was there at the bottom of the staircase, waiting. Mother, who all my life had hated this island and had given me the dream of other places, other people, now blocked the door.

"You'll go nowhere tonight," she said. But even after she had locked me in my room, I managed to climb from my window to the hall window and then into the branches of the fig tree. But first, I shouted lies at her through the door, lies about Mad Manólis and Old Petros—imagine the thought of doing anything with such awful men—but she believed me. That paid her back for the slaps she had given me on the stairs, for the laundry bag I left behind there so that when I went down the tree, I had no clothes, no money, nothing to take to Nels but myself.

As I ran through the archway of the fortress, he called out. "Is good you're here." He was standing beside the tent. "They came again." Waving his flashlight around the courtyard, he showed me where his belongings had been thrown. The guitar lay smashed over in the weeds. His clothes were scattered and torn among the books and papers. The little burner and the plastic bottle of kerosene were to one side.

"Oh, Nels." I stood there, beginning to tremble. "Someone spat at me in the marketplace today."

"Spat? What means this?" I showed him. "Oh, that

is nothing. They do not break your things as with me."

I knew then that I had to say it. I could feel the words there on my tongue and I couldn't just go around them and pretend they had already been said. The wind was moaning over the fortress walls and was strong tonight. It pushed at me as if urging me forward, insisting. Perhaps that was all it could do now, the centuries having left it mute, the sacred word, whatever it was, forgotten. The wind slapped me hard on the back of the head.

"Take me with you."

"What?"

"You have to leave. You understand that they've broken your things, they may come back for you. I'll help you put these things in your pack. We'll have to walk to the harbor because there's no bus tonight. But the ferry is already there at the dock and we can get on it now without anyone seeing us. When it has pulled out tomorrow morning, we can pay for our tickets then. No one will care."

"I don't understand. Is crazy; everything is crazy here. I know what they want. But they do not find it and I am not leaving."

"What who wants?"

He looked at me for a moment before answering. "All right, come here. I'll show you."

I followed him to a corner of the courtyard where there was a depression in the ground, overgrown with weeds, not easily seen. He aimed the flashlight into it. I made out an encrusted half circle of pottery, the handle of what once must have been a water jug. Nels bent down and lifted it to one side. There were other pieces—more handles, more pottery fragments, all encrusted with shells and stones. "I bring them up," he said excitedly. "Are hundreds of them under the water in that cove. Old, so old. Some are not broken but are far out. I try each day to go deep but is hard this, with no equipment for breathing."

"But why? It's just a lot of broken water jugs. Why do you want them?"

"Don't be a fool," he snapped. "I can sell them."

My mind was so filled with the need for us to leave that I couldn't understand what he was talking about. "Sell them? Where? Who wants to buy broken things?"

"In the antiquity shops of the marketplace in my town or in cities anywhere. Much money. When I sell these, I will not have to work in the print shop, not even in summer. I'll be free. For this I came here, to find such things."

"For this?"

The voice of the *Tselapétina*: *Treachery, betrayal!*

Now you see! the dragonfly shrieked.

We said nothing for a minute. And then the other places he had visited went through my mind. In every place there probably had been someone to distract with talk of stars, someone who would point out little-known sites where he could find things to smuggle out of the country. This was what he meant when he talked of being free, this and what happened in the tent.

"This is what you do everywhere? Find someone like me who can help you steal things that you'll sell later?"

He stood up and smiled, then laughed, brushing the hair off his forehead. "Is so bad this? No one wants these things here so is not stealing. And everywhere I go people like to help. What can I say?"

What could anyone say? I stood there looking at him standing by the wall. Behind him and below stretched the village, its lights, streets, houses. I can't go back there now,

I thought, back to Mother, back to my bedroom, to the classroom. Leaving mattered more than Nels and always had. I had been a fool to think otherwise.

"All right," I said. "I've helped you. Let me go on helping you. It will be dangerous for you to stay. I'll get you on the ferry tonight and by tomorrow morning we'll be away from here."

"Oh no. I need still a few days to try for one not broken. No, Amalía, you are very kind, very sweet. But when I go, I go alone, always."

"Take me with you! You can't carry all these things. I'll help you . . ." I was talking rapidly; my voice had gone up and I was frantically gathering up his scattered belongings, rushing around the courtyard, picking up clothing, books, dropping things, picking them up again. "You're right—we're not civilized here. But it will be all right. I'll help and I won't cause you any trouble. We'll be on the ferry soon, you'll see, Nels, it will be all right . . ."

"Don't," he said. "Just leave those things." He was kneeling again, putting the fragments of pottery back and covering them with dried grass. "You stay here," he said. "You're young. Who knows? Maybe you will marry that boy, what his name is? Nikos, oh yes. Maybe he is not so bad."

"Please, Nels," I called out, my arms full of his belongings. But he said nothing as he bent over his pieces of pottery, his stupid pieces of pottery, and there was silence except for the gods.

Fire will clean, fire will keep you here.
Burn, burn!

It was then that I saw the kerosene bottle and a box

of matches by the little burner in the weeds. Quickly I dropped everything and picked up the bottle, ran to the tent and poured the contents on the canvas. Nels turned at the sound.

"Stop this! Is crazy." But before he could reach me, I had lit a match and thrown it on the tent. There was a great *whoosh* as flames jumped up, lighting the whole courtyard, reaching above the walls. I was startled to see the fire, as if there were no connection between it and me.

"They're not ancient," I blurted out, tears running down my face. "Those stupid pieces of pottery you found. Everyone knows that Panos takes the jugs that get broken or cracked in his shop and throws them away in the cove. They're worthless."

"Is not true," Nels said beside the tent, his face lit up by the fire.

"Yes, it is. They won't let him throw pottery with the other rubbish because it won't burn."

"Are covered with old shells, stones . . ."

"When they've been there for a year or two, they look the same as if they were there for thousands of years."

"Is lies, this."

"It's the truth, Nels," I sobbed. "Nikos and Andréas didn't come here for broken water jugs. They came for *you*. I'd catch that ferry tomorrow, if I were you."

In the ditches in the hills the donkey bones still lay, empty of marrow, in the late-winter sun. From one ditch I had taken the skull the day I frightened the housegirls and in the long night after the fire I found it again where I had hidden it, under my bed. When day came, I took it from its hiding place and returned it to the hills with the rest of its poor bones. I liked to touch them; they were clean and smooth and had holes in them, tiny holes. They pleased me. I brought wildflowers and made wreaths for them, filled eye sockets with narcissi and nostrils with anemones. Some had died in uncomfortable positions so I rearranged them, made new creatures far more handsome than the old ones, with heads both front and back so nothing could surprise them. Gathering thyme and oregano and rosemary, I stuffed the long, hollow leg bones so they gave a sweet, clean smell to the air when I waved them in the wind. There were bones on the beach too, washed up in the sand, huge ones, like those of prehistoric animals or perhaps of serpents that really did exist at the bottom of the sea, no matter what the books said. I dug them out of the sand and put them with the donkey bones. They had little holes in them too. That's how I felt then—full of holes, stripped of all flesh, white and hard.

I kept my resolve that no one would read anything in my face, not Mother, nor the old women, nor my classmates. I stared into the mirror each morning and smoothed my face with my fingers, made it as blank as bone. When I walked past the cafés and one of the men held his glass up, smiled and bowed as he would to a foreign girl, his rudeness did not bother me. Nor did the backs of the women who continued to turn away when I passed them in the street. Mother's voice bounced off my hard surface and the eyes of classmates looked full into mine, then away. The teacher called on others though I was perfectly prepared to recite, in fact I had never been better prepared. The sunlight stirred dust across the classroom floor.

I went back to the fortress one day and the pottery was still there. I don't think Nels took even a single piece.

Perhaps he should have, for as I looked at it more carefully, I saw that some was not from Panos but was of much older design. The sea bottom is full of pottery fragments—there are more of them than fish. Most are new but the sands shift in winter storms, revealing, concealing. I had not thought of it that night when all the pieces looked the same in the flashlight beam. One by one, I threw them back into the water.

Ach, Nels. I thought of him walking through a tunnel of ice. And in spite of everything, I longed for his coolness, his blandness. I wanted to die when I came back to my room after the fire. But death was no longer such an easy thing to take into myself as a line of ants on a wall, crickets on lemon leaves. During the night while Mother snored on the other side of the door, I felt another presence. When I was desperate and weeping, I felt Death come, felt her sit down beside me like the ancient mother she is and say, *Shh, shh, everything will be all right tomorrow. Just hold on to me.* But I wanted neither the one mother nor the other then and the next day I took the skull into the hills where it belonged. I could not hear the gods; perhaps my staying calmed them. It rained for centuries, it seemed, all through those end-of-winter days and I often ran to the hills to touch the bones that I felt protected me, wave them in the rain as water ran off my head, until winter was folded up, packed away and Carnival was taken out.

"Bravo, Amalía!"
"Bravo, girls!" called the teacher.
I repeated the step across the schoolyard, the other girls following as the record played on the old phonograph in the schoolroom window. My last year to lead the dance

in the square, my last year to lead the rehearsals. Spyros Galánis was home from his travels and had begun to visit the school while we were rehearsing in the yard. What a fuss the headmaster made over him.

"Maria—bring a chair for Mr. Galánis. Philio, coffee from the café."

"No, no," Spyros always said. "I'll just stay a minute. It's been years since I've seen the dances of my own village." He had come back recently, full of money and plans. Papa's closest friend. Did I remember him or did I only seem to? He didn't look at all like Papa—he was broader, stronger looking and dressed in all the latest foreign clothes—yet there was something of Papa about him. Maybe it was just knowing that they had been like brothers. I always tried to dance especially well when he came to a rehearsal.

I like dancing for its order and control. Usually you know what will happen next. And yet when the music catches you up, there is an opening for the wild turn, the unplanned leap. But you have to be ready. You have to be precise and well practiced in order to recognize the opening when it comes. You have to earn it.

These other girls who dipped and bowed behind me thought the dance was all leaps and turns. They never learned the precision that led to the leap and made it perfect. They had no control. They gave themselves up completely to the music and because of this they were bad dancers. But they didn't care. Those who were not already engaged, danced only in hope that boys would notice them and arrangements between families would be made.

"Is there anyone?" Mother asked me from time to time.

"No."

"You must be thinking of what you want to do when school ends." But I didn't want to do anything. Whatever happens will happen, I thought as I drifted through the days, looking out from behind my smooth bone face. "There are good language schools on the mainland," Mother kept suggesting. But it was she who had locked me in my room when I tried to leave, she who had taught me of other places, then stopped me at the bottom of the staircase. No matter that she had been right about Nels. That just made me dislike her more. No, I would not please her by leaving for some dull school. Just as strongly as I once wanted to leave, so I now felt that I was of this place. She would not get rid of me so easily.

At least my name was so bad, I thought, that no one would bother me with talk of marriage agreements. But fathers still knocked at the door; they just had less to offer. Sons with one bad leg or a stutter. Little land, mostly chickens. They all knew that my dowry had not changed. Only my good name was no longer so bright which meant that families who would not have thought of such an alliance before, now sought it. Mother sent them away.

And the dance moved on. Spyros watched us closely as the line passed in front of him and the scratchy music came to an end. "Wonderful!" he shouted. "Just wonderful." And the headmaster at his side, taking his arm, trying to lead him into the school in the hope, no doubt, that Spyros might be interested in contributing to the repair of cracked blackboards and broken desks.

He didn't come to every rehearsal but he did see many of those that took place in the schoolyard. Later, we began to rehearse at night in the square, where we were to perform. These night rehearsals usually lasted until late, but one went so well that the teacher let us all go early and, arriving home sooner than expected, I found Mother and Spyros on the sofa in the parlor.

"You must have come in late last night," Mother said, munching toast the next morning. "I didn't hear you. Was it a long rehearsal?"

"Long enough." She moved back and forth across the kitchen, making coffee, putting dishes in the sink for the girls to wash later. Just as always. I thought she would explain what I had seen and heard last night. But what needed explaining? I didn't know. Nothing, probably. And everything. How could she just go on moving breakfast things around the kitchen?

Spyros had arrived the night before while I was getting ready for the rehearsal. As I came downstairs, I thought I saw him and Mother pull away from each other. But it was Carnival time, after all, when everyone called on friends and family and embraced and wished one another luck. Spyros was in pirate costume and had brought some sweet wine. I sat with them a minute but Mother kept reminding me I was going to be late, so I went off to the square.

When I came home the house was dark and I went up the back stairs. It wasn't until later, while crossing the landing to go to the bathroom, that I heard noises in the parlor. But standing at the top of the stairs, I could see nothing below in the darkened room. As my eyes became used to the dark, I made them out, Spyros first, then Mother, half-hidden under him. I don't know how long I stood there but it seemed to go on and on. Or maybe it didn't; maybe I went back to my room at once and it only seemed like a long time of listening to the noises that grew stronger until they broke, like a kind of wave, and turned to sighs.

"I wonder who'll lead the dancing next year," Mother said at the kitchen table, "when you're out of school."

"I don't care."

"I've heard that Maria is good. And Chrysoúla. Are they?"

"Not very."

"Sometimes I wish I had learned more dances. There was so little time when I was young. And then the fire. Ach, how old I am." I watched her stir her coffee.

Not so old, I thought, not too old for the right kind of dance.

"Where are you going?" she asked. "You haven't finished your breakfast."

"For a walk before school."

But everywhere I walked in the next few days, Spyros was there. If I went outside the village, he was riding his horse through the fields and waved when he saw me. In the marketplace too, he talked with village men, his arms full of blueprints. He nodded to me and always I turned away and moved on as quickly as I could. I was restless and nervous and when I closed my eyes, I saw them again on the sofa, rocking against each other.

Mother had gone to visit Old Lilliána. Poor thing—she no longer cared much for herself. She might not have eaten at all if Mother and I hadn't taken her food from time to time. Sunday night was Mother's time to go. I was upstairs brushing my hair after having soaked it with laurel oil, washed and dried it, when there was a knock at the garden door. My hair was all undone, hanging over my shoulders nearly to my waist as I went downstairs in my robe.

Spyros was there, startled to see me instead of Mother. I reddened. Couldn't they plan better than this?

"Katína is not here?" he asked.

"Mother is at Lilliána's house."

"There was some business we planned to discuss. Perhaps she forgot."

"I suppose so."

"I'll come back later."

"Yes."

"When?"

"She should be home in about half an hour."

"Good. Thank you." And he left. But she was still not home when he returned fifteen minutes later.

"Oh, come in," I said. "It won't matter. It's late now, everyone is asleep and she'll be back in a minute." I held the door open as he stepped inside. The hall was narrow and his eyes seemed bright as he passed close to me. Then as I was closing the door, he said something I didn't understand.

"The seawall, meet me at the seawall." I turned from the door to ask what he meant but we were so close together that I could see all the tiny hairs that curled up out of his shirt around the base of his neck and I couldn't say anything. I knew what was going to happen but when he pressed me against the door and stopped me from speaking with his mouth on mine, I was surprised and couldn't do anything at first. His breath was sweet and he was touching me, but not gently as Nels had done, pushing his hands roughly under my robe. "Oh, God," he kept saying under his breath, "Oh, God." And then I was pushing him off, kicking out at him while he kept talking in this low voice, running everything together, saying he'd die if I didn't let him go on. I pulled away just in time and started up the stairs as Mother came to the door.

"Oh, Spyro," I heard her say as she came in, "I'm sorry to be late. Lilliána won't eat, you know. You have to treat her like a stubborn child."

"Good night!" I shouted down to them and slammed the door of my room. Leaning against it, I waited to get my breath back, waited a long time. I felt sick to my stomach. Papa's best friend. Now would he make love to Mother but think of me? I held myself to stop trembling. It was all horrible, the way he used his hands—I wanted to kill him, I had liked it that much.

That much. The voice of the *Tselapétina.*

You're back?

You brought us back, hissed the dragonfly. *You can't live without us.*

Yes, I can. I have for some time now.

But you're still bad, the *Tselapétina* said. *You liked it.*

Yes, yes I did.

The music of the professors blared under the half moon in the square and we danced beneath the trees. The whole village pressed toward us, along with visitors from the mainland and other islands. I looked for Mother and Spyros, expecting to see them discreetly on separate sides of the square. But they were not to be seen. The empty house, I thought, the sofa without me there, the bedroom upstairs.

Nikos and his friends were right in front. He was to climb the fig tree later, to come into my room. "I had to come here," he would say.

I loved the look in the eyes of the women as we passed because I thought they were remembering the days when they too had worn the velvet dresses of their mothers and grandmothers. It was their youth that danced past to the badly played music. The men cared little for our skill, our grace, our antique clothes. Their eyes roamed our figures. But the women noted each step, watched for the mistakes of the girls who might become future daughters-in-law. The music paused; the line reversed direction.

"When you stopped in front of me," Nikos would say later, "I understood." Understood what? For in fact I had looked past those in front to see someone who looked like Spyros, then wasn't and the line had moved on. The same music, the same steps as in all the other years. People nudged one another and pointed to various dancers as details of dowries, of families were discussed. There was much nodding and talking in the crowd; arrangements were being made, but not for me. I didn't care, but I longed to be away from Mother, to be out of the house. If there were only a cabin somewhere in the hills where I could read and take walks. But it was impossible; I would not be left alone. There was only one idea about single women who lived so. Everyone knew of Katia who was visited by men at night in her little house at the edge of the village.

What would I do? It wasn't fair that Mother should have what she wanted and I have nothing. The village told people what they could and could not do, but Mother was doing as she liked. Back and forth the line moved and Spyros definitely was not there, was not anywhere around the square. And then I remembered what I had not thought of since Sunday night: Seawall, meet me at the seawall. I had gone over everything else that had happened countless times but the words had somehow dropped away and only now came to mind.

"Bravo!" cried the crowd among whistles and cheers, as if they knew my thought and applauded it. But they were saluting the dancers as our line moved out of the square, into the street and my last Carnival came to an end.

"We are the village," Nikos would say, his eyes dark and crazy. "We can do as we please."

"So, Amalía, what do you think? Will the new harbor be good for the island?" Spyros asked. He waved his hand out from the seawall toward the beach and water where I could see men new to the village studying charts and gesturing as they talked. "You see the new quay will be there . . ." He pointed and went on explaining about piers and moorings and sandbars. "The banks are full of American money. It is like candy." He had been down below when I first saw him, talking with the other men. I stood there a long time until he noticed me and then came up to the wall.

"I suppose the new harbor is good," I said. "I don't know."

"You're trembling."

"Am I?"

"Yes." He touched my arm.

"I have to go." But why then, had I come? He had only said to meet him, but not when or anything else at all, as if I would know what he meant. My legs had walked me there and I waited.

"My house is just near, you know, Amalía. Perhaps if you drink some water. The sun is very hot today."

James William Brown

It's nothing to do with the sun, I thought, but already he was leading me along the street. "No, really I'm fine," I said as we went along. It was time for everyone's afternoon sleep so no one was around. I felt weak and lightheaded, a little silly.

The *Tselapétina* was perched on the balcony of a house we passed. *Danger*, it whispered. *Deception*.

The dragonfly swooped over our heads. *Turn, flee!*

No, I said. *Not this time*.

I once read somewhere in one of Maroula's film fan magazines, I think it was, about a film star who took women strongly, wildly. That's how it was with Spyros. We were no sooner inside the house than he had my school uniform off and thrown on the floor, his arms around me, his mouth on mine. He seemed crazy, he wanted me so badly. This is how I had thought boys would be, how Nikos might be. Not Spyros who was so much older, who had been everywhere and done everything. But then what did I know? He wasn't like Nels, anyway. He pulled me onto a kind of narrow bed in a corner of the parlor—the house had almost no furniture in it yet. He took off my underclothes quickly and then I thought his heart was going to stop the way he looked at me and kept saying, just as Nels had said, "My God, oh, my God," while he pulled off his own clothes. I covered my face then. I couldn't stop myself from doing it even though it was something a child would do. But he pulled my hands away and made me look at him and then I said, "Oh, my God," too, and for no reason at all burst into tears. He paid no attention to me but went right ahead, all wild and noisy and in a minute my tears had stopped.

He wasn't selfish, the way I had thought men would

236

be. He wanted me to enjoy everything as much as he did. What he wanted, I came to want too, and after a while a voice that I didn't recognize as mine came back to me from the blank walls.

I went there nearly every day in the next weeks. I would tell myself that I wasn't going to go again but then I would go. My body never completely lost the smell of his, the feeling of his weight. I learned that memory is not just something that happens in your mind—for I'd sit in school not thinking of him at all and then suddenly parts of my body would remember and I thought I'd go crazy until I could be with him again. There was so little in my life to look forward to but this was new and seemed to give meaning to everything else. I felt my face soften, felt the bone fall away. I was even thoughtful around Mother now that I saw to it that Spyros had little time to see her.

All this was nothing like what had happened in the tent with Nels. If I said to Nels, Don't do that, he didn't. And something in me didn't want his gentleness. Spyros did as he pleased. There were the marks to be covered with makeup stolen from Mother. The careful web of excuses to be made at school, at home. We made love in every room of the house, and even in the old walled garden behind it.

"Ach, here is what I like about you," he said one afternoon, lying on his side facing me, his head resting in the crook of his arm. "You have your father's ways. He always used everything up completely—whether it was a big sale in the shop, a trip to the mainland with me, dancing in the taverna—no matter what. You're like that too. You burn yourself up, like a good bonfire."

"That sounds more like you," I told him. Spyros reminded me of the way I imagined Papa when he was young but Spyros was still that way in spite of his age. I had seen him tear mattresses from the bed and throw them down on the floor when he wanted me there. Or lift me as if I weighed no more than a pot of geraniums and carry me into the garden where he set me in the crook of the old plane tree. Its thick leaves hid us and softened our cries.

"No, no," he said. "I'm not like Grigóris. No one is. All those years away from here I thought, Well, why go back? With Grigóris dead and my wife dead, no family left here anymore. And I would think of him, our jokes on each other, how we danced in the taverna. Ah, Amalía, I have never felt so alive as I did in those days, except when I am here with you."

You are pulling away, the *Tselapétina* whispered to me.

Lost! the dragonfly sang. *Lost and lost and lost. But I am still beautiful. See my beautiful wings.*

Leave me alone.

Not as beautiful as my feathers, said the *Tselapétina*.

Go away.

We never spoke of Mother. She looked strained and I wondered about the excuses Spyros was making, but I didn't ask. Spyros and I talked of nothing that might cause bad feelings between us. Mother and Nels, the village, the world, all were kept outside his house. Only Papa was let in for he was a love we shared. We seldom spoke but when we did it was always of him. Spyros's eyes would grow moist. I understood, finally, that it was not really me he wanted, and not Mother either. It was his friendship with Papa that Spyros wanted to get back to, his youth dancing in a smoky taverna, drinking coffee in Papa's shop.

"But you can't get anything back," Spyros said, "once it's gone. You might as well tear the past up and make something new out of it. For this I came back to the island. Someday you will understand, Amalía. I have plans, such plans!"

It was on Easter Eve as I stood in church with Mother, holding an unlit candle and waiting for the Holy Fire to descend at midnight, that I realized I was carrying Spyros's child. Everyone was there, the whole village, and the smell of incense was making me dizzy. The priest droned on; people whispered and shuffled their feet. I felt myself swaying and Mother turned to look at me strangely. I won't faint, I thought, I won't, not here in front of everyone at the highest service of the year. It was the only time we ever came to church, for the service was beautiful and I didn't want to miss it, although I had been feeling odd lately. I fixed my eyes on the great icon, the oldest in the church, Mother and Child, which had once been said to weep, to heal, though it had done neither in my lifetime. As I concentrated on it, and especially on the Child—though for no particular reason—I was suddenly filled with the desire to have a baby, to come into my whole body and have a child of my own. I had never felt this before, had never wanted a child, had always thought babies messy and stupid. But as I looked at the baby in the icon, I longed for one of my own.

And then it came to me—of course, that was what the dizziness meant. The nausea I had felt the day before when passing Maroula's shop where naked chickens hung upside down by their yellow feet. They had never bothered me before. But then my breasts had never felt so sensitive and swollen before; I had never wanted so much sleep, so much food. A child!

We are the only child you need, the *Tselapétina* said.

You gave birth to us. We are a part of you, the dragonfly insisted.

You are me, all the sharp and jagged parts of me. But not my children. Just leftover pieces of my growing up.

Leftover pieces! screamed the dragonfly. *Pieces of your seeing!*

Feathers of your wing, said the *Tselapétina*.

It was true. Talking to them was talking to myself. They had gone away when Nels left. When the long, boring days held nothing I could be blamed for. And when Spyros came, they returned with the new possibility of guilt, of blaming. They were the vain, guilty, cowardly parts of me, born in the black days after Papa's death. They could only live in such dark corners.

All through the rest of the service, I grew more certain that all this was true. As excitement grew around us when midnight approached, so grew my wonder. Then the lights went out; the priest went behind the screen. Silence fell on the restless, whispering crowd as it waited for fire. The voice of the priest cried out from the screen, "Christ is risen, truly risen!" He came forth with the single lighted taper as everyone pressed forward with unlit tapers to take their light from his.

Mother and I managed to get home without the night breeze blowing our flames out—a good omen, we both agreed. I felt strong, even joyful as I climbed down the fig tree later when the village was asleep. I let myself into Spyros's house and upstairs.

"I want to marry Nikos," I announced to his sleeping form.

"What? Who?" He sat up in bed, groping for the light. "What's wrong?" he asked.

"Nothing's wrong. I'm going to marry Nikos. You're his godfather, aren't you? It should be easy to arrange but you'll have to encourage him—he thinks I won't have him."

"But why do you want to marry him?"

"Everyone else is getting married. I want to get married too."

"This is not like you. I don't understand."

"Do it anyway. Do it for me."

The dragonfly leaves the shoulder of the priest, circles once above us as the choir repeats:

> "The morning comes,
> and also the night."

The wedding bread is baked. The old women came into our garden the day before yesterday to knead the dough. I watched from an upstairs window and thought, It's my life they're kneading in their wooden troughs, squeezing between their fingers. Maybe we're all molded by their hands, little bread figures rolled out of dough, our arms outstretched, heads unbaked.

Certainly my classmates looked so as they wobbled around the garden this morning on their seldom-worn high heels, shrieking and giggling. Some of them are married now; others will be soon. Mother set up tables where they could prepare the wedding favors, could gossip as they cut out squares of tulle and shaped them into little bags to contain a few candied almonds, all tied up with a blue ribbon. They called up to me, offering to help me get dressed, but I stayed upstairs alone, took a long bath and dressed carefully, without help from anyone.

The dress was Mother's choice. A little too elaborate for me with its satin train and all the lace. I would have liked something simple but I really didn't care that much and the selection, ordering and final adjustments of my dress and hers have kept Mother busy these last weeks, as I hoped they would. Hers is dark blue silk and suits her nicely, I thought a moment ago, as I glanced around at her beside me, just before the priest picked up the two wreaths of blossoms.

"The Lord's servant Nikos engages the Lord's servant Amalía," he says as he touches our foreheads with the wreaths, joined by a ribbon. Mother is studying me, staring into me, her eyes asking why.

"I can't stop feeling that you're marrying this Nikos to get at *me*, somehow," she said a few days ago.

"There are easier ways to get at you, Mother." She will never tire of trying to find out and it will keep her busy through the years as together we raise this, her first grandchild. She will help me and I will welcome her help, for I know little of such things and Nikos will be no use at all with the child. Men never are. And in spite of everything, I know that Mother is the only woman with any sense in the village and I need her. If she comes to understand, she will curse me but always love the child and hold the truth close to herself, that the village may never see. Spyros will return to her (perhaps he already has) with an excuse she will believe, but when he is with her, he will think of me.

"In the name of the Father, the Son, and the Holy Ghost," the priest says, crossing himself three times for Nikos and three for me. Then Spyros, dutiful godfather behind us, takes the wreaths and passes them back and forth over Nikos's head and mine, crowning us each with one. He has done well, our Spyros, has arranged the negotiations neatly.

"Nikos's family has always wanted this match, but now I don't know," he told me those early hours of Easter morning. "There was all that talk about the foreigner, you know."

"I was foolish. It's nothing."

"But it may be something to them."

"You can change that. Everyone respects the opinion of a godfather, especially if the godfather is you."

"Katína has always said that one day you will leave the island."

"Ah, but I still will. An island woman marries an island man—this does not mean the world out there goes away. You will give Nikos a job, yes? And you have offices and contacts all over Europe. I am good at languages; Nikos will be good with people. You will see."

"Something has happened to you."

"Of course. I've decided to marry—that's what has happened." He did not ask more, though questions hung there between us. It would do him no good to know. Spyros and I could never marry—Mother would kill me first. And Spyros would love the child too much. No, this is to be my child. It needs a father like Nikos, someone who adores me, whom I can make do as I wish, once I have bound myself to him here in front of the village. His pride is too great for him ever to suspect the truth and his coloring is much like that of Spyros. Even if either of them realizes, he will never let anyone know after Nikos has presented the child to the village as his own. Nikos will act the good father but the child will be mine, my sweet secret.

"I won't come here again," I told Spyros just before I left his house.

"I know you won't, daughter of Grigóris."

"It would be easier if I left the island, wouldn't it?"

"Ah, we shall see what is easy in this world and what is not."

Now the priest gives Spyros the rings and he passes them back and forth over our hands, not meeting my eyes, slipping them onto Nikos's finger and mine. "What God has joined together, let no man put apart," says the priest, and he separates Nikos's hand from mine, showing us what no man must do. From the altar he lifts the heavy chalice of red wine and holds it to my lips.

Poison, screams the dragonfly, still hovering.

Don't drink, the *Tselapétina* calls down from the dome.

I have already done so.

Who will protect you now? they ask.

It is my time to protect new life. This is what I choose.

The priest begins to lead us through the Dance of Isaiah, a walk three times around the altar as rice and rose petals are thrown and so we are sworn to each other for life. Three times for love, some say, as if love comes first, second and third.

I remember when Maroula and I used to read foreign magazines and books, how everyone wanted to be in love all the time and to be loved too, as if they were children all screaming, Me! Me! It is an idea of those other countries, I suppose, that love is all. Pah! Love didn't save Papa or help Mother get through all these years without him. It didn't protect Maroula from her family, save the peacocks for Nels, or take me on the journey I once wanted. And it won't give Spyros back the past that he longs for.

No, first must come a child and second, years, I think, time. Love comes third, if it comes at all. Mother has always said it is foolish to expect love early in a marriage. But if Lilliána was right in saying that island women are fated to love men seeking things not to be found, perhaps one day I will reach out to Nikos. And then, like the light from Acrux—old light from a twin star—love will come as a reward for waiting. It will be something we have earned.

There are rose petals in the thick hair of my bridegroom as we circle the second time, the third. The faces of the village smile on the other side of the shower of rice and petals.

Keep us with you, says the *Tselapétina*.

I cannot.

When we cut, when we bit, we still loved you, the dragonfly sings. *We loved before they did.*

I know.

Good-bye, then.

Good-bye.

"You have sworn before God and man," says the priest. "And thus it will be for all time."

V THE MEN

From the door of the café we watch Nikos come out of the church with his bride on his arm. He stands with her on the steps as her girlfriends lift the long back part of the wedding dress and the little boys who carried the tall candles in the ceremony dance around them saying something that makes everyone laugh. Then Spyros comes out and Widow Katína, followed by the parents of Nikos and the rest of the village except for us, as we are too old for this throwing of rose petals, for the smile on Nikos's face that says, See, I have won her. We smile too, for we once stood on those same steps with our own proud brides and we know now what we did not know then: it is woman who casts the net, sits quietly and watches the water. Health to you, Niko, and to your bride.

She looks as juicy and delicious as a midsummer peach. We lick our fingers over her beauty and say, What bad luck, Nikos, that the foreigner probably had the first bite. Never mind—what will it matter in a few years when she has drawn children from your loins and your house is filled with the screams and smells of babies? Amalía will grow fat while her voice becomes shrill and you will find your way here to the café where there is only the sound of good talk and cards slapped down on tabletops. Here where we swear and lie and unravel stories, then tangle them again, away from the words of women that confuse everything.

Ach! If there is a café for any of us to go to, that is, after Spyros has his way with the island. We hear that he has a surprise gift for the couple that will be announced tonight at the wedding feast though tongues have wagged already and what we have heard is no gift to the island of our grandfathers.

But look there, how the bride and groom are coming down the steps of the church, leading all the others into the sunshine of the square where the professors are tuning their instruments. What a picture it is as the breeze catches Amalía's veil and the sun flashes from the whiteness of her dress. Nikos beside her, proud as a warrior, and the priest there now too, the gilt threads of his robes sparkling in the light. The others follow them into the square in a kind of procession. How like that other procession, someone says from inside the coffeehouse, the one years ago that was made up only of children. That one, yes, we all remember and agree.

Amalía and Nikos couldn't have been more than seven or eight at the time. Even then Nikos was the leader of all the other children in the village. Well, someone—a cousin, was it?—gave Nikos a little pig for name-day gift. No one ever raised pigs on the island then so most of the children had never seen one and they all wanted to play with it. Nikos would allow no one other than Amalía—always his favorite friend—to touch the pig. She and Nikos would put a dress and bonnet on it and carry it around the village, pretending it was their baby. It was something new in their lives, something exciting, this pig in a bonnet. But we said things should look like what they are and a pig is not a baby. If an animal doesn't feed you or clothe you or work for you, why have it at all? And it was always getting away from them. Everyone would laugh as it went squealing down the street with its bonnet strings trailing in the dust.

How Nikos's parents hated that pig! It rooted around in their garden until it had ruined all the good vegetables that Nikos's mother raised. "I'll see it roasted on a spit over charcoal!" Nikos's father would shout every time he caught it in the garden. But the pig had been a gift to Nikos so they couldn't take it away from him. Then one day it rooted up something that made them forgive it! A rotten old leather bag with four gold sovereigns in it. Who knows how long it had been there or where it had come from? Perhaps from the time when pirates sheltered in the many coves. The coins were a gift from the island, we said, and Nikos and Amalía were very happy. Their baby had brought them great luck. We all went to touch the pig in the hope of getting some of its luck, but no one else found any sovereigns. Nikos was a generous boy so he gave one sovereign to his parents, one to Amalía and kept one for himself. The fourth, he said, was for the pig.

"For the pig?" his father shouted. "Don't be crazy, Nikos. What will a pig do with a sovereign?"

"I don't know yet. But the pig found the sovereigns so one is for the pig." His parents let him alone about it. He was a strong-willed boy and what could they do?

"We'll wait until Nikos and Amalía have spent their sovereigns," they told everyone, "and then we'll see how long they let the pig have the other one."

But before this could happen, the pig ran away from the children one afternoon just as a cart loaded with vegetables was coming down the road. Amalía had put the bonnet and dress on the pig that day and when the cart wheel finished with the animal, it was something terrible to see. It could have been a real baby for all you could tell. And Nikos and Amalía shouting at the driver that their baby was dead and he was a murderer. Isn't that the way of things? we said. The pig brought them money but because they kept trying to make it into something it wasn't, it ran off and got itself killed.

That wasn't the end of it all. Before long the children got the idea of giving the pig a funeral. You know how it is when you are at such an age in a quiet place—even death gives you something new to do. They found a box and put an old pillow inside, then shoveled that poor mess of an animal onto it and took it all to the priest's house.

"Our baby has died," Nikos told the priest. "We want you to give it a funeral." The priest looked into the box and drew back, furious.

"Wicked children to suggest such a thing!" Our priest was new here then and much younger, ach, as we all were. We didn't know him very well yet but through Nikos and Amalía, we would come to see him then as the man he still is today. "Not only is it not human," he shouted as he slammed the door and his voice boomed from inside the house, "it's also not Christian!"

Most children would have given up then and taken the pig off for a funeral of their own making, such as you sometimes see them giving a dead kitten or a bird. But not our Nikos—he always gets what he wants. He and Amalía talked about the problem for a while and then he went back to the priest's house by himself. But the priest refused to open the door. "Blasphemer!" he shouted from inside. "Heathen!"

"But wait," Nikos called out. "Listen to me. My pig left a will."

"Spawn of the Devil! Go away."

"There is something in the will for you. Look. I have it here. One gold sovereign."

There was a silence and the door opened just a crack, wide enough for the priest to see the heavy gold coin in Nikos's hand. Now in those days a sovereign was worth more than a village priest would make from any number of weddings and funerals. The door opened wider. "Uhm, in his will, you say, Niko?"

"Yes, sir."

"Come in, Niko."

The women said afterwards that the idea of the will was really Amalía's, though we still think it was Nikos's. What does it matter? Together they got the funeral they wanted, though not a big one, not one held in the church because the priest was afraid the bishop might hear of the bell tolled for a pig. Nor was the animal buried in the cemetery with good Christians. But there was a procession into a field outside the village with incense and singing and Holy Words. All the children of the village went, Nikos and Amalía leading them. We were mending nets when we heard the noise and went to see the children who were dressed in black cast-off adult clothes, passing with the priest and the banners of the church. It looked like a real village funeral, if everyone had shrunk except for the priest. And a kind of chill went through us as it sometimes does when you see your children dressed up in your own clothes and you're reminded of the end of things, and of their beginnings. Amalía shrieked and threw herself into grief, just as our women do and little Maroula and the other girls held her arms to keep her from throwing herself on the box that contained the pig. Nikos beat his breast while the priest chanted. They did it so well that we said grieving for a thing lost must be something we're just born knowing how to do. We crossed ourselves as they made their way back to the village as if their loss were ours too.

Now they stand in the square, Amalía and Nikos, receiving the good wishes of the children of the village grown up like the rest of us but we have grown far older. Spyros and the priest are talking to one side; they must be settling the price of the wedding for Spyros looks angry and the priest has raised his hands to the sky to imply not his will but God's, a sure sign he has asked four times what the ceremony was worth. Most priests are thieves and this one knows that Spyros can pay anything.

Spyros will say tonight that after a while, after he has taught Nikos the business, the managing of the fields, he will transfer Amalía and Nikos to other places, to his mainland office, even to foreign countries. For Amalía knows languages and Nikos is clever at mathematics. Spyros says he needs people such as these in his many offices, now that our tomatoes are sent around the world. Amalía and Nikos and others of our young people will be sent away to work in distant places, as Spyros mostly trusts those from this island of his birth. But who will till the fields, we ask, who will do the work in the new harbor? The tomato saved us from the barren sea and from the dynamite that tore the limbs off our bodies. Now the tomato gives us this new harbor. But if our youth all sail away, who will raise each year's crop and do the other work? Who will live in our houses after we're gone, who will wear the shoes that we haven't yet worn out?

He says he will bring in outside workers. They are cheap and easy to find for the dog's work in the fields and harbor. Why waste our own good men on it? Spyros asks (though *we* were not too good to waste). Ach, this is not all. In Spyros's office there are plans for a new island, for hotels huge and gleaming. All the old houses along the waterfront will be pulled down, houses that have been there longer than we can remember. Inside the fortress will be a casino. And there will be a yacht harbor, restaurants, souvenir shops. Most of the village, even the old marketplace, will be pulled down to make way for this new island to be built on the back of the old one.

We'll be rich, some say. We will live better than the king who built the fortress whose walls will contain the new casino. Pah! You will be poor, we say, for this smells to us of death. This is something new in your lives, something exciting but you're like Nikos and Amalía dressing up that pig. You may come by some money in all this but these things go too far, run away from you and the result is death. Have we not heard of other islands where this has happened? Places where outsiders run hotels for the holidays of outsiders and all that is left of the old village are a few houses tumbling down, a few old men like us gossiping in the doorway of a café while foreigners take our photographs. Or perhaps the houses are painted fresh again but when you peer through the window to see what's on the stove, po-po-po—it's not a house at all, just the frame of one. Inside it, badly made weaving and clothes brought in from other places are sold where someone's kitchen used to be.

No one listens to us. There is nothing we can do. This all began long ago, the day Widow Katína, then a young woman, arrived here. It is she who started the wheel turning that will crush the old bones of the village, may the earth rest lightly on them. Had she not come to the island, not walked about with the sun playing over her long hair, her full body, our Grigóris would have married one of our own. And our Spyros would never have seen Katína and burned for her, though promised to another. When Spyros buried his wife, poor skinny Froso, we said now he will leave the island so as not to look on the wife of his friend Grigóris, but one day he will come back for her. So because of Katína he left, became rich and returned for her and the shop of Grigóris she now owns. He burns for Amalía too, of course—ach, don't we all—and who can say, maybe it was he and not the foreigner who had the first bite of the peach. Today he wisely marries her to his godson and later he will send them away, but not until we have had a careful look at the first child born of this union.

Well, this is what comes of letting outsiders live among you. The good dog stays in its own kennel. Before there were outsiders here, everyone knew what everyone else was doing, what your neighbors ate for dinner last night, who made love to his wife and who didn't, what each saw in his dreams later. Miracles happened as easily as bread rises. Icons in the church wept for us and wise women knew the secrets of healing. We will have to heal ourselves these next years for even Old Lilliána met her hour the day before the wedding, may the earth rest lightly on her too.

Now foreigners take their clothes off on our beaches, have our daughters in their tents and photograph the icons whose eyes no longer weep at our envy and our greed. It was such a foreigner that Amalía used in order to make Nikos want her. On the day of the sea turtle, he claimed what had always been his from the time long ago when he walked with her out of the village, leading that dark procession. And now, as we watch Amalía and Nikos prepare to lead the village in their wedding dance, we can see them still, all in black behind the banners of the church, crossing the field to bury a pig. Perhaps that is why a chill passed through us, as if it were the village being buried, as if it were ourselves. For there may be no one but outsiders to give us the simple rites that the children, in their innocence, and the priest, in his greed, did not deny a lowly pig. And our lives will slip by, finally, without leaving a trace.

Ach, there the priest and Spyros have agreed at last for they are shaking hands and turning to speak with Widow Katína who stands under the trees our great-grandfathers planted. The first squawks of music come from the professors' instruments and men line up to pin bank notes to Amalía's dress that they might be among the first to lead her in the dance, after the groom has had his turn, and his godfather.

The music begins. Thanks to God only part of our hearing remains. Nikos takes Amalía's hand and leads her and the others in a line around the square. Everyone sways along behind the bride and groom, laughing, bumping into each other, now moving faster. The awful music calls us too and just as the line bends and almost becomes a circle, we hobble into the square and call out, "Health to you, Niko, and to your bride!" We take the hands of those at the end and join the old dance of the people of our blood. It now moves almost faster than we can stand. Though some of us have forgotten the steps, everyone has the feeling of the dance.